BETRAYED TRUST

DRUGS, CRIME AND SHATTERED LIVES

TOM HAIR

First published in Great Britain in 2025

Copyright © Tom Hair

The moral right of the author has been asserted.

All rights reserved.

This book is based on true events. Some names and characteristics have been changed, some events have been compressed, and some dialogue has been recreated

No part of this publication may be reproduced, stored in a retrieval system, or transmitted, in any form or by any means, without the prior permission in writing of the publisher, nor be otherwise circulated in any form of binding or cover other than that in which it is published and without a similar condition including this condition being imposed on the subsequent purchaser.

Design, typesetting and publishing by UK Book Publishing.

www.ukbookpublishing.com

ISBN: 978-1-917329-83-5

DEDICATION

To my wife and daughter who are patient,
supportive and understand me.

ABOUT THE AUTHOR

Tom Hair is a Sunderland born author who began his career with Newcastle United Football Club as a professional footballer in 1984.

Following a handful of appearances in the first team, his career was ended after a series of knee injuries at the age of 19.

He later became a Detective Constable working in the northeast of England where the majority of his career was spent in intelligence running Police informants.

CHAPTER ONE

Simon Cohen made a big mistake.

That mistake was moving his camera shop from the centre of Sunderland to outlying Easington. Sure, it reduced business costs, with lower rent and rates, but it also condemned *Cohen's Cameras* to a slow, miserable slide towards insolvency and, in the shorter term, it brought Simon a nasty concussion and a trip to A&E.

Simon's dad, Manny, had built the business. Manny had held a head for business. Simon didn't, hence the ill-judged move to Easington. Once a pit village which had housed well-paid miners, it was now – post Thatcher and Scargill – home to a demoralised and aimless population, who enjoyed the services of a bookie's, a couple of charity shops, a kebab house and a specialist camera shop, which nobody could afford to patronise.

This explained the overdone smile and cheery welcome with which Simon approached the first person to walk through the shop's door late on that Thursday morning in August 2002.

"Hi, you okay there? Can I help at all?"

Not only was this punter looking at a camera that was ticketed at £899 and so locked in its glass display case, but she was, as Simon noted, quite fit. Probably mid-twenties, slim, verging on skinny, but with a nice shape which was shown to advantage in blue jeans, hair tucked under a woollen beanie hat, dark shades and a pretty elfin face.

She smiled, which made her look sweet.

"I was just interested in this camera."

He stood beside her, perhaps closer than strictly necessary, and looked over her shoulder.

"The new Nikon Coolpix 5700. What can I tell you? It has an 8 times Zoom-Nikkor lens with 8.9-71.2mm coverage and 5.0 megapixels. Only been on the market a couple of months. It's a step up from the Coolpix 5000 and its only real competition is Minolta's DiMAGE 7i or and Sony's DSC-F707, but, to my mind, this has the edge."

"Right," she said, drawing the word out. "Could I have a closer look at it? I mean, see what it feels like."

"No problem."

The key was in his pocket, attached by a fine chain to his belt. He unlocked the cabinet and handed her the Coolpix. As she took it in delicate, hesitant hands, somebody else entered the shop.

Tall, baseball cap and grubby bomber jacket. Simon did a swift appraisal. A charva, a wrong'un who was never going to buy anything, probably wanted change, or directions to the bookies. Simon gave him a brief nod and a half smile and turned back to the girl. The charva paused to examine a display of camera bags. "It's not as heavy as I thought it might be," said the girl, hefting the camera.

"No, it's a nice weight. Is it for you?"

"For me boyfriend. A present."

"He's a lucky bloke," said Simon, in a sly drawl.

She looked at him, fluttered her eyelashes and tittered. Simon smiled. She held the camera up, unclipped the lens cover and looked through the view finder towards the door.

She was called Eva. Through the camera, she saw the door and, through that, the street beyond. She walked towards it and the image on the screen grew larger. She took a couple more paces, passing Jordan on her right, who was examining camera bags. Then she made longer, more purposeful strides. Her free hand was pushing the door open, when she heard the guy's voice behind her. "Er…excuse me"

It ended with a gasp. Then there was crunch. She recognised that, she'd heard it before. It was Jordan head-butting him. She didn't hear him drop to the floor because she was out of the shop, thrusting the camera into her bag and striding down the street. But she soon heard Jordan's footsteps running after her.

§

The evening of that same day, in Eva's flat in Washington's Sulgrave Estate, Jordan swung between conflicting moods. Neither mood was much influenced by the flat, which was furnished with a mixture of second hand furniture in synthetic fibres, largely browns and oranges, and a formica-topped table. Eva's home-making femininity was reflected in the bunch of dusty plastic roses thoughtfully arranged in a chipped plastic vase on that table and by the fact that the well worn carpet was significantly less littered with dirty plates, pizza boxes, mugs and soiled clothing than if it had been Jordan's flat alone. You could, after all, still make out some carpet.

No, his moods were driven by that morning's events. On the one hand the camera they'd lifted in Easington, which had been marked up at nearly nine hundred fucking quid, had only fetched them three hundred from Gus Walton on the other side of the estate. Tight bastard. But, let's face it, beggars can't be choosers and with two hundred and fifty of those three hundred notes, they'd scored an eighth of smack. Two of those wraps had allowed them to idle away a euphoric afternoon, which still, on the whole, left him with a feeling of well-being and contentment.

There was a good chance that the camera shop had CCTV, but they'd worn headgear and she'd had shades. They'd be fine.

On the other hand…

He contemplated Eva, sitting on the carpet opposite, her back resting against the sofa, eyes closed, a half smile on her lips. He swore under his breath. He didn't want to spoil her mood, but he had to tell her sometime. Maybe he should have done it before they'd shot up.

Bollocks. He'd tell her now. Then they could score some more smack.

He stretched out his own foot and prodded her. She grunted. He gave her a gentle kick.

"Eva."

"Aye, what?"

He rubbed his chin, searching for the words.

This time, she kicked him. "Frigging what man?"

"I've something to tell you."

She closed her eyes and sighed, seemingly not anticipating anything of interest. "Yeah?"

"Thing is…"

"What?"

"It's that…er…I've heard…"

"What?"

"He's getting out."

Now she opened her eyes – wide. Then she started screaming.

§

Paul Gibson was an important man. He told himself that. He was, after all, the governor of HM Prison Bradford, the UK's largest high security prison, and, since last year, the first in the country to have one of the new Supermax security units for the most dangerous cons.

Even his office testified to his importance: oakpanelled, a classic, large, twin pedestal mahogany desk – well, mahogany effect. It had space for a leather sofa, matching chairs and coffee table and, against the wall facing him, files and books on shelves behind glass doors. Yes, definitely the office of an important man.

Who the hell was he kidding?

Importance implied power and Paul Gibson was all too well aware that he didn't have any, not real power. No, that lay elsewhere – with a Home Office that was in thrall to political correctness and liberal criminologists, to an interfering prison inspectorate, to a truculent and unionised team of prison officers and, let's not forget, to the prisoners.

Oh yes, he'd long since given up pretending that the real power in his prison, known throughout the system as the Monster Mansion, lay with anyone other than with its inmates. They called the shots, dictated procedures and ensured its smooth running, unless you pissed them off, by restricting their supply of drugs, or mobile phones or visiting rights. In that case they ensured violent mayhem, riot squads, national TV coverage and the effective end of the career of one Paul Gibson.

Not that the prisoners exercised their power democratically. They didn't all have an equal say. The nonces, for example - of which the Monster Mansion had more than its fair share, had no voice. As the lowest of the low, they were anxious only to be kept out of the homicidal reach of the fellow guests of Her Majesty. It was the other end of the spectrum that had the voting rights, the aristocrats of criminality who included armed robbers, senior gang members and non-sexually motivated head cases.

Gibson sighed. It was a sigh of resignation, not depression. He'd come to terms with his powerlessness. What else could he do? He couldn't change it. His ambition now was limited to keeping a lid on things until he reached retirement, or managed a move to the Home

Office where he'd no longer be on the front line. Until then, keep his head down and make the best of a bad job.

He picked up his glasses, put them on and opened the file on his desk. Karl Wrathall. He skimmed the front page summary and sighed again. He pressed a button on his intercom.

"Send him in Sarah," he said.

The door opened and a man with a face matching that in the file entered, accompanied by a prison officer. The officer, his hair whisked up in the latest style that made it look like a Mr Whippy, closed the door behind them and they stood before the desk.

Gibson contemplated Wrathall, a big man, six foot two, according to the file, broad shouldered, but, Gibson noted the thin wrists and the trousers that hung loosely, betraying a greater interest in heroin than food. Not something that Gibson wanted to dwell on, given that Wrathall was just finishing five years in a prison, nominally under Gibson's supervision and supposedly drug free. Wrathall looked back in return, his eyes were dark and their gaze was intense but brief. After it had fixed Gibson with a penetrating and disconcerting stare, it flicked away, and, for the rest of the interview, it was never aimed at him directly again, as if Wrathall had appraised him in a second and had dismissed him as not being worth any more eyeball time.

The governor cleared his throat with a loud harrumph, preliminary to gaining control of the interview, or at least give the impression that he had, not so much to convince himself or Wrathall as Prison Officer Wells. "So Wrathall," he said. "Not a pretty record. It goes back to your childhood, nearly quarter of a century ago. Starts with the usual petty stuff but soon we're on to the big time. Threats to kill, firearms offences, conspiracy to rob and jail-breaking. Thanks to that, a large part of that quarter of a century has been spent inside. Wasted."

He looked at Wrathall, who stared expressionless at a corner of the ceiling behind the governor's head. Gibson continued. "Tomorrow you're being released back into society. You were sent here for ten. You do realise, don't you, that if you go down again, with this record, you could be looking at double that?" Wrathall muttered something.

"What?"

"I said, yeah, I realise that."

"Good, I'm glad you do. Next time you get out you'll be well into middle age. Your life will have been completely wasted. From what I read in these pages, you're not an unintelligent man Wrathall. You could still make something of yourself, so long as you stay off the drugs."

Which, thought Gibson, you've almost certainly been getting access to, possibly supplied by the glassy-eyed Wells standing behind you.

"I'll stay clean," said Wrathall, in a low voice. "Good, I'm glad to hear it. When you leave here, you're going back to Sunderland? Where will you stay?"

"With me dad."

"Good, is that on your probation details? Oh, they're not in the file. Just a minute." He pressed the intercom. "Sarah, do you have Wrathall's probation docs? Good, let him HAVE his copy would you?" He ended the call and rose to his feet, his hand extended.

"Well, good luck Wrathall and don't let me see you again."

Wrathall contemplated the governor's outstretched hand as though it was attempting to hand him a Jehovah's Witness pamphlet, then took it and shook it without evident enthusiasm. As they released each other, the door opened and Sarah, brunette and buxom, entered holding papers.

"The probation docs you wanted Governor."

"Oh, thank you Sarah, you could have given them to him on his way out, but never mind."

Wrathall turned to face her and took the papers with a nod. Then all three left the office, leaving the governor alone. He shook his head and dropped back into his seat. When Sarah had handed Wrathall those papers, she'd given him a dazzling smile and Gibson, who saw Wrathall's face reflected in the glass bookcase, could have sworn the prisoner winked at her.

No, there was no doubt who was running this bloody place.

CHAPTER TWO

Detective Constable Dan Kilford pulled his Fiesta into the kerb and switched off the engine.

He sucked on a tooth and cast an unenthusiastic eye around. Even on a cloudless Friday morning Sunderland's Villette Road Estate wasn't going to lighten his mood. A 1950's settlement of red brick semis, clustered in crescents and closes, it had long been used by the city council as a dumping ground for its worst tenants: the workshy, feckless and plain criminal, who were placed in houses rather than flats, by virtue of being families with children.

The house Kilford had parked opposite, number 52 Cairo Crescent, was much like its neighbours. The front gate was hanging from a hinge, the garden was an overgrown tangle of grass and bramble and an old tan leather sofa sat surrounded by empty Fosters cans. Condensation glinted on the insides of the windows whose curtains were mismatched, grubby and half drawn.

Kilford shook his head. He was in a bad mood and that wasn't like him. He was normally of a sunny disposition. He liked his job. In fact, he loved it. He lived and breathed the job and, if it didn't always put a spring in his step and a smile on his face, he at least didn't share the world-weary cynicism of most of his colleagues. That's why they nicknamed him Alf – Annoying Little Fucker.

It wasn't Villette Road that had dampened his spirits. His day had taken a turn for the worse at home in the kitchen over breakfast when he and Vicki had a row. No, not really a row. Row implies give and take. This had been purely one-sided. Her giving, him receiving. Kilford worked in the Sunderland Area Command Dedicated Source Unit, an intelligence gathering operation that was responsible for, among other things, managing informants: grasses, narks, snouts. It was a job that took a lot of time and Vicki felt that at least some of that time was owed to her and their daughters, Natalie and Beth. Two things had brought matters to a head. Last night, Vicki had got home from visiting her mother in her care home to find Kilford lying next to three-year-old Beth, on her bed, story book in his lap, but him fast asleep and a tearful Beth trying angrily to prod him awake. He might have got away with that had not that same day Natalie's head teacher sent them a letter informing them that their thirteen-year-old had been part of a gang caught drinking cans of cider and then she had spent much of the afternoon in the infirmary being sick.

Kilford shut his eyes as he recalled Vicki's face, pale with anger, shaking forefinger jabbing in his face. "You're never bloody there for them Dan! You're just never bloody there for any of us!"

He groaned. Up until then he'd faced an alliance of two daughters ganging up on him to bully him into getting a dog. That he could handle, but now it was him versus all three of them.

Because he'd been so demoralised when he'd reached the station that morning, he'd been talked into doing this job by DS Tam MacFarlane, the Glaswegian who headed up the Reactive CID Team.

"Och, it's just a tiny favour wee man."

If his own DS, Cliffy White, found out about this wee favour there'd be hell on, but Kilford had allowed his arm to be twisted.

So, here he was, sitting opposite 52 Cairo Crescent to do a job that should have been down to uniformed branch. He was to interview Mr and Mrs Ray Nixon, to confirm that they no longer wished to press assault charges against local hard man Tom Betts, whom Ray had so rashly offended late one evening in The Red Lion public house.

Get it over with.

Kilford got out of the car and crossed the road to number 52. He opened the gate, careful not to detach it from its one remaining hinge. He walked up the path and noticed that behind the pram was a dog. A mangy German Shepherd, its coat matted and one ear hanging, scratching itself. It looked at him, wary.

"Hello old son," said Kilford.

The dog gave its tail a hesitant half wag and lowered its shoulders, submissive. Kilford knocked on the door, which was opened by a fat man with a bald bullet head and thick neck which sported a spider web tattoo. Kilford noted the man's knuckles bore the letters ACAB (All Coppers Are Bastards), a common saying among a certain Sunderland social set. He also wore a pair of joggers and a stained vest.

"Ray Nixon?" asked Kilford.

"Aye."

"DC Kilford, Sunderland police."

Nixon gave the proffered warrant card a brief glance and stepped back.

"I suppose you'd better come in."

As Kilford stepped over the threshold, something brushed his leg. He looked down to see the dog had followed him and it accompanied them into the living room. Despite it being a mild day, the heating was on and the place stank of fried food and nicotine and something worse. The room was littered with papers, broken toys and dirty mugs. A woman, pasty faced, pinched and clearly much put-upon, introduced by Nixon as "our lass" and a boy of maybe four or five, "the bairn", sat on a sagging sofa and stared. Nixon joined them. Kilford eyed a squalid armchair facing them and, with deep misgivings, sat in it. The dog ambled over to the threadbare rug before the gas fire, circled it a couple of times and flopped down and also fixed Kilford with an unwavering stare.

Kilford pulled a notebook out of his jacket pocket.

"You'll know why I'm here."

"I reckon it'll be about that Betts carry-on."

"That's right."

The interview proceeded on predictable lines. Nixon confirmed that he wanted to drop the matter, evaded Kilford's attempts to get him to say why and was unmoved by the policeman's arguments (half-hearted because he didn't believe them himself), that it would be in Nixon's best interests to pursue the complaint.

Kilford went through the motions, out of professional pride and a sense of obligation to Tam MacFarlane, but he knew he was on a hiding to nothing. As Nixon whined out some excuse, Kilford's attention was taken by the dog, which paused in its scratching to stand up and then, crouched and trembling, proceeded to crap on the rug. Kilford was transfixed, not so much by the dog, as by the Nixon family, none of whom spared it or its evacuations so much as a glance. Nor did they seem much to notice the subsequent stench that soon had Kilford gagging. Oh God, he thought, I've got to get out of here. He brought the interview to a hurried conclusion, stuffed the notebook back in his pocket and got to his feet.

"Well, Ray, I strongly advise you to think about what I've said. And, if you don't take this any further, I strongly advise you not to waste our time in future.

You might be hearing from DS MacFarlane."

Nixon nodded and stood to walk him to the door. Kilford stepped out into the fresh air, or as fresh as air ever got on the Villette Road, then drew a grateful breath. He headed down the path, negotiated the gate again and was half way across the road to his car, when he heard Nixon's voice behind him.

"Oi, coppa!"

Oh Christ, now what? Reluctantly, he stopped and turned.

"Ha'way man. You've forgot yer dog."

§

Graham Morrison ('Bob Marley' to his friends, thanks to his dreadlocks), sat in the Black Diamond sharing a midday pint of snakebite with Callum Wright. Callum was a sort of friend. Not a mate exactly, but someone worth knowing – because he knew one of two other people worth knowing. Bob's circle of friends wasn't as wide as it had once been. People he'd known at school or back in Biddick had grown wary of him and the kind of company he kept, the kind that hung out on the Sulgrave Estate, for example.

They sat in companionable silence. Callum gnawed at his thumbnail and Bob shredded a beer mat.

Callum broke the silence.

"Oh, fucking hell!" He had his back to the wall and was facing the pub's front door.

Bob swivelled on his stool to follow Callum's gaze, to see a tall, well-built figure entering. He was dark, unshaven and with penetrating eyes that darted around the pub's interior. Cautious instinct made Bob avoid them, instead he looked at Callum.

"Who the shit's that then?"

"It's only fucking Karl Wrathall."

"Who?"

"You din't want to know. Horrible, nasty bastard."

Broke out of Darlington nick once."

Bob covertly observed Wrathall, who'd taken a seat across the room and was already in conversation with some guy Bob only vaguely knew.

Callum stood. "I'm going for a tab." Bob nodded.

Callum walked out, then Bob's Adam's apple jerked as the man Wrathall turned and stared at him, before rising and approaching. His expression was forbidding, but as he drew near a brief smile appeared. It wasn't convincing. Bob ran a nervous hand up the back of his neck, teasing his dreadlocks.

"You Bob…Marley?"

Bob nodded. Wrathall took the stool that Callum had vacated.

He held out a hand. "I'm Karl."

Bob shook his hand. He swallowed.

Wrathall's eyes fixed on him, unblinking. "You owe Barry Fenwick for some brown: is that right or what?" Bob nodded.

"I bought the debt off Barry. You owe me now Bob." Bob didn't like the way this conversation was going. He eyed the door of the pub, gauging the distance and his chances of making it before this bastard had time to react. Not good.

"I can pay. I'll get you the money - no bother." Wrathall shook his head. "There's no rush. I'm a patient man."

"Oh. Right. Er…nice one…"

"I might want you to do me the odd favour though."

Bob swallowed again. "What sort of favour like?" Wrathall rubbed his jaw and looked around the pub. "I hear you've got a car?"

"A Polo, yeah."

"It's legit and the bizzies haven't got it marked, is that right?"

"Yeah."

"I might want you to drive me on a few jobs."

"What sort of jobs?"

Wrathall shook his head. "Not the sort of jobs I can talk about here man. And not the sort of jobs you can talk about anywhere – ever. Not if you don't want to get badly hurt that is, very fucking badly hurt. Do you follow me Bob?"

Bob's Adam's apple did another dance.

He gave a couple of eager nods.

"Yeah, yeah. No prob."

Wrathall's smile made a brief reappearance.

"Good, we're okay then. You're from Biddick?"

"Yeah."

"Nice place. Dad got his own business, that right?"

"Yeah. Taxi firm."

Wrathall nodded.

"I hear you knock about Sulgrave?"

"A bit."

"Know people there?"

"One or two, aye."

"Ever met a red-haired lass called Eva Devlin?"

"Er… I know Eva, yeah."

"Give me her address, Bob."

§

Kilford parked the Fiesta behind the station. An unlovely, functional 1970s block of concrete and glass, it was the home of Sunderland Area Command of Northumbria Police and it was his place of work. After making a detour to the dog pound, he entered the front office, nodded at the officers behind the desk and climbed the stairs, at the top of which, on the other side of a landing, was the door to the DSU, Dedicated Source Unit. The door was kept locked, and, as per protocol, he had to knock and identify himself before being allowed in. Protecting the identity of a source was a matter of life and death and the fewer people who might see papers in that room or overhear telephone conversations, the better. Even the DI needed permission to enter, as it could be that members of the unit might be engaged on a sensitive case, perhaps reporting directly - and only to - the Command's Chief Superintendent.

Kilford's partner and loyal friend Bull opened the door. Bull's wife and family knew him as Matthew Miles, but to his colleagues he was Bull, short for Bullhead, due to his claimed resemblance to the same. Kilford believed Bull wore his hair in a severe crewcut to downplay the size of his head. It wasn't just the head: Bull was thickset, but, for all that, he was surprisingly nimble on his feet. He was also quick-witted and dry: he was no fool. From Kilford's experience, when he did have something to say, it was worth listening to. They exchanged nods and grunts and Kilford closed the door. The office was barely large enough for the five desks and accompanying filing cabinets it contained. Accommodating the five detectives of the DSU, and with a large glass window on one wall, it made for an uncomfortable working environment in winter and an unbearable one in summer. With distaste, Kilford noted that the occupant of one of the desks, Shifty Blair, was, as usual, sweating copiously from the back of his head, as he concentrated on his rapid, staccato one-finger typing. Older than the others, in his late thirties, ginger hair, thin and shabby, Shifty was an experienced officer but with a doubtful reputation.

Kilford's expression softened as he acknowledged Shifty's partner, DC Angela Hartnack, Knackers. She'd only been with the unit for a few months and, a blonde, she was easy to get on with, as well as being easy on the eye.

The fifth member of the team was its leader, DS Cliffy White. Well over six-foot and a keen rugby player, he shared one physical characteristic with Bull, hence his nickname Blockhead. Kilford gave him a wary glance, gauging whether he had any inkling that one of his DCs had spent the first half of the morning on a time wasting job for Tam MacFarlane, but Blockhead, engrossed in paperwork, didn't seem to notice him. Kilford slung his Reebok jacket over the back of his chair and sat. Knackers laughed.

"What's so funny like?"

She gestured at her computer screen.

"I've just got the IS screen up. Looks like the boss has been at it again. In bother, on the drink at the weekend and visited by the uniformed lads. The job's not been closed off. Look!"

Chairs were scraped back, as all four male detectives crowded round Knackers' desk to look at the incident screen on her computer and to laugh at DI Steve Scarratt's latest adventures. The head of Sunderland Area CID, Scarratt (known out of earshot as Rocky), was an old fashioned cop, who ruled his detectives with a firm hand, but who'd defend them to the hilt against the senior ranks that he despised. To Rocky Scarratt – hard-bitten and hard-biting – the world was not separated into sheep and goats, but rather into arseholes and fucking arseholes and, while he could just about tolerate the former, he'd no time for the latter. He was of that generation of cops who worked hard and played hard and playing hard for Rocky often resulted in savage physical retribution from Mrs Scarratt or in fisticuffs with some fucking arsehole he'd got into heated discussion with in one of the pubs or clubs of North Tyneside.

"Aye, his face is scratched again," said Bull. "Looks like he's been scrapping with his lass. Says he's fallen in the roses again. Same shit as last month."

"He's unbelievable," said Kilford. "Where's he at now?"

"He's upstairs with the Super, getting his arse kicked," said Blockhead.

Kilford left them laughing. He slipped out of the office, turned right down the corridor and made his way to the gym. He entered, found what he was looking for, and then continued round the corridor until he reached the DI's office. He tapped lightly on the frosted glass. There was no reply, he looked around, then depressed the door handle and peered inside. Empty. He darted in, placed the boxing glove he'd collected from the gym on Rocky's desk, chuckled and left. He continued following the circuit of the corridor until he came to the Intelligence Unit office, which ran all along the west side of the building. This housed the LIOs, or local intelligence officers, mainly civilian researchers, and FIOs, or field intelligence officers, who were cops, who developed the intelligence provided by the DSU officers. On that morning, it also contained an IT technician whom Kilford vaguely recognised and who, he noted, was wearing a blue Reebok jacket identical to the one he's left over his chair back. Kilford nodded at him as the technician dropped to his knees to tinker with the wiring under one of the desks.

Kilford walked along between the desks, exchanging words with the various occupants. At the end of this office was a second door into the DSU and en route sat an FIO, Liam Hall. Kilford stopped by that desk to discuss a report Hall was compiling on the basis of intelligence supplied by one of Kilford's sources. That done, Kilford knocked on the DSU door and, this time, Knackers opened it for him. He thanked her, savouring her smile, when suddenly an almighty roaring came from the far end of the Intelligence Unit.

"Right! Where the bastard hell is he? Where's he at, the little arsehole?"

It was the unmistakable voice of Detective Inspector Steven Scarratt. Rocky in full cry. Kilford, fearing he might be the subject of Rocky's wrath, squeezed himself further into the DSU, struggling against his colleagues who had rushed to the door, craning to see what was happening. Kilford peered round that door to see Rocky charge into the Intelligence Unit.

Dark haired, dapper and normally impassive, he was now raging, his face red and in his hand he clutched a boxing glove.

"Where is the little - ? Ahh..."

He stopped and surveyed the IT technician who was still kneeling, impervious to the noise, working on his cabling: an IT technician who was wearing a Reebok jacket identical to Kilford's and whose backside was presented to Rocky.

The DI vigorously rubbed his hands together.

"Right, you twat, pay back."

He ran the three paces that separated him from the prone figure and landed his elegantly shod foot on the technician's arse with a force and follow through that would have impressed Jonny Wilkinson. There was a stunned silence, relieved only by the crack of the technician's head contacting with the underside of the desk. The LIOs and the FIOs and the members of the DSU, still crowded in their office doorway, all looked on, mesmerised.

The spell was broken as Rocky noticed the DSU detectives and, in particular, Kilford, who was still trying to squeeze behind the door. Then Rocky looked back at the technician, rubbing his head and struggling to his feet.

Several things happened at once. The technician hurled himself at the DI's throat. Two FIOs standing nearby had the presence of mind to grab him and keep him, spitting and snarling, away from his assailant. "Oh my God," gasped Rocky. "I'm really sorry mate. I thought you were him."

He pointed at Kilford. He continued pointing at him and, above the roars of laughter that now reverberated through the entire first floor of Sunderland nick, Rocky could be heard bellowing.

"You! In my office! Now! You fucking arsehole"

§

Dan Kilford received the third bollocking of the day and his second from Vicki, when he arrived home for tea.

It wasn't meant to be like that.

He'd made a special effort to get home early, to cut the lawns surrounding their neat semi, to help Natalie with her homework and to read Beth a bedtime story without dropping off to sleep while they watched her favourite programme, The Tweenies.

Vicki had a point, he knew that. He did work long hours and, when he was off duty, he was seldom off his phone. He didn't have to do it, they didn't need the overtime and it wasn't like he didn't have a happy home life – though Vicki was starting to make it a bit bloody fraught. No, he just wanted to be the best copper he could be. This career was important. His last one, as a promising professional footballer, just making Newcastle United's first team had gone down the toilet with a knee injury. He was buggered if this one would. As a budding football star, he'd been somebody special. That had been a good feeling, and he wanted to feel, at least some of that, again. It's not like he hadn't explained this to Vicki, but she couldn't – or wouldn't - understand.

Still, tonight he had a peace offering. He'd got the girls a dog hadn't he?

Keen not to spoil the surprise, he opened the kitchen door quietly and, finger to his lips, he motioned Vicki to come out to the driveway where he'd parked. Wiping her hands on a tea towel and looking puzzled, she did as she was asked. "What is it Dan?"

"I've got the girls a present."

He took her to the back of the car and, with a "ta daa" flourish, opened the hatchback.

Looking out at them, tail wagging tentatively, was the German Shepherd Kilford had adopted that morning. Bull, having given free range to his creative imagination, had christened it Crapper, but Kilford was keeping that to himself.

He looked from the dog to Vicki. She looked from the dog to him.

"What's this?" Something in her voice stilled Crapper's tail and made him cower back into the car.

"It's a dog…for the girls, like. They wanted one. You all wanted one."

"This" she jerked a thumb at the car "is not what we had in mind."

"What's wrong with him?"

"I really don't think you know, do you?"

"What?"

"We thought a puppy, you know, like a sweet little Lab, the kind that runs off with the toilet paper. Not some bloody flea-bitten, scabby backstreet mutt like this. What kind of a man…? Oh God give, me strength."

"But…when he's had a bath…"

She slammed the hatchback, cutting short a whimper from Crapper.

"Get it out of here before the girls see it."

Kilford sighed. He didn't seem to be able to do right for doing wrong.

§

Jordan Ratcliffe was walking through Sunderland's Mowbray Park, towards the Winter Gardens. His hood was up, his shoulders hunched and moving rhythmically back and forth as he walked. He was no longer conscious of it, but it was a walk he'd adopted, it said something about him: that he was street-wise, nobody's fool, an image reinforced by his habit of always talking out of the side of his mouth, letting his words out into the world with miserly care. He was Ratty and he knew the way the world worked, he'd been around. He'd certainly been inside a few times – the fruits of a career of shoplifting, burglary, robbery and drug dealing.

Knowing what was what, earned you respect.

Eva respected him. She looked up to him. He taught her stuff and looked out for her. She was from some poncy family down South, been spoiled in some ways. Innocent – that was the word. But he looked after her, taught her what was what, and she respected him for that.

He liked looking out for her. She was canny, for all her prissy ways, and he liked her. He liked her a lot actually – a fuck of a lot.

His phone trilled in his hoodie pocket. He pulled it out.

It was Bob Marley.

"Bob. How're ya doin' mush?"

"Ratty!" Bob's voice was urgent. "It's Eva. She's in the shit man."

"What yer on about?"

"Know a bloke called Wrathall?"

Ratcliffe felt a lurch in his stomach.

"I've heard of 'im"

"He's been asking after Eva."

"Yeah?"

"I'm sorry man. I think I've dropped a bollock. I've told him where she lives."

Ratty took the phone away from his ear and looked into the distance, barely aware of Bob's voice babbling away in his hand. He jabbed the end call button and returned the phone to his pocket. He started walking again, faster now, towards the bus station. He had to get back to Washington, back to the Sulgrave. It took him the best part of an hour. He made his way into the estate – distinguished by being the cheapest housing in the UK – through its labyrinthine concrete courtyards and stairwells until he reached Eva's flat.

The door was unlocked. He walked in.

She was sitting on the sofa, head down and she didn't look up. In the centre of the room was a tall, broad bloke. He stared at Ratty. Ratty had never seen him before, but he knew this had to be Wrathall. There were no formal introductions. Wrathall looked Ratty up and down.

"Who the fuck are you?"

"I live here."

Wrathall smiled and shook his head.

"No, you don't. Not anymore. I live here now. See, me and Eva go back a long way. Don't we pet?" She sniffed.

"I said: don't we pet?"

She looked up and nodded and Ratty took in the tear filled eyes and the split lip.

Wrathall jerked a thumb at the door. "Now you'll fuck off if you know what's good for yer." So Ratty fucked off.

CHAPTER THREE

Kilford tapped on the door of the DSU. Knackers opened up and smiled a greeting. Kilford entered, nodding to Blockhead and Shifty.

"Bull not in?" he asked Knackers, removing his jacket. "Rang in, he's got a dentist's appointment. Monday morning of all times! He'll be in shortly. Here, I've made you a coffee. It's probably cold by now."

"Thanks pet. Aye, I had to go over to the pound, see to Crapper and give Pooch half a bottle of scotch to keep him sweet."

PC John Booth had responsibility for the station's dog pound and, as a consequence, was fondly known as Pooch. He liked dogs – which was fortunate in his role – but was growing increasingly pissed off at the new lodger foisted on him by Kilford. Kilford wasn't too happy about the situation either, as he'd have to spend part of his lunch break walking Crapper.

"Why'd you bother?" asked Knackers.

He shrugged.

"I dunno. I suppose 'cos I know what it's like being in the doghouse."

She laughed.

"You mean with Rocky?"

He shook his head, sat at his desk and swallowed some coffee.

"Rocky's the least of my problems."

She shot a quick glance at Shifty, who had his head buried in a filing cabinet, and at Blockhead, who was engaged in a heated telephone conversation. All the same, she leaned conspiratorially over the desk towards Kilford. As she did, his eyes were drawn to the cleavage revealed by the open top two buttons of her blouse.

She lowered her voice.

"Domestic trouble?"

"You could say that. Y'know, pressure of work, not enough time at home."

"Tell me about it. My bloke and I split over it."

"I didn't know you'd been married." She shook her head.

"We just had a place together. But when I was doing training, he found he was no longer centre of attention and the rows started. So, I know what it's like, so…if you need a shoulder to cry on…"

Kilford's gaze flitted between her shoulder and her cleavage. He cleared his throat then jerked at a knock on the door. Grateful, he leapt to his feet to open it.

It was Bull.

"How y'doin' man?" asked Kilford.

"Im all bloody numbed up." Bull gestured to his cheek. Bull settled behind his desk, which Knackers now vacated, volunteering to make him a coffee. Bull and Kilford exchanged less small talk than usual, as he struggled to talk through his numbed mouth. Drinking coffee also proved challenging and a thin stream of the liquid was soon dribbling down his cheek. Kilford grinned and settled down to his paperwork. This included a faxed report from the Force Intelligence Bureau, based at HQ in Ponteland.

He waved the sheet under Bull's nose.

"Seen this?"

Bull peered at it.

"Wrathall? Oh aye, they rang about it Friday, while you were out."

Kilford read the report. It informed them that one Karl Wrathall had been released from HMP Bradford. It carried a summary of his record and stated that his residence on release would be with his father and gave an address in Sunderland. It also carried a photograph. Kilford studied it. The face that stared back was similar to mug shots anywhere in the world, the hint of defiance in the thousand yard stare, the badge of a professional criminal.

"Know 'im?" asked Kilford.

"Naah. Seems like a nasty bastard though. Robbery, firearms offences and a prison break-out." Kilford wrote out a summary for inclusion in the uniform shifts' briefings: day shift, back shift and then night shift. Another copy would be attached to the bulletin board. All to flag up that one of the more serious players – and a nasty bastard to boot – had, once more, been released onto the streets. "Shifty," he said, when he'd finished. "Will you type this up for us?"

"Stick it on the pile."

Shifty Blair had many shortcomings as a detective. He was untrustworthy, unreliable, lazy and often strayed onto the wrong side of that fine line which divided perks of the job from corruption. They'd lost count of the times his transgressions had led to him being ejected from CID and put `back in blue', but, his inexplicably good relationship with the Chief Super, always led to reinstatement. However, for all his shortcomings, he was an accomplished one-fingered typist and there was an unspoken agreement in the unit that he escaped part of the burden of more demanding police work in return for the loan of that skill.

Kilford skimmed the sheet onto Shifty's desk and looked up at another knock on the door.

He opened it, this time to reveal George, the station handyman. A squat, ex-miner, with a shaven head and no neck, George had been patching up the station's jerry-built fittings for a few years, but, cynics noted, his experience never seemed to add to the durability of his own handiwork. He was holding a shelf and an electric drill.

"Alright George?"

"Aye."

"What y'after?"

"I've come to put this shelf up. Where d'you want it?"

"On the bloody ceiling mate," said Bull. "It's the only bastard space left in this shithole." Kilford stepped back to let George in.

"George, y'sure it's for in here, mate?"

"It'll be to store Blockhead's dinner plates – fat twat," offered Bull again. "Or his overtime forms." Blockhead didn't look up, but raised two fingers in Bull's direction.

"It's for the sex offender files, or so I'm told," said George. "The DI sent us."

"Ha'way George man," said Bull. "You must be wrong."

"Hang on," said Kilford. "I'll have a word with the DI." He squeezed past George and made his way to Rocky's office. He was thankful for an opportunity to re - establish amicable relations with his DI, following Friday's unfortunate arse-kicking incident. He tapped on the door's window and interpreted the answering grunt to be an invitation to enter.

"Boss, George is in our office with a shelf."

Rocky, seated behind his desk, looked at Kilford over the top of his reading glasses.

"Huh uh. Aye, that's right, it's for those sex offender files – forty two of 'em."

"Sex offender files? What d'you mean?"

"Aye, you're in charge of 'em. As of now?"

"You're joking! How's that like?"

"'Cos I said so, so get on with it."

"Boss, how am I supposed to look after this? I've got snouts to run."

"Tough shit, Look, I know you're busy, but there's no one else. You and your chubby mate can have overtime to look after them – twenty hours a month.

Now shut the door."

"We'll never keep on top of 'em."

Rocky threw his pen onto his desk and pulled his glasses from his head, his voice rising.

"Right! Forty hours and that's it. Shut the door. Here –" he opened his drawer and took out a bound document. "Get your head round that."

He tossed the document at Kilford who caught it and looked at the title: *Sex Offenders Act 1997*

"Thanks a lot boss."

"You're fucking welcome."

Kilford closed the door and swore. Forty hours overtime! Oh Vicki was just going to love this.

§

Ratty had his pride.

But he also had a well-honed survival instinct. So, although the former had been dented by Wrathall's unceremonious ejection of him from Eva's flat and her life, the latter made him cautious. Sure, he didn't want to take it lying down but, he'd no illusions, if he challenged Wrathall directly, he would he lying down, in intensive care – or in a funeral parlour.

And it wasn't just a matter of pride. Eva had come to mean a lot to Ratty and he was missing things about her, things he'd never noticed when she was around: the way she smiled, the way she talked – shit like that. It also gnawed at him to think what she might be going through at the hands of that bastard Wrathall. No, Ratty had to do something. But, whatever it was he did, he wasn't going to do in a hurry. No way, Ratty was too fly for that, he wasn't going to go jumping in like some wanker. No, sooner or later, there'd be an opening and then he'd be in like a rat up a drainpipe.

Until then, he'd watch and wait.

To do that, he had to stay on the Sulgrave, so he wheedled and cajoled and bribed his way onto kipping on a couple of mates' sofas who lived on the estate. That was enough. He didn't need to mount an elaborate surveillance operation to find out what Wrathall was up to. Wrathall's presence on the Sulgrave soon made itself felt – in every corridor, walkway and piss stained stairwell.

Wrathall's reputation as a hard man and a head case cowed the estate's residents enough to make it easy for him to establish himself as top dog within days of his arrival. This meant he could extract regular tributes of deference and of drugs. The more foolhardy dealers tried to avoid the latter, but Wrathall was ruthless in his taxing. This could be painful for dealers who'd keep their stash concealed in their anuses, even more traumatic, if they secreted it further up – on the second shelf. As for those who kept a couple of wraps behind their foreskin…

It pained Ratty to see that this not only allowed Wrathall to feed his own, and Eva's addiction, but also to dole out the odd reward to those who did him favours. One of these, Ratty was annoyed to observe, while peering over the edge of a walkway balcony, was Bob Marley. He watched Bob take what was obviously a wrap off Wrathall, cringe in thanks, and then scuttle away. Ratty's mood wasn't improved the following morning when he bumped into Eva.

He intercepted her when she was hurrying back from the Spar, clutching a plastic carton of milk, head down against a buffeting wind that whipped round the corners and into the gullies of the Sulgrave, wet from a light rain.

"Eva," he said, stepping in front of her.

She looked up startled.

"Oh, hi Ratty." She looked round, her eyes darting, clearly afraid of witnesses who might report back to Wrathall.

"How's it goin'?" he asked and offered her a cigarette, which she took, with quick nervous fingers.

"'S'all right," she said and accepted a light.

"D`you…er…fancy getting together sometime…just for a natter, like?"

She took a deep drag, looked around and again, gave a thin smile and shrugged.

"Eva?"

She looked him in the eye, then down at her trainers. She took another draw on her cigarette, supporting her elbow in her cupped hand.

"Look Ratty, I don't want to do anything to piss him off."

"You scared?"

"It's not just…Look…he gets me smack…y'know?" She took another drag, so intense the end of the fag blazed into fierce life, and then she tossed it into the litter strewn bushes.

"Sorry Ratty, I've got to go."

She elbowed past and scurried towards her stairwell. Ratty made to follow, then stopped. He swore, then watched her disappear into the building's gloom. He took out his phone and dialled a number.

"Bob?" he said, when a familiar voice answered.

"Aye, canny. Listen man, we've got to meet."

Ratty met Bob that afternoon in a café in Southwick, far enough away from the Sulgrave that there'd be little chance of being seen by anyone who might know them. It wasn't the kind of place that employed smiling baristas – rather a sullen Polish woman with forearms like hams and a hacking cough. Ratty bought Bob a coffee and they chose a table in a far corner, as far from the window as possible.

"Thanks for the coffee," said Bob. He took a slurp and scalded his lip. "Balls!"

Ratty was in no mood to smile. He waited while Bob finished dabbing at his mouth.

"So," said Bob, at last. "What d'you want to see me about? What's up?"

Ratty shrugged. "Just a catch up."

"You sounded like it was urgent."

"Just wondered if you'd seen Eva lately."

"Off 'n' on"

"How's she doin?"

"Seems a'right. Y'know she's shacked up with that Wrathall now? He's taken over her ken"

"How could I not shagging know that, seein' as how I used to live there me self?"

Bob muttered something apologetic and studied the froth on his coffee. Ratty breathed hard through his nose and toyed with a sugar sachet.

"What's the craic with Wrathall mush?" he asked. "He's top dog on the Sulgrave, man. Everybody's shit scared of him. He's taxing every fucker that has any H, he –"

"Yeah, I know all that. Tell me something I don't know."

"Like what?"

"I've been watching him. I've seen him talking to people. I've seen him talking to you. What's he up to?" Bob eyes darted left and right and he rubbed his hand through his dreadlocks.

"Frigging hell, Ratty, he's a hard bastard. I don't want to –"

"He'll never know. Not from me. We're not exactly on speaking terms."

"Suppose not." Bob rubbed his forehead and licked his lips.

"Come on Bob, man. What's he up to?"

"He's bringing gear up from the Boro. He's got a supplier down there." Bob looked round again, and then leaned over the table, excitement in his eyes. "You'll never frigging guess what the bastard wants me to do…"

§

Barbara glanced at her watch: ten to ten. She looked out over the counter and through the glass door of Seaham's Connor's Mini Market. It was dark outside. She could close in ten minutes, cash up and lock up, take the five-minute walk home, get in, draw the curtains, have a light supper and get to bed. She preferred working the late shift. After Tom had died four years ago, she found the loneliness biting hardest in the evenings. Working for Bill Connor's convenience store didn't just help her pension go farther, it kept her from climbing the walls. Tomorrow would be a good day, though. Aye, she was looking forward to it: a pub lunch with her daughter Tina. The thought cheered her.

The door chime went off, she looked up. It was a young man, wearing one of those hoodies, which shaded his face, but she could make out some hair, done in that awful style, like a black person – dreadlocks or something.

"Good evening," she said.

Just a grunt from him. He walked down the far aisle to the back of the shop. Probably after drink. But, within a few seconds he reappeared, empty handed.

"Can I help you pet?"

Another grunt and a head shake and he left the shop, door chiming again. Barbara shrugged. Barely five minutes to go now.

§

Wrathall was in the passenger seat of Bob Marley's Polo, staring across the road at the brightly lit shop front of Connor's Mini Market. Bob appeared in the doorway, opening it. Wrathall was opening the car door even before Bob gave a discreet thumbs up. They crossed in the middle of the road, Bob heading for the car, Wrathall for the shop.

"It's empty, just an old biddie, on her own" muttered Bob.

Wrathall said nothing. As he reached the shop door, he pulled down the ski mask that was covering his hair so that it now hid his face.

This was the apparition that Barbara saw, as she looked up as the door chimed again. Her mouth opened in an O shape and she put her hands up to her face. Wrathall took his right hand from inside his leather jacket – it held a long kitchen knife. The old biddie gave a whimper, which might have forced its way out into a fully-fledged scream had not Wrathall reached the counter in two swift paces to give a back hander with the fist holding the knife. She gasped and reeled and then he grabbed a handful of her curly grey locks and pulled her close to him, her terrified face looking into his. He gripped her and raised her, by her neck, a couple of inches from the ground. She gurgled and he put the knife point under her quivering chin. "Open the fucking till. And put everything you've got in a carrier bag. Make a shagging noise and you'll get some of this."

§

Bob sat behind his steering wheel, car engine running and his heart pounding. He kept looking round, hoping fervently that no last-minute shopper was going to patronise Connor's. Then the door opened and Wrathall was sprinting across the road. He pulled the passenger door open, tossed a carrier into the back and dropped onto the seat, pulling up the ski mask.

He slammed the door shut.

"Get the fuck out of here!"

But Bob had the car in gear before he'd finished speaking.

Inside Connor's Mini Market, Barbara lay behind the counter, releasing great gasping sobs, along with the contents of her bladder, oblivious as yet to the pain from the broken nose the masked man had given her – even after she'd given him the money.

Back in the car, Bob felt his stomach doing somersaults and he fought an urge to put his foot down. The last thing they needed now was to get pulled for speeding. He was aware of Wrathall on his left rummaging in the carrier bag he'd brought from the shop.

Then the big man spoke: "Right Bob, pull over as soon as you can, so we can count our score."

"I just want to get the fuck out of it. I'm shittin' meself man."

"Do as you're told and keep a fucking lid on it. Are you listening?"

"Yeah, but"

"No buts. Do as you're told "

Once out of Seaham, Bob pulled into a car park at the head of a path down to the beach. His was the only car in it. He hoped to Christ, no passing bizzie would stop by to make inquiries.

"Turn the light on," said Wrathall.

"What?"

"The inside light! Hasn't this thing got an inside light?" Bob reached up above the rear-view mirror and flicked a switch, illuminating the inside of the car, Wrathall's gaunt face and staring eyes and – Bob realised - with his stomach going like a spin dryer – advertising their presence to any curious patrol car driver.

He watched Wrathall rifle through the bag.

"I can frigging tell you now, this is no good," he said.

"This is shite, we won't get an eighth of gear for this."

"What we goin' to do then. I don't want anything. I just want to go home."

"Won't be happening. We go again."

"Oh for Christ's sake!"

"You'll do as I bastard tell you, or else. Got that, you snobby prick?"

Bob swallowed.

"Well?" demanded Wrathall, a dangerous light in his eye.

"Yeah…yeah."

"Right, get this car down to Peterlee. I'll keep you right I know a good score, but get your foot down; this one shuts at half ten …two old biddies, it'll be easy. Now go!"

CHAPTER FOUR

Kilford became aware of the insistent chirping of his mobile. It was getting louder. He woke up. He was in bed, beside Vicki. One of his mobiles was ringing, he couldn't remember which ring tone it was. "Oh for God's sake!" hissed Vicki. "Just answer the bloody thing."

"Sorry," he whispered and scrabbled out of bed, grabbing both phones from the top of his bedside drawers. He stumbled out onto the landing, trying to close the door gently behind him, while juggling the phones. He had his own personal mobile and a police phone, the number of which was given to informants. It wasn't an arrangement that Kilford or his colleagues were happy with; if an informant's phone fell into the wrong hands, a detective's number could be found on it. Not only that, but if two snouts knew each other and one suspected the other of being an informant, they could confirm it by checking the other's phone.

The system was fraught with danger.

It was his police phone that was ringing. As he hurried down the stairs, Kilford saw the name of the caller: John Henderson.

All informants were given a pseudonym and this one belonged to Terry Armstrong, a small time drug dealer and petty thief. Kilford answered the call as he reached the foot of the stairs and headed for the kitchen.

"Terry, why, in God's name, are you ringing me at half three in the bloody morning?"

"Only time I can get to me self, like." Kilford turned the kitchen light on, pulled a stool from under the counter and hoisted himself onto it. He rubbed his eyes with the thumb and forefinger of his free hand and released a heavy sigh. "You still there Dan?"

"Yeah man, go on then."

"I've summat to tell you, about Del Whitehouse and Butch Watson."

"What?"

"They're planning to drop some nice cars for the alloys. They've eyed up a BMW on the Sulgrave."

"Is that happening tonight?"

"No, I just wanted you to know. I've been a bit quiet lately, haven't I?"

"Nae bother. We'll speak tomorrow Terry."

"It's just me contract's coming up for renewal. I wondered if you'd put in a word with Mr Scarratt for me."

It was the DI's role, as official controller of informants, to draw up initial contracts with them and he was responsible for their annual renewal. Terry had proved to be an increasingly erratic snout over recent months and probably realised that Rocky was coming to regard him as unreliable and unproductive.

Breathing hard, Kilford said: "We'll speak tomorrow mate, okay?" He hit the disconnect button and shook his head. He was pissed off with Terry for having woken him and Vicki for something that could have waited, but also disappointed. When he received a call on this mobile, a call from a snout, it always got the pulse racing and the adrenalin flowing, at the promise of some quality intelligence, something that would lead to something significant. Shit!

He left his phones on the kitchen counter and headed back to the stairs. At their foot, he saw that the landing light was now on and Vicki was leading Beth by the hand towards their room. Beth was rubbing her eyes and whimpering. He'd woken her too. Shit!

Vicki glared at him. "What time did you get in last night?"

"I dunno. About eleven."

"More overtime?"

"Aye, there's a lot on."

"You did eighty hours overtime last month. Looks like you might beat that this month. By the way, let me introduce you. Dan, this is Beth. Beth, meet your dad."

"I'll sleep on the couch."

"Good idea."

§

Kilford sat at his desk the next morning, stifling a yawn. He was tired and had a headache and was in a bad mood. He'd left home after a hasty breakfast of coffee and toast taken in an oppressive silence, broken only by Vicki clattering pots in the sink and banging them on the counters.

Bull seemed to detect his mood and said even less than usual. Knackers also busied herself in writing up interview notes, her early attempt at conversation with him, asking after Crapper, having been politely but firmly rebuffed. God, didn't he have enough domestic complications at the moment?

He had to come up with some way of mending fences with Vicki. Flowers? No, she'd throw them at him.

Take her out for a meal? When was he likely to get a free evening?

His desk phone rang. He picked it up.

"DC Kilford."

It was the front desk.

"There's a Ralph Wilkinson down here to see you."

"Just a sec." Kilford put his hand over the receiver and looked at Bull. "Who's Ralph Wilkinson?" Bull shrugged.

"Hang on, I'll check the CIS."

Bull was skilled at navigating the highways and byways of the Criminal Information System and within seconds was peering at his screen and reading across to Kilford.

"He's a sex offender, just convicted. Right little perv by the looks of it. Keeps feeling women's arses. Can't help himself."

"Takes all sorts I suppose. Right, let's go down and meet him. Bring the file mate. Oh, and one of those SOR1, Sex Offender's Registration Form, he'll have to sign one of those."

Once convicted, a sex offender had five days to attend a police station and register a home address. It was Kilford and Bull's responsibility to document this, do a full interview with the offender to be typed up and to make arrangements for a home visit.

Kilford took his hand from the receiver and said: "Okay Jean, we're on our way down. By the way, don't turn your back on him."

Knackers tittered. Kilford smiled at her, cleared his throat and followed Bull out of the office. Down at the front office, Kilford surveyed the people sitting or standing in the reception area.

"Ralph Wilkinson?" he asked the assembly at large. A short, frail man, looking nearer to seventy than sixty, with thin wispy grey hair and wearing a grimy, tan overcoat, got to his feet and took a couple of nervous steps towards them.

"Come through this way please," Kilford said and he and Bull led him to an adjacent interview room, where he was invited to sit, while they took two chairs on the opposite side of the table.

Kilford introduced himself and Bull. Wilkinson responded with brief, birdlike nods and with a squeaky, but educated voice,

"Pleased to meet you."

Kilford took the file and opened it while Bull took out a pen and began filling in the form.

"Where are you living Ralph?" asked Kilford.

"Flat 14, Trafalgar Walk. It's on the Sulgrave Estate"

"Nice."

Ralph gave a wry smile. "It has…character."

"Is that what you call it? How long have you been there?"

"I've just received the keys."

"Okay, we'll need to be down to visit you." Ralph raised his eyebrows.

"It's the law," said Bull.

Kilford talked through the details of Ralph's conviction and his record of sidling up to unsuspecting women of all ages, at bus stops, in shops and even in a church, and stroking their bottoms. For some time, the police had been receiving complaints about a phantom groper and eventually he'd been detained by an enraged husband. The relatively mild nature of his offences had initially resulted in a caution, but Ralph's urges were too strong and he'd been unable to resist a fondle too far. Sadly for him, on that occasion, he'd selected an off-duty policewoman for his unsolicited attentions.

It felt strange to Kilford. He and Bull had conducted scores of interviews and interrogations in this room, or ones like it. They'd sometimes had to deal with likeable rogues and, at others, with violent low-lifes, but there was always a certain familiarity in the conversation. It might be on a level of jokey banter in some cases, or scarcely concealed antagonism in others, but there was common ground, a common language. With Ralph, on the other hand, laughable though his crimes might be, it was like operating in a different sphere.

The conversation was formal, almost proper. "The magistrates warned you about your behaviour Ralph," said Kilford.

Ralph gave a solemn nod.

"If you offend again, you're going to jail. You know that, don't you?"

"Yes Mr Kilford, I realise."

"Good, well, we'll be in touch in a few days to see about popping round to your flat."

They got him to sign his form, then escorted him back to front office and saw him out of the building before making their way back upstairs.

"What d'you make of that then?" Kilford asked Bull.

"Frigging weirdo."

§

Back in the office they joked about Ralph and updated his file. Kilford looked at his watch: half eleven, soon time to walk Crapper before he went to get some lunch. What was he going to do about that bloody dog? Hadn't he got enough on his plate? He could only imagine Vicki's reaction if he told her he wasn't only doing eighty hours or more of overtime a month, but was also spending more than an hour a day walking the mangy hound she'd rejected so vehemently. His mood, which had been lightening, darkened again.

Then the phone rang.

He snatched up the receiver.

"DC Kilford."

Front office again.

"It's Jean. There's a Jordan Ratcliffe down here, says you've got some property for him." Under his breath he muttered: "God's sake, there's never a dull moment." Then louder: "Jean, is it still busy down there?"

"No, it's gone quiet."

"Okay, tell him to take a seat. We'll be down in two minutes."

It was 'we' because the procedure was that two detectives should always be present at an interview, not only to corroborate what was said, but also because it wasn't unheard of for some aggrieved citizen to visit the station with the sole intention of assaulting a particular officer. He looked at Bull and whispered: "Ratty's in the front office to see us." Bull reached for his pad and pen.

"Wonder what he wants."

"Dunno, but he shouldn't be here. Best let the boss know. Grab those tracky bottoms in that plastic bag." Informants were never supposed to come into a station voluntarily: the risks of being seen and word getting back to those who might suspect them of grassing were obvious, or should have been. If they did come in, tradecraft said they had to have a cover story, preferably a simple one. In Ratty's case, it was usually that he wanted to collect property that had been seized from him during some previous encounter with the police. Ratty was constantly being arrested, often for burglary and that involved the confiscation of his clothing for forensics. For these eventualities, the DSU team kept a collection of spare clothing and shoes, POFP property other than found property, much of it scrounged from the Property Office.

The pair made their way to the Detective Inspector's office, knocked and entered at the bellowed invitation. Rocky looked inquiringly at them over the top of his glasses.

"Boss," said Kilford, "Wayne Langley's downstairs and wants to speak to us."

Even with the DI, who knew every informant's real name, outside the DSU office, the pseudonym had to be maintained. Too many people could overhear and information had a habit of leaking out of police stations.

"What the hell's he doing, walking into a police station? The fucking arsehole."

"I don't know, I've not spoke to him yet."

"I know that, you arsehole. He shouldn't be just walking in here, it's frigging dangerous. Get his arse kicked when you see him."

"Okay boss, will do."

"Let me know the score after you've spoke to him."

As they were leaving the office and closing the door, Bull made a quick wanker motion with his right hand.

Kilford grinned.

"Oi!" Came a shout from behind.

"Don't you two arseholes be pulling faces or making cheeky shagging gestures." They laughed. "`Course not boss."

"How does he do that?" asked Bull.

Two minutes later, Kilford and Bull were once more sitting in the interview room, this time opposite Jordan – Ratty – Ratcliffe, aka Wayne Langley.

Bull had his notepad on the desk, a pen in his hand and, on the way in, he had placed a cigarette behind his ear. He'd given up smoking years ago, but it was a useful interview tool. Ratty was sitting back, swinging on the rear two legs of his chair, nervous.

"You're not supposed to be here Ratty," said Kilford. "You know that, don't you?"

"Aye, I know mate. I'm sorry."

"You'll be a shit sight sorrier if word gets out that you're talking to the bizzies. You won't be much of an informant with your jaw wired up and taking your meals through a straw."

"I'm sorry mate, it won't happen again."

"Okay. Right, before we get onto anything, before we start, what are you like at the minute?"

"I'm using a tenner bag a day, our lass is alright, we're cush."

A tenner bag was a wrap. Acceptable enough, if true, so as not to cast more than the usual doubt on the word of a snout. Kilford studied Ratty closely: he wasn't twitching, he didn't look to be off his head. He let the silence hang, let Ratty sweat. This one was sly and had been known to call an interview like this solely to gauge how much the police knew about one of his own jobs. Bull, playing along, yawning.

Ratty gestured towards the fag behind Bull's ear. "Can I have a tab like?"

Bull handed it to him, reached into his pocket for a lighter and leaned forward to light the fag. "You shouldn't be smoking in here, mind," he said. "Keep that tab under the table or you'll set the smoke alarm off."

Ratty took a deep drag, exhaled over his shoulder and darted his hand holding the fag under the table as told. Bull wafted at the smoke with his note pad. "Could I have a cup of tea with three sugars?" asked Ratty.

"No!" said Bull. "Frigging get on with it, You've got yer fag. Ha'way, what d'you want? We've got stuff to do.

What yer after?"

"It's good, but I want to know how much is in it for me."

"We can't say," said Kilford. "If it's good, you'll get looked after, y'know that."

Bull straightened his pad on the table, pen poised. Ratty took another pull on the fag before sticking it back under the table. This time he flapped his own hand to disperse the smoke.

"Y'know he's out? That mush Wrathall."

"Aye?"

"He's blaggin' and it's bad." The detectives looked at each other.

"Go on," said Kilford.

"He's done a couple o' blags o' shops. Y'must've heard of 'em."
"Where are they at, like?"
"Seaham and Peterlee."
"That's not on our patch mate, but go on."
"He's got a kid drivin'. He's legit, you'll know of him. Bob, Bob Marley."

Bull and Kilford exchanged another glance.

"Bob Marley?"

"Aye, a white Rasta kid, his father's got a taxi firm and he has a proper nice ken down in Washington Village."

"What's his real name?" asked Bull.

"Graham…er…Morrison." Bull scribbled it down.

"Why Bob?" continued Kilford.

Ratty became animated, the front legs of his chair hitting the floor.

"He's fucking shot nervous mate, he's well petrified of Wrathall, every bastard is, to be honest. He's crazy man, the bloke is a proper radgie. And he's sellin' some bad shit. Bob owes Wrathall's pal Barry Fenwick for a few bags, so Wrathall's took the debt. Bob's legit, he's not known to any of the bizzies."

Kilford suppressed an urge to lean forwards. He forced himself to sit back in his chair, anxious not to betray any eagerness. Likewise, Bull stared at the ceiling. "What's the craic with the job then?"

"He's done at least two in the last couple of days. Bob goes in first, walks round, eyes up the shop. He reckons he's fucked as the shops got cameras. He walks in and Wrathall goes in wearing a balaclava, fuck off 12-inch knife, he rags the staff, old biddies, drags them out of the back o' the shop. Bob's got the car runnin' outside, he's nae choice, he's terrified, he's absolutely shittin' it. Wrathall's taxin' people in Sulgrave. We've got nae choice. So, he's been busy mate."

"How d'you know this Ratty?"

"Bob's rang me. He's well shittin' it. Honest."

"Who else knows?"

"No-one else knows. Honest."

Kilford said nothing, contemplating Ratty, but his mind was racing. This was good stuff, if true. He rubbed his cheek and crossed one leg over another. Ratty took another drag, dropped his fag on the floor and crushed it under the toe of his trainer. His gaze darted from Kilford to Bull and back.

"So where's Wrathall living Ratty?" asked Kilford.

"Like I said, he's on the Sulgrave."

"Big place. Where exactly?"

Ratty's eyes flickered from side to side and he gave an embarrassed cough. "He's in my ken."

"What?"

"Not with me. He's kicked me out and moved in with our lass."

"So, this is personal is it Ratty?"

Ratty shrugged. "I want this Wrathall sorting. I'm kipping in a few pals kens in Sulgrave. I'm okay, honest."

Kilford rubbed his jaw, as if weighing the odds, before speaking.

"We know about Mr Wrathall. We know about his past. But, to be honest, what you're telling us is news. I'm going to have to make a few inquiries and a few phone calls and speak to our contacts in Durham Police. If it's right, it'll be a good earner for you."

"That's fucking cush, but what about getting me a few quid now, even a tenner?"

"I'll have to speak to the boss, you'll have to wait here a minute if you want any money."

"Bollocks to that man, I've got stuff on." Kilford shrugged.

"Suit yourself. I'll be in touch Ratty. Now, you try and get out of this station without being clocked and remember what you've been told about coming in.

Here, grab these tracky bottoms."

They filed out of the interview room, Bull stooping to pick up and pocket the cigarette butt. As soon as they'd seen Ratty leave the station, hurrying away, hood up, head down, darting glances to left and right, Kilford turned to his friend.

"Right Bull, I'll go and get the Boss, you go and let Blockhead know."

"Aye. Hey, this looks bloody good if it's true. That Wrathall's a proper target, this could be a right earner for us."

"Too right, but let's not get ahead of ourselves. Looks too good to be true."

Kilford made it to Rocky's office almost at a run. He knocked and his boss had barely finished his 'come in' before he had the door open and his head through. "Boss, we've just finished with Wayne Langley. Have you a few minutes to do a debrief in our office?"

"Looks good does it?"

"Yes Boss, he's on about Karl Wrathall. Reckons he's blagged a couple of shops in Durham's area and he's kicked him out of his flat and is living with his lass, Eva Devlin..."

Rocky rubbed his hands together vigorously. "Wrathall? That bastard? Brilliant! I'll be along in a minute, get everyone together. Oh, and good lad." A minute later, Kilford was back in the DSU office and told the team that the DI was on his way. Bull had briefed Blockhead, and Shifty and Knackers had been brought up to speed, so there was a palpable air of excitement. This was partly because of the prospect of a significant and high profile investigation and partly because of the enhanced overtime such an investigation would inevitably bring. Bull took from a shelf the team bugle. This had been acquired years ago, under long forgotten circumstances, and it was the custom to blow it through a window of the office, so that it could be heard by the nearby Proactive CID team, to taunt them with DSU's overtime windfall. The team grinned as Bull made for the window but Kilford's face was strained. More overtime! More grief on the home front.

As Bull was unlatching the window, there was a knock at the door, Blockhead unlocked it and Rocky entered. "I'll stick that trumpet up yer arse Bull, put the bloody thing down," was his opening pleasantry. "I've told you lot before, don't go out of your way to wind up everybody in the frigging nick, especially the Proactive team."

He grabbed the nearest chair and sat. He looked from Bull, to Kilford, to Blockhead.

"Right, get on with it, arseholes."

Blockhead signalled to Kilford to brief the DI on the Ratty interview. Kilford ran through it. Rocky asked a couple of questions, the last being: "Did you bollock the fucking arsehole for coming into the station?"

"Yes boss."

Rocky looked at Blockhead. "What d'you think?"

"Could be a load of shite but somehow I don't think so, that Ratty is normally cock on, the devious little bastard."

"Good." Rocky gave his hands a rub. "Right, you take charge of this and get onto Durham to find out if it's on the level. If it is, let's sort out a joint meeting here. We'll run the source side of it, but, if it is right, they'll look at the crimes; it's their patch."

"Okay boss, we'll ring their FIO and take it from there.

Shifty, get onto Durham and see what they know."

"Aye no bother, will do. I'll bell Budgie Burrows, he's got his finger on things down there."

Rocky gave his hands another quick washing and got to his feet.

"Right, get on with it arseholes and keep me informed.

Good stuff boys."

He left. Shifty closed the door behind. The team looked at each other for a few seconds, giving Rocky time to head back to his office. Then they looked at Bull.

"Tally fucking ho!" he said and sounded a resounding note on the bugle.

§

Wrathall opened the door and slid into the passenger seat of Bob's Polo, which had pulled up at one of the entrances to the Sulgrave Estate. He looked at Bob, who was staring straight ahead through the windscreen.

"You took your time," said Wrathall.

"I had to make a phone call. I was supposed to be having lunch with my folks."

"Lunch! Fucking listen to 'im. Were you going to stay on for tea and scones?"

"Very funny. What is it you want? Not another job? It's broad daylight, for Christ's sake."

"I need you to take me to Farringdon. And stop crapping yerself, it's not a job. Not yet."

Bob released an exasperated sigh and drove, through Sunderland, across the Wear and towards Farringdon, south west of the city centre. As they drew close, Wrathall began to give directions, until they pulled up on a quiet residential street of semis. "Wait here," he said. "I won't be long."

He got out of the car and crossed the road, to one house, that, though respectable, looked as if it had seen better days. He paused at the garden gate and looked at the building. There were a lot of memories associated with this place – not particularly good ones.

He walked up the garden and rang the doorbell. He waited a few seconds and nothing happened. He swore and pushed the bell for three long, continuous rings. Then he heard movement inside and detected a blurred figure through the frosted glass. The door was opened to reveal a short, thin man of late middle age, in cardigan and shapeless jeans. He was balding with strands of greasy dark hair combed over his crown.

"Karl," he said in a reedy voice.

"Dad."

Wrathall stepped past him into the hallway. His nose wrinkled at the musty smell, the smell of the home of an old, single man who'd long since stopped giving a shit. His father closed the door.

"You're out then?"

"Still on the ball. Yeah, I'm out and, if anyone asks, I'm staying here."

The other gave a glum nod. "Shall I put the kettle on?"

"Yeah, do that." Wrathall pushed open the door to the lounge. He was about to enter, but stopped on the threshold, staring into the room.

"Oh for shit's sake! Not again! What the fuck are they doing here?"

CHAPTER FIVE

Knackers was pressing up close against Kilford, her bare forearm warm against his, her long blonde hair, so close he could smell it. This intimacy was enforced; the DSU office was crowded, containing not only the whole team, but also the DI and DC Colin – Budgie - Burrows, a Durham Constabulary FIO, or Field Intelligence Officer, based in Chester-Le-Street. Budgie, good looking, dark-haired, in his late thirties, was sitting with a video player and screen set up on the desk in front of him. Leaning forwards on the desk to his left were Kilford and Knackers, to his right were Rocky and Blockhead and, behind him, craning over his shoulders, Shifty and Bull.

It was mid-afternoon of that same Tuesday. Following the debrief on the Ratty intelligence with the DI, Blockhead had phoned Budgie to ask whether Durham might have had a couple of nasty robberies that week.

"We have, really nasty. Please tell us you've got something."

"Source reported today. I think we need to get together."

"On my way."

Budgie had brought with him CCTV footage from robberies in Seaham and Peterlee. They had all reviewed the first tape of the Seaham job in silence. Budgie ejected the tape and inserted another. He fast forwarded, stopped, rewound and hit play. They could see the grainy black and white footage of the interior of a minimarket.

"Fraser's Convenience Store, Peterlee," explained Budgie.

The camera was focused on the store's till area. Two women, late middle age or early sixties, wearing some kind of light coloured tabards, stood out against a backdrop of shelves of cigarettes. They appeared to be bending over the open till drawer, cashing up. Then a corner of the screen was obscured as another figure entered the shot, revealed as he approached the till, as the rear view of a tall broad man. He swiftly approached the women. Something about him struck Kilford.

The two women look up, then eyes and mouths open in a silent movie scream. A long gleaming blade can be seen brandished in the man's right hand. Right up to the two women now, he deals one a backhander with his left hand and she goes down. He shifts the knife to his left and grabs the other woman by the back of her head.

"Oh God," gasped Knackers. "He's picking her up, he's lifting her off her feet."

He shakes the woman like a terrier shaking a rat, drops her, reaches down and grabs the other by the collar and drags her to her feet. Then he pushes and drags both women though a door behind the till. In the DSU nobody spoke. It was as though nobody was breathing.

After a minute the man appears in the doorway behind the till. For the first time they can see him from the front, but, as in the Seaham footage, with his hood up and with the quality of the film, his features are indistinguishable. He's clutching a carrier bag. He stops by the open till drawer, reaches in, grabs a handful of notes and stuffs them into the bag. He hurries to the front of the shop, towards the camera. The detectives crane forward to see his face, but nothing is clear in the shadows of his hood – apart from the intensity of his eyes, glaring straight into the camera lens, intense, malevolent.

Kilford however, as before, is struck by something that jars, but it's not the man's face. What is it?

He can't put his finger on it.

The man disappears from view. Budgie stops the recording. The time registers 22:35.

Budgie leaned back in the seat. Everybody in the room seemed to breathe out at once in a collective release of tension.

Budgie looked around at them.

"At Seaham he took barely three hundred quid. In this last one, he got away with a couple of hundred from the till and nearly another two thou' from the safe.

Three ladies are in hospital: Barbara Daniels, from Seaham, is recovering from a broken nose and shock. From the Peterlee job, Gaynor Anderson has concussion and a fractured cheekbone sustained in the back office when the robber kicked her in the head because she fumbled over opening the safe. The other lady, Julia Finn, is being treated for shock. None of them are going to get over this in a hurry."

"Bastard," breathed Knackers.

"Any descriptions?" asked Kilford.

Budgie shook his head.

"Useless. They were too traumatised for anything but vague shit. Can't even talk to Gaynor yet and I'm not optimistic. Otherwise, we've a witness reports seeing a VW Polo parked outside at the second job. Can't remember the colour and no idea on plate. Anyway, that's what we've got at the moment. What've you got for me? Got a name for this bastard?"

"We have," said Kilford. "We've got a snout today reporting that the main offender is Karl Wrathall."

"I've heard of him."

"I'll bet you have," said Rocky. "He's got some right form."

"Can we look at the tapes again?" said Kilford. "A few minutes before Wrathall goes in."

Budgie restarted and rewound the tapes as Kilford directed. This time they watched another smaller, hooded figure enter the shops, march in a few paces, turn and leave. In the Peterlee tape, as he was leaving, facing the camera, Kilford asked Budgie to freeze the frame. They contemplated the fuzzy image of a face, largely shaded by a hood.

"See there," said Kilford, leaning over and pointing.

"That's long hair at the side of his hood."

"Looks like dreadlocks, but he's not black," said Shifty.

"Let me present Mr Bob Marley," said Kilford.

Budgie looked at him blankly.

"The snout reported that a kid nicknamed Bob Marley, a white Rasta, is the driver on the job and recces the stores." Kilford glanced down at his notes. "Real name: Graham Morrison."

"Morrison? I wonder if he's anything to do with Harry Morrison," said Rocky.

"Who?"

"Before your time. Harry was a hard man in East Sunderland. Had his own gang. You crossed Harry Morrison at your peril. Did a couple o' stretches, came out, met a lass, got married and went legit, started his own business, taxis I think."

"Snout said Bob's dad has a taxi firm and lives in Washington Village."

"That'll be Harry." Rocky shook his head, as if in wonder at the resurfacing of this name, then he snapped himself back into the present with a gleeful hand rubbing. "Good stuff this lads, we need to get on top of this." He grew serious. "I mean it. We've all seen these tapes, this bastard's dangerous and, if he's allowed to carry on, some poor old lass is going to end up on a slab. I want everyone on this job until we get those two bastards locked up. Wrathall is one clever, sly, evil twat who's escaped from jail before now, so we need to plan. Y'know what I'm always telling yous?" Bull muttered under his breath: "It's the worst it's ever been."

The DSU team hid grins. Rocky swivelled to stare at Bull.

"What d'you say?"

"Er…nothing boss, just thinking aloud, talking to me self like."

"Don't, or I'll send you for frigging counselling. What I'm always telling you is, fail to plan, plan to fail. I want Wrathall and this numpty, Bob bloody Marley or Graham Morrison, or whatever the hell you call him, housed A.S.A.P. Find out where they're living and arrange a TSG team to lift 'em and turn their places upside down. Cliffy can arrange that with TSG. Budgie, we'll run the snout side of the operation and your lot will have to pick up the arrest and interviews, unless things change." Budgie nodded.

Rocky looked at Kilford and Bull.

"Are we happy about the provenance of this intel? Are we confident that fucking arsehole Ratty wasn't in on the job, wasn't him doing the driving?"

"Don't think so boss," said Kilford. "But, you can't be sure with him, he's a slippery bastard."

"Something here boss," announced Shifty. He had moved to sit at his own desk and was looking at his computer screen. "On the CIS. Graham Morrison has form: possession and theft. Last address at his dad's place in Washington Village. You're right, he's Harry Morrison's lad. And, recently seen driving a VW Polo."

"If it's his car, he'd have been driving it," said Kilford. "We know he did the recce, so that doesn't leave a role for Ratty."

Rocky nodded.

"Okay. One other thing: until we get these bastards locked up, this intel isn't to leave this office, I especially don't want anybody in on it upstairs." Kilford suppressed another grin, upstairs resided the superintendent and he and DI Scarratt had an uneasy relationship. While the Super respected Rocky's abilities as a cop and a leader, he was exasperated by the more unprofessional aspects of his character – the scratched face following differences of opinion with Mrs Scarratt or the recent arse-kicking assault on a blameless IT technician. Rocky, for his part, despised all authority, apart from his own.

"There's a 'nice to know' and there's a 'need to know'. And he doesn't bloody well need to know," Rocky concluded, not for the first time.

He was getting to his feet.

"Er...boss," said Kilford.

"What now?"

"It's the Sulgrave we're talking about. We can't just go storming in with the TSG. Y'know what it's like." Rocky sat down again with a heavy sigh.

"Aye, you've got a point."

"Fail to plan, plan to fail," murmured Bull and dodged the stapler the DI hurled at his head.

"What's the problem?" asked Budgie.

They explained the Sulgrave to him. An estate with the dubious distinction of having the cheapest property in the country, it was a fortress of several acres in Sunderland. Flats in blocks of up to four stories, linked by walkways and staircases, surrounded a series of courts, patches of muddy grass. It presented formidable obstacles to a raid. The walkways were obstructed by piles of refuse bags, old sofas and shopping trollies. There were metal gates on all levels, all with different locks and past experience taught that it was next to impossible to get all the necessary keys. Identifying a particular flat was another challenge: all the doors were the same drab grey and the residents, in their anxiety to avoid unwanted visitors, such as bailiffs, debt collectors, the police, or the mothers or fathers of their children, had been careful to remove almost all the door numbers. Nor was it straightforward to work out the location of an address from the few surviving numbers, as the estate's numbering system seemed to be utterly without sequence or logic.

"Unless we know exactly where we're going, we'd need an army to do the job and Wrathall would be on his toes before we got anywhere near," said Blockhead, "We know he's shacked up in Ratty's old flat, with his lass," said Kilford.

"What's the address?" asked Rocky.

"Eighty seven Trafalgar Walk," said Shifty, eyes on his screen.

"Alf," said Bull.

Kilford looked at him.

"That perv we saw this morning, the groper, didn't he say he lived on Trafalgar Walk?"

"He certainly did," smiled Kilford.

"So, we pay him a home visit and do a sly recce to find out exactly where Wrathall's holed up."

There were nods and murmurs of approval. It was agreed: they had a workable plan.

Rocky got to his feet again.

"Right, get on with it tonight. I want an update in the morning. Now I'm off to the pub. Cliffy, give me a bell if there's any problems." He paused at the door and turned. "Y'see, y'pair of arseholes. I knew giving you the sex offenders' job would pay off. Wasn't I right?"

"Yes boss," came the defeated, weary reply.

§

After the DI's departure, Budgie Burrows also left, to return to Chester-Le-Street to report to his own DI that he was working with Northumbria Police, a 'foreign force', on a planned operation. This was being put together on the basis of information received from a

CHIS, or Covert Human Intelligence Source, and this intelligence was rated B,2.1, or damned near as good as it gets.

Of those remaining in the DSU, without being asked, Shifty got to his one-fingered work typing up the notes of the meeting and generally looking after the requisite paperwork, while Blockhead got on the phone to the Territorial Support Group, TSG, based in South Shields. This was a unit of specialist officers, trained in handling public disorder, raiding premises and fingertip searching. Blockhead booked for two teams to attend briefings in Sunderland at five in the morning that Thursday, immediately prior to raids at two locations to be specified during the briefing. Then he started to organise for two warrants to be sworn out and made arrangements to get a name for an operation order – a document to be read out at the briefings, detailing the purpose of the operations and what was to be achieved.

Bull volunteered to spend half an hour getting the sex offender paperwork up-to-date, freeing Kilford to take Crapper for a quick walk. As he made for the door, Knackers got to her feet.

"Mind if I come with you? I could do with some fresh air."

"Er…sure, if you like."

They walked to the dog pound, Knackers talking animatedly about the robberies and Kilford replying in monosyllables. He didn't know what she was playing at and he wasn't at all sure he was up for it. Upon being released from custody by Pooch, Crapper bounded joyfully at Kilford, panting and whooping. Knackers smiled while Kilford petted the dog, who was, he noted, looking increasingly respectable under Pooch's regime. Not that that would cut any ice with Vicki. Once her mind was made up…

"He's very fond of you," said Knackers.

"He knows which side his bread's buttered." He slipped a lead onto Crapper and they headed for the adjacent park. Neither spoke. Kilford felt awkward and nervous. Where was this heading?

"You're very keen on this job aren't you?" she said suddenly, eyes still on the ground in front of her.

"What, these robberies?"

"No! I mean the job. Being a cop."

"I dunno, what makes you say that?"

"You always seem so keen, like it really matters to you."

"Well, I suppose it does."

"Is that 'cos you want to make the world a better place or something?"

Kilford laughed. He bent down to release Crapper to hide his embarrassment. He watched the dog go running off after a couple of gambolling spaniels. "Or have you got something to prove?" she asked.

He looked at her. "Only to myself."

She studied him, head tilted, questioning.

"Did you know I used to be a professional footballer?" he said.

"Really!"

"Yeah, I made Newcastle's first team squad."

"You never told me that. You are modest aren't you." Kilford gave a shy smile and shrugged.

"I'm impressed," said Knackers. "So how…?"

"Did I end up in the police? I got a serious leg injury and that put paid to that career."

"That's tough."

"It was. For a lad like me, from the north side of Sunderland, being in a top flight team was like a dream come true. It wasn't just the money. I was somebody, somebody special and I was bloody good at what I did. That's important to me, if I do something, I want to do it well. I don't necessarily want to be the best, but I have to be the best I can be. D'you see?" Knackers nodded, her expression serious. Kilford coloured.

"Anyway," he said hurriedly, "that's water under the bridge. Crapper! Here boy, c'mon, time we were getting back."

They headed back towards the station, in silence again, until they had dropped Crapper off back at the pound. Then Knackers flashed him a dazzling smile. "I enjoyed that. It's nice to chat outside work, maybe we could go for a drink one night."

Before he could reply, she turned and, with quick steps, walked back into the station ahead of him. He watched her go and swallowed.

§

Knackers wasn't smiling later. She was sitting in a car being driven by Shifty, on their way to recce Bob Marley's house, the family home, owned by his father Harry Morrison on a private estate in Biddick. The car was a Primera, one of the cars reserved for the DSU, tucked away in a separate car park at the back of the station, unmarked and unknown to the criminal community and lacking the tell-tale radio antennae usual on CID vehicles. It was a hire car, with not many miles on the clock, but it had lost its new car smell, overwhelmed by the stale perspiration produced so prolifically by Shifty. Knackers wrinkled her nose and lowered her window an inch, despite the drizzling rain. "Should be just round this corner," said Shifty, making a left turn and, sure enough, the sign for the Chatham Estate came into view through the wipers. "We're looking for number six, Laurel Crescent," said Knackers.

"Here we are, number thirty, it must be just up there on the right. How about we pull over opposite and make out like we're a courting couple?"

He turned to treat her to his most salacious leer, but it was stillborn by a look of withering revulsion on her part.

"In your dreams Shifty. We'll do it the normal way.

Now, slow down."

He crawled past the house, a large detached with a double garage, standing in a generous garden. Knackers cast a practised eye over it: front door handle on the right side; no porch; only outbuilding a small shed; no kennel or other signs of a dog. She scribbled details in her notebook. She finished and looked up to see a car coming towards them in the gathering dusk. It passed them and she looked over her shoulder to follow it.

"Turn round when you can and go back," she said.

Shifty shrugged and did a three-point turn into the next junction, before coming back down the road towards number six, now on their right.

"That's it parked outside," she said. "A VW Polo and it's Bob's plate."

Shifty switched his leer back on. "You're not just a pretty face are you pet?"

She sighed. "Piss off Shifty."

§

Bob Marley parked the Polo and hurried indoors. He saw his father going into the kitchen. Harry Morrison was a big man and, although well into his sixties, his back was still straight and his shoulders still broad. He grunted at his son and gave him a penetrating and disapproving glare from under his beetling grey brows. Bob had worn his dreadlocks for a couple of years now but they still wound Harry up.

Bob gave him an answering nod and ran upstairs to his bedroom, slamming the door behind him. He sat on the edge of the bed, trembling.

"Christ," he moaned. "Christ Almighty, what have I got myself into?"

He felt into his pocket and took out the wrap Wrathall had just given him. God, he needed it, but he couldn't use it now. If he used smack at home and the old bastard caught him, he'd throw him out, after he'd kicked the shit out of him first, that is.

He sat, his head in his hands, rocking to and fro.

He'd just pulled another job with Wrathall.

In Wingate. In broad, shagging daylight!

Bob had gone in first to check out the store, an offy up a side street with just the usual old biddy behind the counter. Then he'd gone to sit in the car until Wrathall came running out, carrier bag in hand.

"Drive!" Wrathall had shouted. "Just get the bollocks out of here!"

Usually Wrathall was cold and impassive, but this time he'd been wide-eyed and excited.

"What's wrong?" asked Bob, turning onto the main street.

"Nuthin'," Wrathall had said, gnawing at his thumbnail. "It's just that old cow. She collapsed. I think she's had a fucking heart attack or summat."

§

At around the same time as Knackers was swatting away Shifty's advances, Kilford and Bull were peering into the darkness at an intercom pad at one of the gates giving access to the Sulgrave Estate. The hoods of their hoodies, worn inside their leather jackets, were up to protect them from the rain, and to hide their faces from any passers-by who could recognise them as detectives.

"What number's Ralph?" asked Bull.

"He said fourteen."

They were interrupted by voices and footsteps approaching from behind. They moved away from the intercom and pretended to be examining Bull's mobile, heads down and in the shadows, as a group of youths walked past, laughing and chatting. They waited until they were clear, before moving back to the intercom. Kilford pressed the button for number fourteen. They listened to the buzz, but there was no response. "The old bastard had better not be out on one of his arse-caressing expeditions," muttered Bull. There was a crackle and a voice from the intercom.

"Yes? Who is it?"

"Ralph, its DC Kilford and DC Miles."

"Yes? What do you want?"

"We're here to do that home visit, we told you about."

"I thought you were going to ring first."

"There wasn't time. We're here now."

Ralph made a twittering sound, then said: "I suppose you'd better come up."

The intercom buzzed and the gate's lock clunked open.

They'd studied the City Council's plans for the Sulgrave, courtesy of a contact in the Housing Department and knew roughly where they were going, and they made their way along the walkways and stairwells, occasionally dimly lit by one of the surviving lights which illuminated the graffiti festooned walls. They negotiated the junk and odd recumbent body. It put Kilford in mind of some nightmarish version of his daughter Natalie's Tomb Raider game, except in this Sulgrave version, a miasma seemed to hang about the labyrinth, made up of a toxic mixture of stale urine, marijuana and fried fat.

They reached a door which, according to their calculations, was number fourteen. After a precautionary look round, Bull knocked. Immediately, there was a scraping of a bolt and the door was opened ajar to reveal Ralph's nervous features peering out over the top of a chain. His eyes widened in fear as he registered the two figures on his doorstep.

Kilford hurriedly pulled down his hood.

"Don't worry Ralph, it's only us."

Ralph unhooked the chain, opened the door and beckoned them. "Come in, come in – quickly." They stepped into the flat. It was sparsely furnished, the curtains were drawn, a television was on with the volume low. The detectives unzipped their jackets. Like so many such flats, it was uncomfortably warm and it reeked with a musty dampness.

"I wasn't expecting you so soon," said Ralph.

"Nobody expects the Spanish Inquisition," said Kilford.

"What?"

"Never mind. Look Ralph, it won't take long. You and I'll just fill in this form together while Bull here takes a quick look round. Can I sit down?"

"Of course."

He gestured at the sofa. Kilford sat at one end and Ralph at the other. Kilford took out a SOR1 home visit form and a pen and began to go through it with Ralph while Bull disappeared into the kitchen, to reappear a few seconds later and then enter what Kilford guessed to be a bedroom. After a minute, Bull's voice came through the door. "Ralph, you got a minute?"

Ralph, accompanied by Kilford, went into the bedroom. Bull hadn't put the light on and was stood in the darkness by the window, one hand pulling the curtain back a couple of inches and looking out into the night.

"What is it?" asked Ralph.

"This window is secure is it? You keep it locked?"

"Of course."

Bull nodded, as though satisfied. Now Ralph was standing by him. Bull pointed out through the window, to a door which could be seen through the walkway railings across a fifty-foot void which separated it from another. Kilford looked over Ralph's shoulder. This was the door they had calculated was number eighty seven.

"Any idea what number that is Ralph?"

"No, I'm afraid not. Why?"

"Any idea who lives there?"

"Let me see. Ah, yes, a young lady. She lives there with a man, a big man, quite a terrifying character from what I can gather. Strange, she seems so nice, she has a lovely…er…figure."

Bull, letting the curtain fall back, sighed and rolled his eyes.

"Ralph," said Kilford. "You've got to try to keep your mind off that sort of thing."

Ralph looked sheepish and nodded. Kilford shook his head. If this poor bastard fondled Wrathall's lass's arse, it would probably be the last arse he ever fondled.

On their way back into the lounge Bull drew his partner aside and whispered.

"Let's get out. It's boiling in here – and it stinks." Kilford nodded. They'd got what they had come for, a confirmation of the location of Wrathall's flat. Asking Ralph had been a risk, but a calculated one. If he was to mention that the detectives had expressed an interest in number eighty seven, he'd be revealing his own contact with the police and that could betray his status as a registered sex offender, which would be a significant social misstep in the Sulgrave.

The pair took their leave of Ralph and made their way back to their car. As they reached the gate, Kilford's mobile rang. He answered, spoke for a few seconds then rang off, frowning.

"What's up?" asked Bull.

"That was Budgie. There's been another job. In Wingate. This time they left the victim in a coma. Doesn't look like she'll pull through."

"Shit!"

They closed the gate behind them with a bang and left the Sulgrave. They didn't notice a slender figure who had been observing them from the shadows.

§

Kilford and Bull returned to the station. By now it was getting on for ten, but Blockhead was still at his desk. They briefed him on the visit to Ralph's and they'd barely finished when Knackers and Shifty arrived to report what they'd seen in Biddick. They asked Blockhead about the Wingate job but he knew no more than the details they'd gleaned from Budgie. It was agreed that the team would reconvene in the morning to prepare for the raids to arrest Wrathall and Bob Marley in the early hours of Thursday morning. Kilford got home to find the house in darkness and the whole family in bed. He stole in to kiss his daughters and tentatively looked into his and Vicki's bedroom. Her steady rhythmic breathing indicated that she was asleep, or at least was pretending to be, so he tiptoed downstairs to spend another night on the sofa. He was up early that Wednesday morning and was leaving the house as the rest of the family were getting up. He just had time to kiss the girls goodbye and promise Vicki that he would he home at a reasonable hour that evening.

"I'll believe it when I see it," was her parting comment. In the office they set to work to put the final building blocks in place for Operation Hammer, as the raid to arrest Wrathall and Bob Marley had been designated. Blockhead went to brief the DI, while the others put together an operation order and a briefing package. Between them these contained two warrants for the arrest of the two suspects, a full risk assessment of both properties, describing the types of premises, details of the doors and which way they opened and any other potential complications. This was considerably longer for the Sulgrave than for Biddick.

The package also contained images of the two suspects, along with their history and any known propensity for violence – in Wrathall's case, considerable.

A phone call from Budgie informed them that Irene Fletcher, aged 67, who had a part-time job in the off licence in Wingate that had been hit last night, appeared to have suffered a coronary and was in a coma. There were signs of bruising to her neck and a cracked rib, probably from where she had fallen. It appeared that the CCTV had not been working properly but a technical team was working on it.

Rocky visited the team and said: "Right, these fucking arseholes could be up for manslaughter now. This is getting really nasty and I want it stopped."

Not that they needed any urging; this was the kind of work they all enjoyed, a welcome respite from everyday admin. It was still filling in forms, but it was filling in forms in preparation for an operation. They worked with an intensity and purpose, there was a buzz in the room and it was light-hearted, despite the seriousness of the task. The radio was on and at one point even Bull started humming along, tunelessly, to Oasis' She's Electric. As one, Kilford, Blockhead and Shifty told him to shut up. Knackers giggled, her eyes sparkled as her glance met Kilford's and she gave him an arch look. He cleared his throat and buried himself again in his work.

By three in the afternoon, they were through. Kilford seized his chance when Knackers went to the ladies.

He grabbed his jacket, said,

"See yous at half four in the morning," and headed off for the dog pound to give Crapper a walk before keeping his promise to Vicki to get home in good time.

§

Eva was sitting in her preferred position on the floor, with her back resting against the sofa, with a cigarette looking at the TV. She wasn't watching it. It was showing a pre-school animated puppet show, which provided her with some colour and sound but didn't demand attention.

Her relaxation didn't last long. The door banged and, without looking round, she knew from the heavy tread that it was Karl. He dropped onto the sofa.

"What's this shit?" he asked and, before she could tell him it was The Hoobs, he'd snatched up the remote and switched it off.

"Is there any scran?" he asked.

"What?"

"Food."

"We had half a loaf but it was going mouldy so I binned it."

He reached into the pocket of his jeans and pulled out a roll of notes. He unfurled a twenty and handed it to her.

"'Ere, go and get us some pizza."

She dropped her cigarette stub into the dregs of her mug of coffee, where it landed with a lame hiss. She got to her feet, lifted her denim jacket from the chair against which she'd been leaning and made for the door, but then stopped.

"I had pizza last night. D'you fancy a kebab instead."

"Whatever," he grunted.

She turned back to the door, then stopped again.

"That reminds me."

"What?"

"When I was coming back with my pizza last night I saw two blokes down at the gate."

"And?"

"I'm sure one of them was that copper – Miller or Miles or something, big fat ugly guy."

"You fucking what?"

§

Kilford surveyed the room.

It was one of the station's parade rooms that had been booked for this dawn briefing of the two TSG teams which were to raid premises on the Sulgrave and in Biddick. The purpose was to arrest Karl Wrathall and Graham Morrison, aka Bob Marley, wanted in connection with a series of recent armed robberies in County Durham and to collect any evidence. Also present were Bull, Knackers, Shifty, Blockhead and Budgie.

The detectives sat at the back of the room, while in the row of seats immediately facing Kilford were the twenty two TSG officers, clad in blue overalls, protective jackets and heavy boots, many chewing gum, some with arms folded across their broad chests, all attentive. Kilford knew they were a tight-knit team, they had to be, because their line of work meant watching your mates' backs. Coppers who joined the TSG tended to stay. Kilford also knew that each team member was a mixture of brawn and, if not brains, certainly some carefully honed skills. Part of their training was in searching premises, painstakingly, meticulously, combing every inch of every room long after the average detective would have given up. But there was also the brawn, they were all big men. Kilford had seen them in action before and knew that, when a front door was smashed open and they went charging into the premises, any occupant would obey their bellowed commands – if not paralysed by shock. When they'd arrived at the station at five in the morning, they had not known what their operation was or its location. They had been taken straight to the parade room and the door locked. Then, Kilford had briefed them, describing the offences and the suspects, photograph images of whom were pinned to a flip chart. They were told about the lay out of the premises, details of doors and windows and any potential obstacles or risks. They were told that the doors at Sulgrave were UPVC, which elicited a groan. They were told what items would be of particular interest in the search, such as clothing the suspects had worn on the robberies, but most important – bank notes or any large knives.

Kilford pointed at Wrathall's image.

"This one's dangerous. He's got a record of violence, has broken out of prison before and uses a knife." Not a flicker from the impassive faces gazing back. If Wrathall drew his knife on this lot, he'd be leaving the Sulgrave on a stretcher.

"Any questions?" he asked.

Glances and shrugs were exchanged. No, no questions – all in a morning's work.

"Right, let's be off then."

Blockhead unlocked the parade room door and they filed out, leaving just Blockhead and Budgie. They made their way through a back exit into a car park to the TSG vans. Here the TSG split into two teams, one to each van and each headed by an officer in charge, OIC. They set off in two convoys, one headed by Knackers and Shifty in their Primera for Biddick; the other led by Kilford and Bull in their Fiesta, Sulgrave bound.

Bull drove. It was still dark but there was a hint of light on the western horizon ahead of them. Kilford was excited. He wasn't afraid. He and Bull would lead the TSG to the flat and then all the action would be down to them. His only fear was the same he always had on these operations: that they had identified the wrong flat and that some upright citizen and his wife would wake to find a TSG team rampaging through their bedroom. Kilford consoled himself with the knowledge that the chances of finding an upstanding citizen in the Sulgrave were slim. No, it wasn't fear but adrenalin that was coursing through him.

There was little traffic and they reached the Sulgrave in twenty minutes. Bull pulled up opposite the gate they'd gone through the night before last. Kilford turned to confirm the TSG van had pulled in behind them. He and Bull were barely out of the Fiesta before the blue clad figures, now wearing helmets with visors, had poured out of the back of the van and were jogging noiselessly across the road. The two detectives followed and, as they caught up, there was a sharp crack and the gate swung open, jemmied by a formidable crowbar wielded by one of the officers.

The OIC turned to them.

"Right, you lead the way."

They followed the path they had taken to Ralph's, only this time much faster. Kilford, the former footballer, who still used the gym, bounded up the stairwells, but he could hear Bull labouring behind him, even over the pounding boots of the TSG. Somewhere, away to the right, a door slammed and there was a scream.

They ran on and, at the top, instead of swinging left for Ralph's, they turned right, across to the opposite walkway.

Kilford stopped, waited for the OIC to draw level and pointed at the door they'd identified from Ralph's. The OIC nodded, turned and signalled for two of his team, who ran forward, one holding a ram. The door, as they had been briefed, was uPVC, not wood, which made the ram prone to bounce off, so the officer wielding it smashed at the lower panel, which splintered with a crack. He followed with two more blows which smashed the panel in. He ducked and crawled though, followed by his mate and then, one by one, the rest of the team, with astonishing speed and dexterity.

"Like big, bastard ferrets," breathed Bull.

From inside they could hear crashing and thuds and shouts of "Police!"

Then the door was opened from the inside and the OIC beckoned them.

"Let's go and meet Mr Wrathall," said Kilford.

CHAPTER SIX

Kilford and Bull looked around the room.

"Shit!" said Bull.

The flat's living room contained some dated and dilapidated furniture and, on the floor, fast food detritus, along with chipped and dirty coffee mugs. It also contained the TSG unit's OIC, who had removed his helmet and visor and was shaking his head. "It's empty lads, looks like they've flown the nest. As you can see and smell, it's a shit tip and a frigging health hazard - needles and crap everywhere, but we'll do a thorough search."

Kilford took in the syringes lying among the debris and nodded.

"Okay, cheers Sarge, we'll just have a quick butcher's then get out of your hair. We'll catch up later at the nick to see what you've got for us."

He and Bull looked into the apartment's kitchen. Some grease encrusted plates lay in the sink, a bin liner was disgorging its contents over the floor. There were more needles, blackened teaspoons and pieces of tinfoil. "Someone tipped 'em off that we were coming," said Bull. "You reckon it was Ralph?"

Kilford shook his head. "I don't see it."

"Naah, me neither."

They wandered into the bedroom, where there were already two TSG officers at work. The technique was two men to a room, starting in opposite corners and working meticulously around the room, bringing anything of any interest to an exhibits officer, who was stationing himself by the living room's coffee table, where he would record and bag any items recovered. Kilford watched them for a few moments and glanced around. There was more evidence of heroin cooking and overflowing ashtrays and other rubbish. The nicotine coloured wallpaper had a big orange stain on one wall but no pictures. Kilford reflected that this was a girl's flat and sighed. Bull, who'd had some dealings with Eva, had said that she was a nice enough kid, obviously from a decent background. According to her record, she was only in her mid-twenties. It wouldn't have been that long ago that she'd been the same age as Natalie. Just out of childhood. Kilford thought about Natalie's bedroom, with its posters of Blue on the wall and teddy bears on the dressing table. He shook his head. Heroin. What a bastard. Especially when it came with a lowlife like Wrathall. Along with sadness at such waste, he felt disappointment and frustration. They'd missed Wrathall and he was convinced it had only been by a matter of hours, if that. Bollocks!

"Alf."

He looked round at Bull's voice. His partner was putting his phone back in his pocket. "I've just been filling Blockhead in. He says to go back in for debrief. Looks like Knackers and Shifty have had more luck."

"That's something, I suppose," grunted Kilford. "Come on then."

§

Harry Morrison was not a happy man.

Sitting at the kitchen table, staring at its oak surface, he tapped his fingernail repeatedly against his front teeth, listening, brooding and waiting. He could hear the cops stomping about upstairs, opening and slamming doors and drawers. His wife, Sheila, was next door, in the lounge, sobbing and wailing about what the neighbours would think. Harry wasn't going to tell her, but he'd already seen the couple opposite, peering out from behind their bedroom curtains, at the sight of his son, that shit-brained, useless little prick, being led down the drive by Rob Blair and another plain clothes cop, a girl with good looks, to be bundled into the back of their car and driven away. Blair had taken him to one side before that; asked him for his mobile number. He'd wonder why he'd done that later, at the moment he'd got enough on his bloody plate. None of this made Harry happy. But he wasn't going to take it lying down. Harry Morrison didn't take this kind of shit lying down.

He was mentally making a to-do list.

First, he was going to ring his lawyer. Ben Raine had got him out of some scrapes in the past, now he could do the same for his son, or at least limit the damage. Then, he'd calm Sheila down. No point attempting it while the police were still in the house, but he'd have to get to work on her, reassure her that the old days hadn't come back. After that, he'd make some more phone calls, call in a few favours, get people asking some questions. The comfortable, respectable life he'd carved out for his family was under threat and that threat had to be neutralised. And, then, somebody had to pay.

§

By the time Kilford and Bull got back to the station, at about half seven, Shifty and Knackers had returned to join Blockhead and Budgie. Shifty told them how they had burst into Bob Marley's house to find him still in bed. Now he was in a cell downstairs.

"When I arrested him, one of the TSG lads had to hold Harry Morrison back from killing him, the old bastard was livid," said Shifty. "Me and Harry go back a long way, he was one of my boys." Shifty winked. "He always did have a bit of a temper. Anyway, Bob's shitting himself. When I cautioned him and locked him up for robbery, he started spouting off that he had nowt to do with the jobs and Wrathall forced him to do it."

Bull snorted.

"If he was forced into it, he had something to do with it, the little bastard can't have it both ways. Anyway, it's tough shit. I hope you got him to sign your notebook, Shifty, because that could be important." Shifty treated them to his annoying, characteristic cackle, like a clucking hen with bad catarrh. "Naah, even better, it's documented on his custody record from when I booked him in and he signed that." Kilford smiled thinly and congratulated Shifty and Knackers, which made her eyes sparkle, so he added hurriedly: "Aye, it's good news, but where are Wrathall and Eva? How did they know we were coming?" He rubbed his chin. "I do hope Ratty's not up to his old tricks. When the boss gets in, he's not going to be best pleased." He'd hardly finished speaking before there was a peremptory rap on the door. Blockhead opened it and Rocky entered, booming.

"Who's not going to be frigging happy? Don't go and spoil my day before it's even started. Eh, this job, it's the worst it's ever been."

He dropped into the nearest seat and surveyed them over the top of his reading glasses. "Come on arseholes, let me have an update, and it better be good, mind."

Kilford described both raids. The DI listened expressionless, although his face did turn a shade darker when he heard that Wrathall had slipped the net. Then he took charge of the meeting, a role he slipped into, his self-assurance and experience lending him authority and his team confidence.

"First off," he said. "Let's get that twat Bob bloody Marley on tape. If he wants to come across, let's not give him time to change his mind.

Budgie, you and one of Tam MacFarlane's Reactive lads can sort that out." There were nods and murmurs of agreement.

"Cliffy, I want Wrathall locating and I want all snouts tasking. This is our priority, `cos we know he's not going to stop. We know from his past that this is only going to get worse and we're going to be dealing with bodies before long. Get Wrathall and Devlin circulated Force-wide and beyond."

"Right boss," said Blockhead.

Rocky looked at Kilford and Bull.

"You two get yourselves down to Wrathall's dad's place and see what he knows, but be careful: he's a weird bastard, if I remember correctly, and, you never know, Wrathall might even be there – stranger things have happened. When you're done there, update Tam, `cos we're going to need more bodies on this job. Tell him I want his full team on it. Right, let's get on with it and we'll meet here again at three to see what we've got."

§

Kilford let Bull do the driving. He took out his work phone and punched a number. It rang a couple of times before being answered. He made sure it was the voice he was expecting before he spoke.

"Ratty, you alright to talk?"

"Aye. See you've been busy this morning – on the Sulgrave."

"Not much gets past you is there?"

"That's what you pay me for innit, listening to the jungle drums and that? Mind you, the whole of bastard Sulgrave knew about it before you'd smacked that door in."

"Did you know about it beforehand and did you mention it to someone?"

"Hey come on man! What d'you take me for?"

"Let's not go there, Ratty. Listen, if you know so much, you'll know Wrathall and your lass are on their toes and we need to find them, like now, especially if you want to keep her out of the shit. I need you to make a few calls, work your magic and get back to me straightaway. Have you got that?"

"You got Bob?"

"Aye."

"Lean on 'im hard, 'cos I know 'im and he's a weak little fucker and his arse will fall out and he'll blow that wanker Wrathall up. Trust me."

"Ratty, just do your job and leave us to do ours."

"Aye, alright. Hey, listen, I can't ring Eva, it's too dodgy. I'll have to wait till she thinks it safe to ring me. If he finds out he'll hurt her proper."

"Okay, just make sure you keep your phone on." Kilford rang off and pocketed his phone as they entered Farringdon. He consulted his notebook for the address and directed Bull. They pulled up opposite the house they were looking for. Kilford leaned over and appraised it through Bull's side window. It looked respectable enough, although it had obviously seen better days. He had no great sense of anticipation. He and Bull knew it was highly unlikely that Wrathall would be there. So did the DI obviously, otherwise he wouldn't have sent them alone. As members of the DSU, they wouldn't normally carry personal radios. There were too many situations where it wouldn't just be embarrassing but downright dangerous to have them crackling into sudden life and they were hard to conceal. On the other hand, without the ability to call for immediate assistance, they could be vulnerable, so Rocky was insistent that the team had regular self-defence training. In Bull's case, their instructor had soon realised he had little to teach a man who seemed to have such a comprehensive repertoire of vicious, underhand, street fighting techniques. That gave Kilford more comfort than a radio could have provided.

Bull echoed Kilford's thoughts.

"This'll probably be a waste of time," he grunted, as he heaved himself out of the car with a grunt. They made their way to the front door of the house and rang the bell. Kilford hung back, taking in all the windows, alert for any sudden movement or sound of opening back doors. The front door was answered by a short, shabby, balding man.

"Mr Wrathall?" said Kilford, producing his ID. "DC Kilford and DC Miles. Can we come in and speak to you?"

Old man Wrathall's features screwed up in petulant expression.

"Is this about Karl? What's he done now?" What's he done now? thought Kilford. Like he might just have been riding a bike without lights.

"We just need to speak to him. Look, it really would be better if we could come in."

"Oh, alright, if you must. But just make sure you keep the noise down. Some of them can be very sensitive you know."

As they stepped inside, Bull hung back and whispered to Kilford.

"What's the old bugger babbling about?" Kilford shrugged and they followed Wrathall Senior along the hallway and into the front lounge. The detectives had only advanced a few feet into the room, when they both froze, staring.

"Bloody hell!" breathed Bull.

They were looking into a room with a twenty-year-old brown Dralon suite, a threadbare carpet and a Formica-topped coffee table. All unremarkable, if not tatty. What was unusual was a baby's bath, full of soapy water that stood on the hearthrug. In the bath was what looked like a small child, but with expressionless, doll-like features. Then, the detectives realised that the little figure, up to its chest in water, was a mannequin. Behind it, a gas fire was on full, making the room unbearably hot. Kilford and Bull exchanged glances. Wrathall senior stood behind them.

Kilford turned to him. He pointed dumbly at the mannequin.

"I'm just washing the baby before I get him ready for bed."

Kilford and Bull swapped another quick look.

"Right…" said Kilford and then words failed him. "Anyway, the water's getting cold. What is it you want?"

"Er…" Kilford shook his head, trying to concentrate.

Bull was still staring at the bath.

"It is about your son, Karl," he said, making a determined effort. "We just need to speak to him. Do you have any idea where we might find him?"

"No, I don't. He's not here, if that's what you're thinking. Have a look around if you don't believe me."

"If you insist, yeah, we will."

Old man Wrathall stood aside to let them through, back into the hallway. He watched them, as they had a quick look in the other downstairs room and the kitchen, but he didn't follow them upstairs. There, they looked into the bathroom, at the stained bath and grimy toilet, a small bedroom which appeared to be used as a junk room full of old suitcases and cardboard boxes overflowing with dog-eared magazines and another bedroom, with an unmade bed and clothes strewn about the floor, which Kilford guessed to be the old man's. They were at the door of the third bedroom, when a voice called from downstairs: "Try not to wake them."

Bull opened the door. Despite it being daylight outside, the curtains were drawn. Bull switched on the light and they saw a double bed with two shapes in it. Kilford walked over and peeled back the duvet to reveal two more mannequins, lying side by side. "What the hell is going on here?" asked Bull. "This bloke is one strange bugger. This is definitely not normal."

"You're not wrong there, Bull. I think this would even make Ralph a bit uneasy."

"Aye, at least he's a normal perv. Anyway, Wrathall's not here – and who can blame him? Let's get out. Apart from everything else, it's bloody boiling, and it stinks."

There was an unpleasant smell about the place and Kilford knew that Bull, in most ways not a fastidious man, had a sensitive nose.

Kilford agreed and they made their way back downstairs.

"I hope you didn't wake them," said Wrathall Senior.

"They're still sound asleep," said Kilford.

Old man Wrathall nodded and went back into the lounge, leaving them to make their own way out. En route to the front door, they a passed a telephone table and Kilford noticed it also contained a bundle of envelopes, stamped HMP Bradford. He pointed this out to Bull.

"Looks like he kept in touch with his old man," said Bull.

"Aye, probably asking after the kids," said Kilford. "Y'say kids, but them mannequins are taller than you Alf." laughed Bull.

§

They returned to the station, where, instead of going to the DSU, they headed for the Reactive CID team's office, looking for their leader, DS Tam Macfarlane. There were only a couple of detectives at their desks, who told them he was attending the scene of an overdose at the rear delivery entrance at the Galleries Shopping Centre in Washington. Twenty minutes later, they had parked at the Galleries and were making their way round the back, to the loading bays, by way of an elevated walkway.

"There's Tam," said Bull.

He leaned over the walkway's rail on his left and pointed to a figure about a hundred and fifty yards away, who was standing, smoking a cigarette over a motionless body curled up in a doorway. "Professional or what?" said Bull. "Potential crime scene and he's smoking a tab over the body."

"Aye, that's Tam for you," said Kilford. "But don't wind him up mate, we need his help."

Tam saw them approaching and waved. An affable Glaswegian, he was in his late thirties, tall, with brown, wavy hair and with a moustache that Vicki, who had met him at a party, said made him look like part of a Village People tribute act. Tam was famed for his love of tea and for cutting corners and ignoring procedural niceties, but, probably because of that, he was an effective copper. In any situation, his instinct was to go in hard and fast, which was at odds with his easy going, jovial manner.

"Och, if it's no DSU's finest," he greeted them. "How're you boys doing?"

"Hello Tam, mate," said Bull. "What we got here then?" Tam gestured at the body with his cigarette. They looked down at a young man, who wasn't going to get any older. He was lying on his side, probably early twenties, brown hair, acne, mouth and eyes open, but with the pupils rolled up into the sockets, a drying pool of vomit under his cheek.

"Another overdosed young bastard," said Tam. "Two kids I've just spoke to say this is John Ashworth, twenty years old. There's some bad shite in Washington at the minute boys. Those two wee bastards say the stuff is called the devil's dandruff. Must be bad stuff boys. Whisper I've heard is that it's coming oot o' Middlesbrough. Yous boys heard anything aboot that?"

"We have and it's linked to the bastard we're looking for," said Kilford.

"Is that right? So, what brings you boys out here?"

"We're after an armed robber, Tam. Hard bastard by the name of Wrathall. He's on his toes and we need your help finding him."

Tam flicked his cigarette end a few feet away from the body and sniffed. "You cleared this wi' Rocky?"

"His idea Tam."

Tam smiled. "Then how could I say no? I'll be back in the nick when I've got this sorted. You get the kettle on and we'll talk about it over a nice cup o' tea."

He turned from them and squatted down by his dead druggie.

§

Eva was weeping uncontrollably, her body shuddering with great heaving sobs. This made it difficult to concentrate on her driving, even though she was doing little more than twenty miles an hour, and this was on a major dual carriageway, the A19.

"Oh for fuck's sake!" said Wrathall, who was in the passenger seat. "Pull in 'ere or we'll get pulled over." Obediently, she steered the Sierra off the road and trundled it into a transport café car park, bringing it to a sudden, juddering halt with the handbrake. Wrathall, whose head came within six inches of hitting the windscreen, glared at her tear-stained face. He'd obviously been too generous with the smack. She'd been completely off her head and now she was coming down heavily, totally losing it – just over the fact he'd been raging at her for the last half an hour. No shagging wonder, she'd just let him down badly at that post office in Ryhope Village in Sunderland. Stupid slag!

She couldn't think straight, that was her problem. Stupid, spoiled, middle-class bitch. He ran his hand over his forehead. He felt weird himself. Maybe he wasn't thinking straight either. He held his hand out and observed the fingers trembling. That new H was powerful. Maybe they'd both been overdoing it.

"I'm sorry Karl," she sobbed. "I'm really sorry. I just couldn't do it."

"Why, what's your pissing problem?"

"I was scared. I don't mind driving for you, but I couldn't go inside."

"That's crap!" He slapped his still outstretched hand onto the dashboard, making her flinch. "You've seen the set-up, just a poxy little post office, not the fucking Bank of England. You didn't complain when we were planning it and when we got those." He jerked his thumb at the bath towels, still in their wrapping, on the back seat.

"I know, I'm sorry. Don't be mad."

He shook his head, disgusted. He unclipped his seat belt.

"What are you doing?" Eva asked nervously.

"I'm going for some fags. You wait here and pull yerself together."

She watched him stride across the car park towards the café. As soon as he'd disappeared inside, she bent down and plucked her handbag from the foot well and took her phone out. She sniffed and brushed the back of her hand across her eyes before selecting a number. She waited until she heard the familiar voice, before she said: "Hi Ratty, it's me…"

§

It was standing room only in the DSU. Crammed into the small office, apart from the five members of the DSU team, were the DI, Blockhead, Budgie, Tam MacFarlane and Sergeant Jim Schofield from the TSG, who had been OIC in that morning's Sulgrave raid. Tam, who was struggling to find elbow room to raise his mug of tea to his lips, said: "It's nice and cosy in here."

This was met with rueful grunts from the others. The packed room was even hotter and more airless than usual. Kilford had to avert his gaze from the sweat sodden hair at the back of Shifty's head, only for his eyes to alight upon a bead of perspiration trickling down Knacker's cleavage. This mesmerised him, until he was brought to attention by Rocky.

"Right you lot," said the DI. "This has gone on long enough. I've just had word that Irene Fletcher didn't make it. So, we've got one person dead and we're looking at possible manslaughter, maybe even murder. The Northern Echo have been on the phone to the press office asking about a spate," he made an inverted comma gesturer with his fingers," of violent robberies in County Durham and they know about Irene Fletcher's death. This is making the fucking arseholes upstairs jumpy and they're giving me grief, so I want it sorted. You all got that?" He looked around the room and his stare was met by a series of solemn nods. "Good. Right, Sergeant Schofield, you have the floor."

The TSG sergeant, a shaven-headed ruddy-faced young man, who, in the words of Bull, was "built like a brick shit house", shuffled forward a couple of inches and cleared his throat.

"Thank you, sir."

He looked briefly at the assembled detectives and then gazed fixedly at his notes as he went through that morning's raids in Sulgrave and Biddick. He listed what had been found in the searches and what was contained in several clear property bags lying on the desk in front of him. These had been duly listed on the appropriate PSR/3 form, which he brandished, as though anyone might have doubted it.

Kilford glanced at the bags. All had labels attached which bore the signatures of the seizing officers at both sites. Through the plastic,

Kilford could make out the drugs paraphernalia and the large kitchen knives that the sergeant was listing. The sergeant finished, cleared his throat again and looked at Rocky. "Thank you, Sergeant," said the DI. "DC Burrows, you can fill us in on your interview with, whatshisname – Bob Marley, or whatever he's called."

"Graham Morrison sir."

"Aye, whatever. Get on with it." Budgie took centre stage.

"I conducted the interview, along with DC Wilson of Northumbria Police, at nine hundred hours this morning. Also present was Morrison's solicitor, Ben Raine."

"Slimy, crooked little twat," muttered Bull.

"I see you've had the pleasure," smiled Budgie. "Anyway, in a nutshell, Morrison confessed to being the driver on all the robberies, but says that, apart from giving the places a once-over before Wrathall went in, he stayed in the car and had nothing to do with the actual robberies. Particularly insistent, as you can imagine, that he was not present when Wrathall assaulted Irene Fletcher in Wingate. He maintains that he was acting under duress at all times, in fear of his safety if not his life. The only reward he received was free heroin from Wrathall to feed his worsening habit. His solicitor has indicated that his client will be willing to admit to his role and make a statement in his own defence, naming Wrathall as the robber."

"Excellent," said Rocky, rubbing his hands. He turned to Blockhead. "Cliffy, you get on the phone to the CPS and clear it with them that we can turn Bob Marley against Wrathall. Assuming they're okay with that, get 'im charged and, Tam, get a couple of your lads to get an in-depth statement out of him, every T crossed and every I dotted, over the next couple of days. In the meantime, we've got to keep the little bastard safe, so Alf, you see if you can get him fixed up in a hotel somewhere out of area."

"I can sort that," said Budgie.

"Just sort it between you. All of you, our priority now is to nick Wrathall. Have you tasked your snouts like I said this morning?" They nodded.

"Good, lean on 'em and let's make it official. I want it noted on their files that all CHIS have been tasked with getting intelligence on the location of Karl Wrathall and Eva Devlin. We'll meet here again at eight in the morning and you arseholes had better have something for me."

Kilford had been on duty for nearly twelve straight hours, so he took the rare opportunity to get away early and, after giving Crapper a quick run round the park, went home.

"Hi!" he said to Vicki as he entered the kitchen.

"Hello stranger."

Was she being sarcastic? He eyed her warily, as he removed his jacket. She smiled at him. No, she was obviously holding out an olive branch. Best snatch it with both hands.

"I was thinking, love. Why don't we all go out for a meal? Brewster's Fayre?"

"Oh, that's a good idea. Why not?"

Result! As she left the room to get the girls, he punched the air.

Thirty minutes later the four of them were sitting in the pub, a big barn of a place in Fulwell. It was popular with families, as it had a kid's ball area, slides and a climbing frame. It also sometimes featured Brewster Bear, when some unfortunate member of staff could be persuaded to don the costume. Kilford was relieved to see that the bear didn't appear to be on duty, as he usually had the effect of sending the kids running screaming back to their parents' tables. Kilford had ordered his sirloin, Vicki her chicken salad, Natalie her burger and Beth her chicken nuggets.

Natalie was being a good big sister and looking after Beth in the ball area and keeping a wary eye out for Brewster Bear.

"This is nice," said Vicki, then added pointedly, "we should do it more often."

Kilford reached over the table and squeezed her hand. "We will, love, I promise. Just as soon as we get this latest job done." He hadn't told her yet about the sex offenders' role he'd been saddled with. Cross that bridge, when he came to it.

"Ah, here we are," he said, as the waitress came into view bearing their meals. "Girls! Come on, your meals are here."

The girls came scampering over and climbed into their seats. Kilford was unfurling the napkin wrapped around his cutlery when his work phone, which he'd placed at the side of the table, started ringing and juddering. He picked it up and looked at the screen. It was Ratty.

"Don't answer that Dan," said Vicki. "We've just got our food. It can wait ten minutes surely."

"Look babe, I've got to take this call, it's really important. I'm sorry, it won't take a minute."

He got up from the table and, without looking at Vicki, phone to his ear, strode out of the restaurant area, towards the Gents, fumbling through his pockets with his free hand for a pen and a piece of paper, while thumbing the receive button with the other.

"It's me," said Ratty.

"Aye, what've you got?"

"They're down Boro somewhere. They're going to be shacked up with a Jamaican who he met in the nick."

Boro? Middlesbrough. That was the second time Kilford had heard the place mentioned today. "That's brilliant mate. Any idea where?"

"They were on their way when she rang me and I didn't want to ask too much. From what she knows, it's going to be like a crack den.

Wrathall's nicked a motor, a silver Sierra and he's going to plate it up. She reckons he's reversed it into another car when he was off his head, so it's damaged."

"Did she say what they are planning?"

"No, but I reckon there's something big and she's terrified of him. He says he's going to get loads of gear in Boro, so she thinks he'll be back up here dropping off to his little fucking joeys."

"Okay…who's his busiest boy at the minute mate?"

"Have a look at Teethy Irving from Donwell. He's busy at the bus stop in the bus link. I reckon he'll meet him near there."

"Good stuff Ratty. Keep your phone on. I'll ring this in and be in touch. Any more calls from her and you ring me straight after, it doesn't matter what time." The call ended. Kilford then rang Blockhead and filled him in.

"Sounds good Alf," said Blockhead. "I'll ring the DI and the rest of the team. Unless you hear otherwise, we'll meet in the office at eight tomorrow morning."

"Okay. Got to go."

Kilford was buzzing as he made his back to the table. With any luck they'd have Wrathall tomorrow and it was down to his snout. What a result!

His excitement evaporated when he returned to find the food still on the table but no family. Vicki had taken the girls and left him. She must be steaming to have done that. Shit!

The waitress approached, as he listlessly forked his steak and chips. She looked curiously around the table.

"Is everything all right sir? Can I get you anything else?"

He sighed. "Just a taxi."

CHAPTER SEVEN

Eva gripped the steering wheel until her knuckles hurt. She wasn't driving, but was parked in Hutton Henry, a hamlet just off the A19 that was little more than its own front street. It boasted a couple of side streets and the Sierra was on one of these, a few doors down from Zak's News, a corner shop Karl had entered less than two minutes ago.

Eva was holding the wheel like her life depended on it, because it was the only way to stop her hands shaking, like she was some kind of frigging demented pianist or something. Oh God, how had this happened?

Less than a week ago, life had been straightforward. It had revolved around H, but that had been okay – mostly. Now it was dominated by him, by the need to keep Karl happy, or at least not make him angry, or rather, try to make him a bit less angry than usual.

And that was getting harder and harder.

There had been a time, in another life, when she'd been drawn to him, fascinated by his dangerous energy, by his exciting edginess. Now he just terrified her. And he was getting worse. Okay, she was getting pretty spaced out herself, but no, it wasn't just her, it was Karl, he was like totally frigging losing it. Could she get out of this shit? Was there any way? Maybe go back to Mummy, if she'd take her back. Try going back to uni…? Yeah, right…dream on Eva.

"Ahh!". She leapt and screamed as the passenger door opened.

"What the fuck?" said Wrathall, getting into the car. "Oh shit, it's you." She put a hand to her chest. "You startled me."

He glared at her. "I had hoped you'd be fucking expecting me. Y'know, like a getaway driver?"

"Sorry."

"Just fucking drive."

He shook his head as she pulled away and turned onto Front Street, back towards the A19 to head south. From the corner of her eye, she saw him take the knife from his jacket pocket and tuck it under the seat. Then he rummaged in the plastic carrier bag he'd been carrying and brought out a roll of banknotes. He unfurled them and counted through them, his lips moving.

"Shit!" he said and stuffed the roll back into his pocket.

"What?"

"Three hundred and seventy poxy quid. That's piss all."

He swivelled in his seat so he was facing her and jabbed his forefinger at her.

"Right, tomorrow we're doing the Ryhope job with those." He jerked his thumb at the towels still in the back. "And this time you'll do as you're fucking well told."

§

Through the window of his taxi, Kilford saw a petrol station with buckets of flowers on display outside the shop. He told his taxi driver to do a U turn, pull into the forecourt and wait for him. He selected the three biggest and most colourful bunches and carried them dripping into the shop.

"Anniversary is it?" asked the driver when he was back in the car.

"Something like that," he grunted in a tone to discourage further conversation.

As they pulled up outside his house, Kilford's eye was caught by something bobbing up, into and then out of sight, on the other side of their hedge. He smiled. Natalie was on the trampoline again. After paying off the taxi, he walked into the drive, but, instead of making straight for the front door, he walked over the lawn towards the bouncing Natalie, who was being watched by an admiring Beth. She stopped as he approached and nimbly jumped onto the lawn by his side. Kilford hoisted Beth onto the trampoline in her place and the little girl began performing her own little jumps, squealing with delight and then falling over in fits of giggles.

Kilford smiled at her and turned to Natalie.

"How's your Mum?"

"She's calmed down – a bit. I think you'd better say sorry."

"Don't I know it. Look, I got some flowers."

"Smart move."

Kilford ruffled her hair and headed off to the kitchen to confront his fate. Vicki was at the sink, her back to him.

"Hi Vick," he said. Silence. "Have you and the girls eaten?"

She replied without turning: "We had some pizza from the freezer." He coughed.

"I...er...got you these...to make up...for the pub, like." She faced him and he handed her the flowers. She took them and he thought he detected the slightest trace of a smile.

"This doesn't make up, okay?"

"How about this?" He took her by the shoulders, drew her towards him and kissed her on the lips.

"Mmm. You're getting there."

"Eugh, per-lease," said Natalie who was standing at the still open kitchen door. "That is so gross." An hour later, Kilford was relaxed on the sofa with Vicki, bottle of Stella in hand, Beth cross legged at their feet watching a video of Dora the Explorer. Natalie was in her room doing homework. The video finished and Vicki tapped Beth on the shoulder with her slippered foot.

"Time for bed, baby girl."

"I'll take her," volunteered Kilford.

He bathed Beth then let her take him by the hand and drag him into her bedroom.

"Story," she demanded.

"Alright. What do you want?" A sense of dread was stealing over him. "Little Miss Chatterbox."

He groaned inwardly, his worst fears realised. This was his daughter's favourite story and one that he'd had to read a hundred times, never having been a big fan in the first place.

Nearly two hours later, Vicki stuck her head round the door to see Beth with her head on her father's shoulder and Kilford's own head was back and his mouth wide open. Both were fast asleep. Vicki smiled and turned the light off.

§

He woke with a stiff neck in the early hours of Friday morning, gave Beth a peck on the top of her head and crept off to his own bed. He woke at six without the help of an alarm; his body clock had long since been set for early starts and, as usual, he was the first into the office, well before the eight o'clock briefing. He had just fixed himself a coffee and logged onto his computer when Knackers arrived.

"You're an early bird," she said.

"Always have been. Goes back to my football days as a youth. It was a tough regime and the days started early. If you turned up late for training, you really knew about it."

"Harder bosses than Rocky then?"

"He's a pussycat in comparison." She laughed.

"I'll bet nobody's called him that before."

"You're probably right. Anyway, what about you? How come you're early?"

"I just woke up and couldn't get back to sleep. That's what comes of having an early night. When you're sitting home alone at night, bored, there's nothing else to do but go to bed."

She gave him one of her arch looks and Kilford was relieved that, at this point, Shifty arrived. They chatted until others came in and soon the office was also packed with Bull, Blockhead, Tam Macfarlane, and the DI.

Rocky looked around the room.

"Right, we all here? Where's DC Burrows?" Blockhead shrugged.

"Dunno boss. Budgie's usually pretty reliable." Rocky shook his head.

"These foreign forces…terrible. Anyway, let's get started. Alf, run us through your call with Wayne Langley."

Kilford told the assembled team about his call from Ratty: that Wrathall and his girl were believed to be in Middlesbrough with a Jamaican he'd met in Bradford, that they were in a silver Sierra, probably with false plates and with rear end damage, and that he was likely to return to Sunderland to supply a dealer called Teethy Irving from Donwell, who was believed to do business at a local bus stop.

"Good, that's very good." said Rocky, rubbing his hands. "Any chance of you and Bull getting a face-to face with Langley? That's worth a dozen phone calls." Kilford shrugged.

"I've tried three times this morning boss, but he's not answering. That's not unusual, he's probably up to some villainy of his own, or off his head on smack. He always does get back." Rocky nodded.

"Okay. Anyway, well done Alf."

Kilford looked down to hide his gratification that his work had brought a result and that that was appreciated by a man he respected. That feeling was Kilford's own drug habit.

The DI continued: "Now, let's...Hello, who's this?"

He was interrupted by a knock at the door, which Shifty opened to admit Budgie, who apologised for being late.

"I was just leaving Chester when I was given a report of a job last night in Hutton Henry. Looks like our man again. A corner shop cum offy. Robber had a knife, took cash estimated to be just shy of four hundred quid. Head-butted the proprietor, an elderly Asian gentleman who's in hospital being treated for shock and concussion. No CCTV, but a witness reports a car parked nearby."

"Silver Sierra?" asked Kilford.

Budgie raised an eyebrow.

"Silver family saloon. How d'you know?"

Kilford filled him in on the previous night's telephone call from his source.

"Hutton Henry?" asked Knackers. "I've heard of it, but where is it?"

"Not much more than a few rows of houses, just off the A19," said Budgie. "There was a bit of a delay getting the report through because it's on the border between us and Cleveland. They got the initial call and passed it on."

"I'll bet that bastard Wrathall knows that," said Blockhead.

"Could be. Anyway, the crime scene's still in place and details are still coming in."

He turned to Rocky and nodded to indicate that he had finished speaking. The DI took over.

"Right, the lot of you, this needs bringing to an end like now, is that clear? The press are onto it and that means upstairs are having kittens. We've got one death on our hands and it's only a matter of time before there's another. Wrathall and his bird, Eva - I'm aware we've not housed them yet, but we'll just have to go with what we've got. Okay?"

He looked round the room, to take in a series of grave nods.

"Right, we'll move on three fronts. First, we'll get onto this bus stop and this dealer, Teethy. Cliffy, have that checked out: which bus stop we're talking about and let's have it watched. Next, let's get onto the car, this Sierra. Langley said Wrathall nicked the Sierra. Let's look through the recent crimes on the VIS to see what we can find. Bear in mind, it's probably doubled up. "Lastly, and this is top priority, see if we can ID this bloody Jamaican kid Wrathall was in Bradford with, then get onto Cleveland and see if they can place him. Whether that gets us a result or not, Tam, get all your team on standby to travel down to Middlesbrough this afternoon with the DSU lads to try and locate the Sierra."

"Excuse me, I'm not a lad," murmured Knackers. Rocky gave her a brief, uncomprehending stare before he went on.

"In the meantime, I'll go and calm nerves upstairs, assure 'em I've got a handpicked, elite team on the job, or some other complete bollocks. We meet again at twelve. You've a lot to do before then, so Cliffy, you crack the whip on these arseholes."

"Yes boss."

The DI, accompanied by Tam MacFarlane, left, muttering: "This is the worst it's ever been."

Blockhead grinned at the closed door and then began allocating tasks. Shifty was given the job of checking out Wrathall's fellow cons at Bradford for a Jamaican who had been released. Knackers was tasked with the finding a likely silver Sierra on the VIS, Vehicle Registration System. He asked Bull to summarise the latest intelligence then to update the Police Intelligence Management System. Kilford made a couple more fruitless calls to Ratty and then started to look into Teethy Irving.

Knackers was the first to find something.

"Bingo!" she said, looking up from her screen. "There was a silver Ford Sierra reported stolen a couple of days ago in Usworth, 1993 reg K736 TNL."

"Nice work," said Blockhead. "Bull, make sure you get that on PIMS with a note that the plates have probably been changed – and don't forget the damaged rear end."

They continued to work on their tasks. Shifty was conducting a series of increasingly acrimonious phone calls with HMP Bradford. He slammed the phone onto its cradle.

"Pissing screws! What a useless bunch of bastards. Anyone who might have any idea about a Jamaican has either left the service, has gone on long term sick or is off shift."

"Just keep at it," said Blockhead.

"I think I've got a result," said Kilford. "The uniformed lads have logged one Ryan Teethy Irving, a convicted dealer, as being suspected of doing business at a bus stop on Druridge Drive in Donwell. There's a note that Proactive were going to follow it up, but nothing seems to have been done about it yet."

"Well that's something," said Blockhead. "Well done Alf. Why don't you and Bull get yourselves over there? Don't be too obvious, but recce it and see if there's a possible site for an OP. Remember to be back here by twelve."

§

Forty minutes later, Kilford and Bull were sitting in their car about a hundred yards away, on the same side of the road as a bus shelter, currently occupied by one old woman.

"You reckon that's Teethy in disguise?" asked Bull. Kilford grinned. They had just checked out Teethy's last known address, it was only a couple of blocks away. They knew he would have memorised the numbers of all his customers and, once he received a call, he would make the two-minute walk to the bus stop where the transaction would be done. It would take a matter of seconds, with hardly any conversation and both parties would then hurry away in opposite directions. The hope was that he would also meet Wrathall there as his supplier, but keeping the bus stop under surveillance, far enough away not to be spotted but close enough to grab Wrathall if he did show, was going to be a challenge. Kilford pointed through the windscreen.

"That house opposite. Look at that bathroom window, that's the best place for an OP. What number is it d'you reckon?"

It was a trim, well-kept semi in a neat garden, which looked like a former council house. Bull looked at the surrounding houses and did a quick calculation.

"Number twenty four?"

Kilford nodded. "That's what I make it."

He took his phone out and dialled a number, which was answered promptly by Blockhead.

"How's it going Alf?"

"We're here, by the bus shelter. The only real OP seems to be number twenty four, Druridge Drive. Can you check the electoral roll, the CRS, Local Housing Department, all that shit, see who lives there?"

"Hang on."

Kilford could hear Blockhead whistling through his teeth as he worked, then he heard him shout some question across the office to

Knackers, which he couldn't make out. A few minutes later, he came back on the line.

"Right, it's a Mr Gareth Down and a Mrs June Down."

Hang on. That rings a bell." Kilford listened as Blockhead called a question over to Shifty.

"Alf? You still there? Aye, I thought so, it's Councillor Gareth Down. He's well in with the Super, probably in the same lodge, very pro police. I'm sure he'll be keen to help. You wait there while I see if I can set something up."

Blockhead rang off and Kilford briefed Bull. They then sat in silence, watching while a bus arrived, the old woman got on and then it left. Their interest was briefly aroused when a young man in a hoodie and was smoking approached the shelter, but he passed it without stopping. Then, after twenty minutes, Blockhead was back on the phone.

"Right," he said. "Councillor Down is up for it. As far as he's concerned, it's just a drugs OP. I told him it wasn't a good idea for you and Bull to go wandering up his garden path, so he says if you get yourself over to Ravensworth Golf Course Club House, he'll meet you in the bar there."

§

Councillor Down was a short man with thinning grey hair, a weathered red face and twinkling brown eyes.

Kilford estimated that he was probably in his late sixties. He and Bull were sitting with him in a secluded corner of the Club House bar. Taking in the handful of other occupants most of whom looked like accountants, or retired accountants, or their wives, Kilford was confident they didn't include any associates of Wrathall or Teethy Irving.

They ordered coffees, exchanged pleasantries and then the councillor leaned over the table towards them and, after looking round, lowered his voice conspiratorially. "So, officers, what's this all about? Your Sergeant White told me it was a drugs matter. Well, let me tell you, in that case, I'm only too happy to help in any way I can. When I see the harm that drugs can do in our communities, families torn apart, young lives ruined…"

Nodding, Kilford let him drone on. This would be a small price to pay for his co-operation.

"…and I don't need to tell you two gentlemen about the damage drugs do to the fabric of civil society and the crippling costs of policing and rehabilitation. Naturally, I see it as my duty to do anything in my power to help you and my wife June will agree."

"We're very grateful Councillor."

"Not at all. Anyway, how exactly can we help? Your sergeant said something about using our house as an observation point of some kind."

"That's right, sir. We have reason to believe that a known drug dealer is using the bus stop across the road from you to sell heroin and, possibly, to buy it himself."

"In the bus stop! Are you certain? It may have its rough edges, but it's a respectable enough area. It's quite a busy road that, you know. Surely we'd see something or somebody would?"

"Believe me, Councillor, these people are very practised at what they do."

Kilford had sensed his partner's growing impatience during the councillor's speech. Never one with much time for politicians, Bull now leaned forward with his own contribution.

"They keep the heroin up their anuses."

Kilford could only be grateful Bull had adopted the word "anuses". He tried to interrupt, but Bull ploughed on, unsparing, as Councillor Down's face lost its ruddiness.

"Sometimes, they'll shove it further up, into what they call their second shelf, like."

The councillor, looking as though he was about to be sick, shot sharp glances over his shoulders, checking that none of his fellow club members had shared the benefit of Bull's expertise.

"Yeah, anyway," said Kilford hurriedly. "So, you see, we can't just rush in and search and arrest. It needs to be a careful operation, photographic evidence and all that…you understand?"

Councillor Down held his hand up and shook his head.

"Do whatever you have to do. The thought of that kind of thing going on next to my house turns my stomach. The idea that June might…it just doesn't bear thinking about. When?"

"Over the next few days. We'll station a couple of officers in your house, it can't be us, we're too well known in the area. It won't be for long, again, a matter of days. We'll sneak them in, as it's important nobody knows they're there, for obvious reasons. So we would ask, Councillor, that you and Mrs Down don't mention this to anybody."

"Don't you worry about that. If I've learned one lesson in politics, it's the importance of knowing when to keep your mouth shut."

Kilford and Bull sat, eyes glazed, while the councillor expanded on this.

§

The midday briefing included four DCs from Tam MacFarlane's Reactive team, making the DSU impracticable, so it was held in a spare parade room. Rocky opened the meeting, but then handed over to Blockhead to provide an update on what had been discussed that morning and some context for Tam's detectives.

"Right, what we've got so far is this. Last night, at nine thirty, we have a knife point robbery at an off licence in Hutton Henry in

Durham's patch. The offender was in possession of a kitchen knife and has ragged the elderly shop keeper about and made off with the takings, thought to be about three hundred pounds. The offender, who was described as tall and well built, was dressed in black jeans and top and was wearing a balaclava or ski mask. The victim, a Mr Abdul Ghaffar, is 68 years old and is now in hospital. No victim statement has been taken, but Budgie's down there now."

"Prior to the job, a witness has described a silver, family sized car in the area. Obviously, inquiries are on-going and we'll get updates as they come in. The shop's closed and we're waiting on any forensics. We'll be setting up a major incident room, based here. "At present, we have reliably sourced intelligence that Karl Wrathall, recently released from Bradford, is active in knife point robberies across the North East. As you're aware, he's currently on his toes for a number of similar jobs where the MOs are identical. This includes one job where the victim has since passed away, thus making it a murder inquiry. Yesterday we received further intel that Wrathall is in possession of a silver Ford Sierra. Our inquiries show one was nicked yesterday from Glendale Way, Usworth. The VRM is K736 TNL "We believe this motor will be on false plates and has substantial rear end damage. We also believe this was the motor used on the job and that the driver would be one Eva Devlin. The flat she and Wrathall were living in was searched with a negative result yesterday and both are currently circulated wanted. Furthermore, our snouts report that Wrathall and Eva are shacked up in Boro with some Jamaican kid he met in nick. Inquiries to find an address for him are on-going but are proving difficult so far."

He then handed back to Rocky who, it struck Kilford, had been listening with increasing restlessness to things he already knew.

"Look, the priority is to get down to Middlesbrough and try and locate Wrathall. It's not going to be easy but we're looking for his silver

Sierra with damage to the rear. You'll go down in pairs and each will have a designated area to search. I know it's a ball ache but we've got to do it the old fashioned way, pounding the streets to look for the motor, then we'll take it from there. Is that understood?" He surveyed the nodding heads.

"Good. Any questions?"

One of Tam MacFarlane's lads, a shaven headed young Yorkshire man, whom Kilford vaguely knew as Adam, asked: "If we do locate this motor outside of an address, are we going to be in a position to get a warrant?" Tam's Glaswegian growl cut in before the DI could open his mouth. "If we locate this bastard we'll no need any warrants. I'll personally identify this wanker at the window as soon as the bloody curtain twitches."

"But, it's another force area"

Tam cut in: "There's no more questions offa my boys." The DI shrugged and closed the meeting. As chairs were scraped back and notebooks folded, Tam MacFarlane beckoned Adam to one side. Kilford passed them on his way out of the room and overheard the DS.

"Look son, I've told you before: if you cannae dance, you better get the fuck offa ma stage. D'you know wha' am saying?"

"Yes, Sarge."

§

After the meeting, Shifty made his way to the station's rear car park, ostentatiously taking a cigarette packet from his jacket pocket as he left the room. Out in the car park, standing alone at the far end, he lit a fag and then, reading a number scribbled on the back of the packet, he punched it into the phone. It rang three times before it was answered.

"Harry? It's me, Rob Blair. You gave me your number. Yeah, sorry about your lad, just doin' me job like. Yeah, don't worry, I'll look out for him, as much as I can. Look, there's something to do with that that might be useful to you. Why? For old times' sake, Harry. Why else? But, we need to meet.

Can't be this afternoon 'cos I'm due down in Boro. Have to be tonight. Late. Say half eleven, same old spot."

§

Eva nodded dumbly, agreeing to whatever Karl was saying, hoping that if she just agreed he'd stop haranguing her, stop jabbing his finger at her. They were in the Sierra, across the road from the post office in Ryhope again. They'd just driven up from Middlesbrough, after staying in a house with one of Karl's mates, a black guy called Dwayne. It had all been a bit of a haze to Eva: a dark house, coloured lights, the smell of ganja, low, droning music and smack - shit loads of smack. She was still feeling the effects and she could see he was too, his eyes even crazier than usual.

"Right, just listen," he said, his voice thick with menace. "Don't even think about fucking this up again. You heard Dwayne last night, he can get me a load of that devil's dandruff shit, but he needs cash. This place just has a pair of old twats in it, we've been sat here for two minutes and no bastard's been in. If you're scared about your face being seen, pull your hood up. Yeah, that's right, like that. We're in an out, like we planned. Right!" She nodded.

"Okay, let's just do it."

Her trembling hand reached for the door, fumbled, found the handle and pulled it. She gasped as Wrathall seized her shoulder and twisted her to face him.

"For fuck's sake! You stupid bitch!" He reached over to the back seat, grabbed the crudely wrapped bath towels and thrust the parcel into her arms.

"Don't forget this."

Eva clutched the package to her chest and hurried along the pavement towards the little post office. She was living in a nightmare and wanted it over as soon as possible. She pushed at the door of the post office and it opened with a merry chime. As it closed, she glanced back and saw Karl hurrying after her, as planned.

She and Karl had checked out this place before. A counter ran along the back wall, the post office part was sectioned off and was fronted by protective glass, with stainless steel troughs on the counter below for passing cash one way and documents the other. From behind the glass, a grey haired lady beamed at her.

There was nobody else in the shop, thank God.

"Good afternoon," said the post mistress.

Eva approached the counter and placed the parcelled towels on it.

"I'd like to send this, please," she muttered, trying to keep her head down and face hidden by her hood. The old biddy said something she couldn't catch.

"Uh?"

"I said, first or second class pet?"

"Oh, first please."

"Just place it on the scales, please."

Eva put the package on the metal plate in the middle of the counter. As she did, she heard the door chime behind her. This was the signal for Karl, who would have been watching through the door.

The postmistress read the weight from a dial on her side of the counter.

"Okay," she said. "Just pass it through here please." Heart pounding and fighting to suppress an urge to scream, Eva watched as the post mistress unbolted the glass partition to one side of the counter and swung the hatch inward, so Eva could push the parcel through. But, she never got a chance.

Instead, Eva was barged roughly to one side, as Karl dived at the hatchway, sent the parcel flying through and followed it himself, wriggling and slithering through, like some monstrous reptile.

§

Betty Matterson stepped back, frozen, as this black clad, black masked figure writhed through the parcel hatch and poured itself onto the floor at her feet. It landed right beside her husband Sam, who had been kneeling there, tidying the Giro documentation on the shelves under the counter.

"What the hell?" spluttered Sam still crouched down. The man in black struggled to a sitting position and punched Sam. Sam reeled, clutching his nose, banging his head against the cupboards. The man stood, pulled a great knife from somewhere and, with his free hand, hauled a still spluttering Sam to his feet, before putting the knife to his throat. Betty clutched at her own throat, croaking, wanting to scream, but hardly able to breath.

The man growled at Sam through his mask: "Safe. Open. Now, or you're fucking dead." Goggling at the knife through his thick rimmed glasses, Sam said: "It's not as simple as that."

"It will be, you old twat, if you know what's good for you."

Sam stared back. Betty didn't know whether he was being defiant or was in shock, but, before he could obey, something seemed to snap in the man with the knife. With a roar, he hit Sam again. Sam slid to the floor and the man kicked him in the head, in the face.

Sam's glasses shattered and blood sprayed.

Betty found her voice.

"Stop! Oh my God, please stop it, I'll open it. Just stop.

Please. Don't hurt him, he's not well to start with." Sam was slumped against the cupboards, his eyes closed, blood bubbling from his nose and mouth.

The man turned to her.

"Sod him. You just open the safe now, or you'll get this." He lifted the knife to her face.

Gibbering and sobbing, Betty bent to open the safe, which, thank God, had just reached its time lock setting.

"Here, get out of the fucking way."

The man shoved her aside, then grabbed a blue cloth cash bag from inside the safe and began stuffing it with neatly wrapped bundles of new five, ten, and twenty-pound notes. But, he spun around as a door at the back of the counter area opened. Betty saw Mark, their thirty five-year old autistic son, drawn by this sudden commotion from whatever it was he did all day upstairs on his computer.

"Mark!" screamed Betty. "Get back!"

"Mum! What's going…?"

The rest of Mark's question tailed off as he gazed down in disbelief at the hilt of the knife thrust into his midriff.

§

Eva had run from the shop as soon as Karl had gone through the hatch. Now, she was back in the Sierra, praying that the sight of his Nikes disappearing over the counter would be the last she'd ever see of him. She'd give him two minutes and then, if he didn't show, she'd shuffle over into the driver's seat, start the car and drive. She'd drive and she wouldn't stop, not until she was back home in Newmarket, in another world - another sodding universe for Christ's sake!

She'd just rest her head on Mummy's shoulder and….

The driver's door opened, Karl hurled a blue bag onto her lap and dropped into the driver's seat. Without speaking, he started the car, let it into gear and set off with a squeal of tyres. She watched him as he drove, hunched over the steering wheel, chewing his lower lip. He kept speeding, then swearing and taking his foot off the accelerator, frequently darting glances at his rear view mirror. He muttered something.

"What?" she said.

"I said, I forgot the bastard towels."

"Do we need it?"

He shot her a swift, disbelieving look, then shook his head.

"Where are we going now?" she asked.

"A19."

"Back to Dwayne's?"

"Naah. North York Moors. I've booked us in a B&B for the night"

"What happened back there?" she asked.

"Eh? It went well. Look in the bag."

She opened the blue bag on her knees and saw bundles of notes.

"How much is there?" he asked.

"I don't know, must be thousands."

"Count it."

It was then that she realised that her hands were wet and sticky. She held one up, it was glistening with crimson.

Eva threw up.

CHAPTER EIGHT

Blockhead squeezed his seventeen-stone frame into the passenger seat of the Ford Mondeo, next to Tam MacFarlane, cursing under his breath.

"What's eatin' you?" asked Tam, reversing out of his parking space.

"You just can't get the staff these days."

"Anyone in particular provoked that wee observation?"

"Shifty frigging Blair."

"Oh him. What's he up tae now?"

Blockhead explained how, in the hurried briefing in the car park, detailing which teams of two would comb which areas of Middlesbrough for Wrathall's Sierra, Shifty had initially been missing only to come hurrying over late, discarding a fag end and stuffing his phone into his pocket.

"He's always doing that, the cunning little bastard, making calls to snouts on the sly. I don't know what he's up to half the time and neither does Knackers, and that's unfair on her."

"Aye, well, that's Shifty for ye, he's always been a bit fly. I'll tell ye something, you never get your dream team in this job, you'll always inherit some shite, or get some shite foisted on ye."

Blockhead nodded glumly, then turned to look over his shoulder, to check that other cars were following in convoy,

"I suppose you're right Tam. At least those two are alright." He jerked his thumb back over his shoulder.

"Alf and Bull, they're in the Primera behind us."

"Aye, they seem like a pair of good lads."

"Bull's sound. He's a good copper: conscientious, honest and never lets you down."

"And wee Alf?"

"I'll be honest, I had my doubts about Alf at one time. I thought he might ruffle feathers."

"How's that?"

"I dunno, maybe by trying too hard. But I was wrong. People accept he's just like that, a perfectionist. You know he was a professional footballer at one time?"

"I didnae know that."

"Oh aye. He grew up with Gaza and played a few games in Newcastle's first team, but then got injured." Tam whistled. "So wee Alf could've been a millionaire, married to a Spice Girl and a' that shite."

"Aye, but think of the job he'd have missed out on." They both laughed.

"Newcastle!" said Tam. "A Magpie working out of a nick in Sunderland? No wonder the little bugger keeps it quiet."

"We're a broadminded bunch. Anyway, Rocky's a black and white through and through and Alf keeps him supplied with autographed kit and stuff."

"How about you? Are you no a Mackem?"

"Rugby's my game, to be honest."

"Rugby!" said Tam. He could hardly have looked more surprised had Blockhead confessed to preferring lacrosse.

They were on the A19 now, heading south towards Middlesbrough. Blockhead checked that the radios were working. For this job, even the DSU team had been issued with personal radios, searching as they were for a violent offender, wanted for murder, in a foreign force area.

Next, he put in a call to Cleveland's Communication Control Room, to confirm that the DI had notified them of their operation and to obtain a designated radio channel. He then contacted the eight detectives from DSU and Proactive in the other four cars in the convoy to pass on the channel details. Ninety minutes later, Tam and Blockhead were walking along Zetland Road in Middlesbrough, casually examining parked cars, looking for a Silver Sierra. It was an area that had become something of a magnet for kerb crawlers, drawn from a wide catchment area of towns and villages in County Durham and North Yorkshire, much to the outrage of the local press and irritation of the police. Tam and Blockhead had debated the likelihood that Wrathall would be there, Blockhead arguing that it was just the kind of area to host a drugs den but Tam doubtful that Wrathall would be comfortable with the stepped up anti-prostitution police patrols.

"There'll be no working girls out at this time," said Blockhead.

"He's no going to be happy in a kip where the police are busy at any time," said Tam. "But, we'll give it a go."

"It's like looking for a needle in a haystack anyway."

"Aye, but dinnae forget, the Cleveland boys are on the lookout."

"There is that." Blockhead was interrupted by his phone ringing. He pulled it out of his pocket, glanced at the screen and put it to his ear.

"Boss?"

Rocky's voice boomed out of the mobile loud enough for Tam to hear and probably loud enough for most of Middlesbrough to hear.

"Get every single one of yous back up here! The post office in Ryhope has just been robbed, the postmaster's son is dead and the postmaster looks ready to follow him. A male wearing a balaclava and a young female have made off with savings from the safe. I knew this would sodding happen, so get everyone back to Sunderland now. Is that understood?"

"Yes boss. We're on our way."

§

When they met in the DSU, at four in the afternoon, the mood was sombre. Apart from the DSU team, the DI was present and Proactive was represented by Tam MacFarlane.

Rocky briefed them on the Ryhope robbery. The postmaster and postmistress's son Mark Matterson, who had sustained a stab wound in the course of the attack, had been pronounced dead in the ambulance on the way to Sunderland Royal and his father, Sam, was currently in Intensive Care. CCTV was being retrieved. It was estimated that the robbers had got away with more than thirty thousand pounds. "I knew this was going to happen and now it has. This bastard Wrathall is a psycho. He's a bad bastard and he's getting worse and you don't need to be Cracker to work out that he's going to escalate things further. Are you all following me?"

He looked at the team individually to be met with nods and subdued murmurs of assent.

"Good. Right, arseholes, there's no more time to lose, we've got to find Wrathall and his woman Eva. What have we got from the snouts so far?"

"Not a lot so far boss," said Blockhead. "Alf's spoke to Wayne Langley a few minutes ago but he's heard nothing from Eva. It's too tight for him to ring her direct as we don't know if Wrathall will answer the phone, so were relying on him coming back to us. He normally comes up trumps though."

"This is a sodding murder and we're going to be well scrutinised," said Rocky. "We can't come out of this looking shite, is that clear? I'm going to be getting well grilled by that lot upstairs, so I need answers - and I don't mean shite ones."

"Boss," said Bull, "We've got that intel that Wrathall will come in and out of the area to supply his little runners and his busiest lad Teethy Irving and we're looking at an obs point in a house that looks directly over the bus link in Donwell where Teethy's reported to be meeting his smack heads and where we reckon Wrathall drops off."

"Brilliant! So what the frigging hell are we doing here then?"

Kilford was tempted to point out that he and Bull had been setting up the obs point before priority had been given to the trip down to Middlesbrough. He thought better of it.

Knackers spoke instead.

"It's tight boss. Everyone in this office is too well known just to walk onto that estate in Donwell in broad daylight. The job would be blown out. We need a couple of unknowns."

Rocky sighed. "What do I always keep telling yous lot?" There was a shuffling of feet and furtive exchange of glances. Rocky had so many time-honoured expressions: it's the worst its ever been; or maybe, fail to plan, plan to fail. Neither seemed appropriate here. "There's no such thing as a problem, only the opportunity to put things right. Right?"

"Yes boss."

"Okay, Alf and Bull, you two finalise this obs point and I'll get you a couple of probationers to man it. Let's get it sorted for first thing in the morning. I want Wrathall locked up ASAP."

"I'll pop in on the obs point house on my way home and make arrangements," said Kilford. "It'll be getting dark by then and I'll park round the corner. I'll ring Councillor Down and let him know I'm coming."

"Councillor Down? It's his house? For God's sake, just don't tread on his toes, I've got enough problems with upstairs as it is."

"You can count on me boss."

The DI closed his eyes, pinched the bridge of his nose and shook his head.

§

Shifty entered the Engineers' Arms, a back street pub in the East End of Sunderland on the road to the port. Standing at the corner of a terrace, it was the kind of boozer that belonged to the era of Andy Capp and Shifty marvelled that it was still open for business. Its survival probably owed something to the fact that, at one time, it had been part owned by Harry Morrison and his criminal associates, who had found its bar a convenient venue and its accounts a useful pipework through which they could pass their own ill-gotten gains. Shifty knew Harry had long since given up his interest, but the Engineers continued to serve a new generation of local criminals.

Shifty found Harry in his usual corner, where he was sitting holding court to three other men, ranging in age, Shifty estimated, from twenty to sixty. Harry Morrison had gone legit, but he still commanded a lot of respect in places such as the Engineers. He had run a powerful gang in his day and had built something of a national reputation for his skill in arranging for the theft, and subsequent smooth disposal of, valuable antique artworks.

A couple of jail sentences and marriage, along with his vehement refusal to have anything to do with drugs, had persuaded Harry that it was time to operate largely on the right side of the law, but he'd managed his retirement skilfully, leaving no enemies around to seek to pay off old scores – or at least none who weren't in wheelchairs.

He saw Shifty's approach and nodded.

" 'Ow's it goin' Harry?" said Shifty.

"Been better." Harry looked at his companions and gave a slight jerk of his head. They smiled, nodded, murmured their best wishes and made themselves scarce. Shifty occupied one of the newly vacated stools and surveyed Harry, who looked maybe a little more gaunt than he'd been a few years ago and whose hair was perhaps a touch thinner, but he hadn't changed much, still looked like a hard, calculating bastard. For many years, Harry had been Shifty's snout, but it had soon become apparent to Shifty that the snout was running the detective and not the other way round. Harry had fed Shifty intelligence damaging to his competitors and, in return, he'd gleaned information on police operations that might have harmed his own interests. Towards the end, it had reached a point where cash passed from the supposed informant to the supposed handler and Shifty had become dangerously tied to Harry, so that his retirement had almost come as a relief to the policeman. But that had been a long time ago, no harm doing Harry one more favour now, surely.

" 'Ow's the lad doing?" asked Harry.

" 'E's bearing up."

Harry nodded, then said: "You said you had something for me Shifty."

"The bloke who put your lad up to it, he's called Wrathall, Karl Wrathall. He's...."

Harry waved his hand dismissively.

"I know all about Karl Wrathall. You think I've been living in a pissing monastery or something? If you want to tell me something useful, tell me where I can find the toe rag."

"Why...er...why do you want to find him Harry? That's our job you know."

Harry flashed a savage, humourless grin.

"Don't come over all Dixon-of-bloody-Dock Green with me now Rob, I know you too well. You know how it works: Graham's a threat to Wrathall and that means Wrathall's a threat to Graham, and me and the wife, even to my fucking Koi carp. It's him or us. So stop pissing me around and tell me where he's at."

"We don't know"

"Oh for shit's sake!" Harry started to rise from his stool. "You're wasting my time."

"Hang on, Harry, hang on."

Morrison sank back onto his stool, eyeing the detective dubiously.

Shifty leaned forward over the table, looked down and began sliding a beer mat back and forth. "We don't know where Wrathall's at, but we've had word that he's dropping off for a dealer, someone called Teethy Irving. Lives somewhere up in the Donwell. You find him and I reckon you'll find Wrathall."

After a quick look round, he reached into his pocket and pulled out a photo of Wrathall and a printout of Teethy Irving's address.

Harry took them. "That's more like it."

§

Kilford parked his car a couple of blocks away from Druridge Drive. He rang Councillor Down to let him know that he was there and to warn him that he'd be turning up on his doorstep with his hoodie pulled well up over his head. These precautions were undermined by the councillor waiting for him with the door open, dramatically beckoning Kilford inside and then casting quick penetrating glances up and down the road before retracting his head and closing the door. "Come on in lad, come on in. Er…do you mind if I ask you just to take your shoes off? By the way, this is June, my wife."

Kilford tugged his hood back and bent to remove his trainers while acknowledging the greeting of the woman standing slightly behind the councillor. June Down was small and trim, with neatly coiffured grey hair. She was friendly and welcoming and, Kilford soon judged, probably brighter than her husband. They took him into the living room and fussed over him with coffee and biscuits while he briefed them again on the operation the police wanted to conduct from their house. The Councillor shot him some significant looks to warn him not to go into the same kind of anatomical detail as Bull. Kilford diplomatically spared June that. Anyway, in this house, it would have been like swearing in church. The place was spotless and gleamed in its beige glory. The carpets had ankle-high pile, the skirting boards shone and there was no item on any of the surfaces that wasn't intended to be there. These included framed photos of a grinning young man, presumably their son, in his graduation robes and of beaming kids, who were, Kilford surmised, the same son's offspring. There were also ornaments – lots and lots of ornaments. "Could I have a look round upstairs?" Kilford asked.

"That's where we'll get a view of the bus stop." The upper floor was similarly pristine: beds neatly made, no clothes lying about and, in the bathroom, towels folded and a bar of soap looking as though it had come straight out of the wrapping. It would have driven Kilford mad to live there, but he found himself warming to them. These were plainly decent people and, while the area was by no means one of Sunderland's worst, it was in danger of sliding and the Downs were doing their level best to keep it respectable. Neither they nor their neighbours deserved to have pond life like Teethy Irving dealing his shit across the road.

The bathroom was the only viable spot for an obs point. Kilford pointed out to the Downs that if the transom window was opened above the toilet, there was an uninterrupted view to the bus stop. "Your boys wouldn't need to stand on the toilet seat would they?" asked the councillor.

Kilford shook his head.

"No, we could easily fit a stepladder in here; clamp a temporary shelf below this window to rest a camera on. It's no problem."

"We have a downstairs lavatory," volunteered June.

"So we could manage."

It was agreed that the bathroom could be used as an observation point over the weekend that began the following day and possibly extended into the next week.

"We'll send a couple of officers over tomorrow," said Kilford. "We'll probably dress them up in overalls and make them look like painters and decorators. That way they can bring in some step ladders and bags with their gear in. If anybody asks, you can say they're working the weekend because they're moonlighting – maybe from the council's Housing Department." He grinned, but the Councillor didn't look as if he saw the joke. June hastened to smooth things over. "That's fine. We're out tomorrow afternoon and we won't be back until late."

"That's right," said the Councillor. "We're going out for a meal and before that there's a party get-to-together to prepare for next week's Planning and Highways Committee. June helps out with the refreshments and I've got to make a bit of speech and she always likes to be there for that."

Kilford didn't need his skills in reading people's faces to detect, in the tightening of June's smile and the flicker in her eyes, a hint that listening to the Councillor's speeches wasn't quite the treat he thought it was.

§

Kilford got up early the next morning. He crept from the bed, careful not to wake Vicki. He wanted to let her enjoy her Saturday morning lie-in and soften the blow when she learnt he was going into work.

He dressed himself, then went to Natalie's room, woke her and cajoled her into getting Beth up and dressed. Then he went downstairs and prepared breakfast: a coffee for himself, cereals and juice for the girls and a carefully prepared tray of tea, toast, jam and juice for Vicki. He took this upstairs as soon as the girls were seated at the kitchen table.

"Mmm, what's this for?" said Vicki, rubbing her eyes. "Why does it have to be for anything?" He kissed her on her forehead.

She sat upright and fixed him with a stare.

"You're going into work, aren't you?"

"It's just for a couple of hours pet, there's hell on."

"You bastard!" were her parting words, as he closed the bedroom door.

When he arrived at the station, he grabbed a bacon sandwich from the canteen, where he bumped into Bull, who'd had the same idea. They'd just finished and were leaving when Blockhead entered the canteen to tell them that they, along with the rest of the DSU team, were wanted in one of the parade rooms.

"What's going on?" asked Bull.

"The Ryhope job's on our patch and has been classed as a major incident and, as we speak, they're setting up the parade room as a major incident room with all the bells and whistles. You two will be vital cogs in this vast and sophisticated piece of machinery." They found the parade room almost as cramped as their usual office, containing as it did more than twenty police and civilian staff, all drafted in, Kilford guessed, from across the Northumbria Force. The police included Detective Constables, a couple of Detective Sergeants and Detective Inspectors. Standing apart from them was a tall, angular man with a grave expression, short greying hair and round wire rimmed glasses, deep in conversation with a short, stocky, bullnecked man, with a shaven head. "That's Detective Chief Superintendent Bob Unwin," said Blockhead in a low voice, nodding towards the taller man. "He's SIO and that's Detective Chief Inspector Jim Lawson, his deputy."

Kilford knew that Unwin, appointed the senior investigating officer, had a reputation as a professional, but also as an ambitious operator, with an eye to becoming Assistant Chief Constable as a matter of urgency.

"And this is us, the Intelligence Cell," said Blockhead, leading them to a far corner of the room where there was a table set apart and, standing around it were Rocky, Knackers and Shifty.

"Good morning arseholes," said Rocky. "As you can see, you're now in the Big Time."

Kilford looked round the room, at the civilians setting up computers, DCs assembling flip charts and senior Detectives trying to look busy by talking urgently into their mobiles. They'd all realised yesterday that the Wrathall robberies would become a major incident, with all the paraphernalia of the Holmes IT system, huge manpower and top brass leadership. Part of him was disappointed that the direction of the inquiry was taken directly out of their hands and that they were to now have a supporting role, but, overall, he was pleased. An inquiry he was instrumental in had become major league. Yeah, like the boss said: it was the big time. Premiership stuff.

"Right you lot, gather round," said Rocky. He jerked his head towards the two senior policemen in the room, still in earnest conversation. "Any second now, the Demon Headmaster and Oddjob over there are going to make one of their rousing speeches and I want to be out of here before they do, so listen carefully. I'm told that yous lot will form the Intelligence Cell for this inquiry – God help us! You'll be tasked with using sources to locate Wrathall and his lass. However, remember your protocols and don't go disclosing sensitive intel. Remember, there's nice to know and there's need to know. At the moment, nobody but us needs to know about our obs point operation, not until it yields something concrete. Got that? Good. Right, Alf and Bull, as soon as you can, slip away, get back to the DSU and get that OP up and running. I've sorted your probationers."

For an hour and a half, the team listened to the briefing from Unwin and Lawson, sat through the introductions, nodded gravely while Blockhead delivered an edited summary of their intel to date and noted carefully the initial allocation of tasks. The whole room watched a compilation of what CCTV footage was available from the raids, including the last in Ryhope. There were gasps at the point where the robber dived over the counter and wriggled through the parcel hatch. But Kilford sat forward on the edge of his seat, staring intently at the screen. There was something…something about Wrathall, but he just couldn't nail it. His attempts were interrupted by the need to brief one of the DSs, an eager young go-getter. Kilford explained to him that Karl Wrathall had been named by a reliable source as being behind robberies which had the same MO as those that had resulted in murder. Blockhead explained that they were pressing this informant, along with all other sources, for the possible whereabouts of Wrathall.

"Okay," said the DS. "Good. Spot on. Regular updates, yeah?" Then he left them and, as soon as he was out of earshot, Bull muttered,

"Wanker." After that, the DSU were left to sort out their own space and field queries from other detectives. Blockhead called Budgie in Chester-LeStreet to fill him in, Knackers and Shifty rang round their snouts and Kilford put in a few unanswered calls to Ratty. Then he told Bull about his meeting the previous night with Councillor Down. They then made a discreet exit to return to their own office to spend the rest of the morning putting things in place for the obs point. This done, Kilford told Bull he was taking Crapper for a quick walk before grabbing a bite to eat and they arranged to meet in the DSU after lunch.

§

Kilford entered the DSU to find Bull alone, leaning back in his chair playing Snake on his Nokia.

"Busy I see," said Kilford.

"Piss off!"

"So, where's our probies then?"

"According to Rocky they're coming up any minute, they're going to report after parading on and it's five past two now."

There was a hesitant tap at the door.

"Ta da!" said Bull and got up to open the door to a pair of fresh-faced young Constables in neatly pressed uniforms and with boots bulled to a gleaming finish. One, slightly taller, introduced himself as PC Burns and his companion as PC Coxon.

"Come on in lads, make yourselves at home," said Kilford. "I'm known as Alf and he's Bull – 'cos he's full of it."

"Piss off, or I'll tell 'em why you're called Alf."

The two probationers exchanged nervous grins and took a couple of hesitant steps into the office. "I see you boys have had lunch," said Kilford, winking at Bull.

"And what leads you to that conclusion DC Kilford?" returned Bull.

"Elementary my dear Bull, you know my methods. You'll observe that PC Coxon's chest is still covered in fresh pasty crumbs, Greggs if I'm not mistaken, but that'll have to await confirmation by forensics."

Bull peered at Coxon's chest.

"Bugger me, it's a Tasmanian Devil Greggs pasty eater. I swear you've got more pasty on yer shirt than in yer mouth mate."

The probationers both laughed, though Coxon blushed and started slapping at his chest with both hands. "Sit your arses down lads and relax," said Bull. "No doubt it's been explained to you that in the DSU we're a highly trained and elite team of crack coppers, operating at the cutting edge of the fight against crime, but don't let that intimidate you. You have been handpicked to assist us in a mega case and your mission, should you choose to accept it, is to dress up in paint-spattered overalls and stand on somebody's bog for hours on end staring at a bus stop."

"They must not, under any circumstances, stand on the bog!" gasped Kilford in mock horror.

By now the two PCs were looking both confused and worried. Kilford put them out of their misery and gave them an outline of the Wrathall case and details of the observation point in the Councillor's house. He explained that they were to dress as painters and decorators in the overalls that currently lay in supermarket bags on the office floor and were to take an old Escort van, which was parked at the back of the station, and proceed to Councillor Down's house on Druridge Drive where he would let them in and show them to an upstairs bathroom. There they were to set up stepladders and observe a bus stop opposite the house.

"You'll be alone in the house until the Councillor and his good lady return home at about half nine. At which point you contact us and, all being well, we'll tell you to knock off until tomorrow morning."

Bull unfolded a map on his desk and pointed out Druridge Drive and the location of number twenty four and the bus stop. The two probationers bent over it and Kilford could sense their excitement and their nervousness. Then Bull spread out photos of Wrathall and Teethy Irving.

"Right," he said. "To recap: Wrathall and Eva Devlin are wanted for murder and a number of robberies and we've good intel that Wrathall is dropping heroin off to Teethy Irving at this bus stop, possibly in a silver Ford Sierra with rear end damage." The probationers nodded.

"All you need to do is watch for activity at the bus stop. You could see Teethy sorting his customers out and, if we're lucky, we might get Wrathall turning up on the plot in the silver Sierra with Eva. Got it?"

"If we see Teethy dealing, do we shout it in?" asked PC Burns.

Kilford shook his head.

"No, Teethy Irving's dealing is not what this is about. By all means take some snaps and log it in this." He handed them an observation log book. "While one of you is watching and describing, the other is to record what's being said. Get it? If Wrathall turns up, then you shout that in over this radio. You're the trigger to give us the heads up.

"Boys, there's naff all to worry about. We've got back up everywhere. If Wrathall turns up we've got traffic and armed response plotted up in the area. Yous just shout it and shout up which way he leaves the area.

We need to know whether he's heading towards Usworth or towards Concord." He pointed at the map.

"Are you both clear? Good."

Bull handed the probationers a police radio and a spare battery. "We're working off channel 87, it's a stand-alone channel just for this job. Take this mobile and we'll ring you every half hour to make sure you're okay."

Kilford looked at the two young probationers. They looked bright enough and eager enough. They'd do. "One other thing lads. Remember, it's not our house, it belongs to a Councillor, so don't go scattering pasty crumbs all over his carpets. Those carpets might be sort of pasty coloured but I'm sure his missus would notice. Right, get into your overalls and we'll show you to your van and I'll ring the Councillor to let him know you're on your way. He'll let you have a spare key, don't lose it."

§

Harry Morrison took the A66 exit off the A1 and, at the junction roundabout, turned into the car park of the Scotch Corner Hotel, a big red brick 1930s building and popular meeting point for those on business. And Harry had important business.

He pulled his Mercedes into a parking space and switched off the engine. He looked at his watch: ten to three. It had taken him fifty minutes to get here and he was ten minutes before time. Tel Firman's boys had to come up from South London, but if they'd made an early start, they'd be about here by now.

Harry had put the call in to Tel last night, after his meeting with Rob "Shifty" Blair. In his wheezing tones, Tel had expressed surprise at this blast from the past, they had exchanged the usual pleasantries and Harry had explained that his retirement had been rudely interrupted and he needed Tel to help him out with a little job. Toot sweet.

"No problem my old son. 'Course, you'll appreciate things are a lot dearer now than what they used to be."

Harry had snarled silently into the receiver but had agreed the fee, which now sat in the form of used twenties in a cheap rucksack in the passenger foot well. He had spent most of the morning putting that together. It was never easy to get your hands on fifteen grand at short notice. The rest of his time had been spent fixing the whereabouts of Teethy Irving. That had been considerably easier. Harry knew a lot of people who either owed him favours or whose sense of self-interest inclined them to do him favours. They, in turn, knew a lot of other people and, given the nature of Teethy's business, it had hardly taken six degrees of separation to run him to earth.

Harry's phone rang.

"Hello?"

"Mr Morrison?" The accent was foreign. Arab? East European?

"Yes."

"I am Besnik. Mr Terry sends me. We are here, in the hotel bar."

"Be right with you Besnik."

§

Danny Burns was uncomfortable. He was standing on a stepladder, squinting through the viewfinder of a long lens digital SLR camera, which was resting on a short plank, clamped across the upstairs bathroom window of number twenty four Druridge Drive. The top of the window was open and through it, and the camera, Danny was watching the bus stop on the other side of the road. He was a tall lad and had been hunched over his camera for an hour and now his shoulders were aching.

He was also bored. Nothing was happening across the road and conversation with his companion in the bathroom, Mike Coxon, was becoming strained. They were probationers together and got on well enough but had little in common. Danny, who was from Newcastle, was streetwise and quick-witted. Mike was from the wilds of rural Northumberland and was more deliberate, even slow. Also, he was always bloody hungry. Danny had been aghast, but not surprised, when Mike had stuffed that pasty into his mouth before going upstairs to the DSU. He hadn't forgotten or forgiven that yet.

He was about to ask Mike to relieve him on the stepladder when he saw movement on the pavement opposite. Somebody was approaching the bus stop. He studied the features through the magnification of the viewfinder.

It looked like, no, it definitely was, Teethy Irving!

He clicked the camera.

"Who is it?" asked Coxon, standing by the toilet.

"Irving."

Then another figure approached the bus stop from the opposite direction, reached Irving, paused, there was some kind of exchange. Danny took frantic shots.

"What's happening Danny? I've got to write it down."

"Er… suspect Irving meets young Asian male." Click. Click. "Irving hands him something… I think… might be drugs. No, don't write that bit." Click. Click. "They've gone. Did you get all that?"

"Yeah, yeah. Was the other bloke Wrathall?"

"I said he was Asian didn't I?"

"Oh aye."

Mike had just finished writing when the mobile in his pocket rang. He swore, rested his log book and pen on the edge of the wash basin and plunged his hand through the opening in his overalls to reach into his trouser pocket. He felt the still vibrating phone.

"Quick man!" urged Danny.

Mike brought the phone out but his hand caught on his overalls. He fumbled, the phone span out of his grasp, he grabbed at it, missed and then, wide eyed, could only watch it spinning, over the open toilet bowl.

Plop!

Danny Burns let his head fall in defeat and groaned.

"Brilliant! Just fucking brilliant!"

§

Kilford held his mobile up and looked at in disbelief.

"It's gone straight to voicemail!"

"The daft bastards haven't switched it off surely?" said Bull.

"They hadn't when we spoke an hour ago."

"I'll get 'em on this," said Bull and snatched the radio up from his desk. Kilford watched as his partner's face worked with the effort of the ensuing conversation and listened to his running commentary.

"What..?" To Kilford: "What the hell is wrong with this radio?"

"What..? Oh change the frigging battery for Christ's sake." To Kilford: "He says the battery indicator's showing full, at least that's what I think he says."

"What..? I'm only getting every fourth bastard word. What..? Fuck's sake! What..? Just try changing the bastard battery and call us back."

The conversation was renewed a few seconds later but the result was little better and all Bull could gather was that the probies had made a sighting of Irving but not Wrathall. He also understood there was an unspecified problem with the mobile. Then the radio went dead.

"Piece o' shite!" said Bull and hurled his own handset onto the desk. Kilford's mobile rang.

"That'll be them! No, it's Ratty! Ratty, where the bloody hell have you been? I've been calling you for days."

"I've been fucking busy man, it's been doin' me head in. I've not been able to get a minute to meself to gi' yous a call."

"That's bollocks Ratty."

"Aw man, I'm sorry, but I've had all kinds of shit going on you wouldn't believe. But I'm here now. What can I do for ye?"

"Ratty, going forward, we'll have to get together and have a little chat about your terms of service. At the moment, there are more pressing matters. Where… is… shagging… Wrathall?"

"No need to shout man. I've been trying. I swear to God I have. But I've told ye, I can't ring Eva. If Wrathall picks it up he'll fucking kill her – and me."

"Ring your contacts, ring your mates. Somebody must know where they are. What about Teethy Irving? You know him?"

"Aye."

"Get in touch with him. Ask him if he's seen Wrathall, ask if he's busy with the gear, if he's likely to see him.

But be careful."

"Fucking right I will. Don't worry man, I'll get yous something, I promise."

"Do that Ratty and if I ring you, you answer or get back to me right away. Got that? Good." Kilford had just ended the call when there was a familiar thump on the door. Bull opened it to let in the DI. Rocky dropped himself into a seat while Kilford told him about Ratty's call. Rocky grunted. "Keep on at the arsehole. What about the OP? Any update there?"

"Yes boss. Teethy's being one busy little lad and he's been clocked dealing, but there's been no sign of that bastard Wrathall."

"It's early days yet. Just make sure we keep in touch with the lads 'cos they'll be shitting themselves. Why are you looking like that? What's fucking happened." Kilford explained their comms problems. "I don't believe this! Phone and radio both on the fucking blink! The equipment we get is such shite. I tell you: it's worse than it's ever been. Ring the Councillor's home number. Surely to God that can't be out of order as well. What are the plans to get them out of there?"

"We'll come up with something boss. We'll give 'em a ring on the landline and then we're going to wait till it's dark and go and get 'em."

"See that you do. We don't want 'em bumping into Wrathall or Irving. If I've sent two probies out to get stabbed it won't look good on my next appraisal."

§

Harry Morrison raised his pint to his lips.

"Cheers," he said, scrutinising the two men opposite him in the hotel bar. Both sitting, he noted, with their backs to the wall from where they could see anyone entering the room. Besnik and Leka were their names. Besnik was huge, his dark hair close-cropped. He had a bullet head, no discernible neck and thick eyebrows that met in the middle; probably in his thirties. Leka, who was a few years younger, said little, was tall and angular with a shaven head, high cheek bones and cold, grey eyes. They both looked like evil bastards. They were Albanian apparently, which didn't surprise Harry. He knew that in London successive waves of immigrants inevitably included some gangsters, who could only compete against established players by being even more ruthless. Tel Firman himself had originally been muscle for a bunch of Glaswegians around Kings Cross but had decided to move South of the River when Jamaicans used guns against the Jocks who were more familiar with knives. Now, apparently it was Albanians and Kosovans, like Besnik and Leka here, who were making things uncomfortable for the Rastas. From what Harry heard, there was even talk now of Somalians putting the frighteners on the Albanians. But Harry was sure this pair would do what was required.

He had made his contacts with London mobsters back in the days when he needed to shift stolen antiques and artworks. It was a world far removed from Antiques Roadshow, you were often talking serious money and that often meant serious violence. This was where the

London connection had been so useful. Sure, you could always hire local muscle, but the North East was a village and people knew each other, so local players were reluctant to go in too hard, were always wary of starting a blood feud, of offing somebody whose brother or son could come and return the favour years later. No, Harry had found that paying London prices was worth it to get a pro who would come in, do the job and not give a flying fart for whose toes they trod on. People respected Harry for that – and respect was important.

"Mr Terry sends his regards," said Besnik.

"How is he?"

"He is good."

Harry nodded. He used his foot to push the rucksack that was on the floor under the table towards the Albanians. Besnik didn't look at it, but reached down for it and put it on his lap.

"You know what the job is?" asked Harry.

"Thees man Wrathall," said Besnik, pronouncing the name with about six Rs. "Karl Wrathall."

"That's right."

"Where do we find him?"

"First you need to speak to a bloke called Teethy Irving." Harry handed over a folded up piece of paper and a photo. "That's all the details you need. He'll tell you where Wrathall is – if you insist."

Leka's impassive face broke into a wolfish smile. "Then you find Wrathall and you make my problem go away."

§

Kilford and Bull were becoming seriously worried. It was getting on for eight and they hadn't been able to make contact with the obs point. They'd repeatedly rung Councillor Down's landline but it hadn't been answered and the mobile and the radio given to the probies both seemed to be still dead. The DI had been half-joking when he'd talked about the probies being stabbed. But what if Wrathall had got wind of the surveillance? The bloke was an obvious headcase.

After another failed attempt, Kilford hung up. "Come on Bull, we'll have to go over there and get them out."

"What's our cover?"

"You'll see."

They got their jackets, left and locked the office and made their way to the back of the station. Kilford explained that they were going to pick up Crapper. He would be their cover.

"We'll be just two blokes walking the dog. People won't take us for cops."

Bull was unconvinced but admitted he didn't have a better idea.

Kilford was relieved that Pooch wasn't on duty. His heavy hints about Crapper overstaying his welcome had given way to an increasing insistence that alternative accommodation be found. Kilford had yet to come up with any solution. Relations with Vicki wouldn't bear the strain of a renewed attempt to bring Crapper into the family home, but Kilford had grown fond of the dog, who greeted him, as usual, with a thrashing tail and pawing at the cage door and, when released he jumped up, trying to lick Kilford's face. Kilford stroked and patted him. The dog was looking good. His fur might not be exactly glossy, but it was no longer matted and mangy and his eyes were bright. He trotted happily along beside the two Detectives and jumped eagerly into the back of the car, panting with excitement.

It was about nine when they pulled up at a quiet street on the top end of the Donwell Estate. Both men were wearing hoodies and they pulled them over their heads before they got out of the car.

"Alf, you sure about this?" asked Bull.

Kilford opened the back of the car and let Crapper out, slipping a lead on the bounding, excited dog. "Will you stop worrying man? No one's going to give us a second look with Crapper on the team? Anyway, we're only going in the house to get the lads out, so pack in twisting man."

They strolled through the estate, trying to take their time and look relaxed, while remaining alert for anyone who might see them and recognise them. Bull nodded at the dog. "He walks canny on the lead doesn't he?"

"Aye, he's a good lad. Aren't you son? You ever thought of getting a dog Bull?"

"Y' can bugger off, he's your problem."

They reached number twenty four Druridge Drive, glanced up and down the road and then slipped through the garden gate. Kilford was relieved to see there was no light on above the door, so they would be well into the shadows. He approached the door and tapped on it. There was no answer. He tried again, louder. Still nothing. Bull took a step back and looked up.

"Bathroom light's on. I bet they're up there, thinking they've been rumbled and shitting it."

Bull went up to the door and squatted down, batting away Crapper who was trying to lick his face. He pushed the letter box open.

"Lads open the door. Ha'way man, it's us."

There was a moment's silence and then the canter of footsteps coming down the stairs. The door was opened to reveal the nervous face of PC Coxon. "Oh, it's you." He opened the door to let them in and as they removed their shoes and entered the hall, Burns came down the stairs to join them.

"We've been trying to ring you on this number," said Bull, pointing at the telephone in the hall.

"We wondered whether it was you. We thought we'd better not answer it, in case we blew our cover like," said Coxon. "We thought we'd better just sit tight." Bull grunted. "Good lads, you did the best thing. Anyway, we're here now and you can jack it in until tomorrow. We'll just take a look at the obs point and get your log book before we go."

Kilford took Crapper's lead off and pointed at him to stay put. The dog gazed up at him, his tale sweeping back and forth over the beige carpet, watching the four policemen heading up the stairs. The four of them crowded into the bathroom. Kilford picked up the police radio which was on the shelf above the sink.

"So, this is on the blink?"

"Completely dead now," confirmed Burns.

"What about the mobile?"

Coxon and Burns shuffled their feet and exchanged nervous glances.

"You didn't have it switched off, did you?"

"No... we... I..." Coxon cleared his throat. "Er... dropped it down the bog."

Kilford looked at the toilet, seat still open under the stepladders, then at Bull and back to Coxon. "Why, didn't you keep the lid down, for God's sake?" Coxon cleared his throat again.

"Er... in case we wanted to slash like."

Kilford looked at Bull. Bull shrugged. Kilford sighed.

"Just get your stuff together and we'll get out of here." The probationers busied themselves gathering up phone, radio, log book and other items and stuffing them into their holdall. They were sheepish and Kilford felt sorry for them.

"You've done a cracking job lads," he said. "We'll go through the log book back in the office now let's Foxtrot Oscar. I'll give the Councillor a ring later and confirm things for tomorrow. Unless he says otherwise, you'll be back at nine in the morning. And tomorrow…" he broke of as he noticed Bull grimacing and sniffing. "What's wrong with you?"

"There's a funny smell, it's like…."

"Bull man! You're obsessed with smells. Every kip we enter you…." Kilford sniffed. "You're right!" His eyes widened in horror. "Crapper!"

They rushed from the bathroom to the head of the stairs and looked down. Crapper was on his back, writhing ecstatically. A few feet to his right was a pile of freshly laid excrement.

They gazed in stunned silence, which was broken by Coxon's throaty chuckle from behind Kilford's left shoulder.

"I reckon that looks worse on the carpet than pasty crumbs," he chortled.

Kilford rounded on him, his finger pointing.

"You two are going to clear that up."

"Lads!" said Bull. "We'll get this sorted. Come on Alf, it's not their fault man."

Kilford sighed, guilty for his loss of temper.

"Aye. Sorry. Let's make this a team effort and quick. Yous two, get in the kitchen, grab some cloths and see if there's any cleaning liquid or something." They went down the stairs, two or three at a time. Crapper, clearly sensing trouble, tucked himself away in a corner. The probationers ran into the kitchen.

Kilford hissed at Bull: "This needs to be quick. The Councillor and his missus are due back any minute. They're not even expecting us to be here, never mind Crapper and his crap."

The probies came out of the kitchen, armed with J Cloths and assorted plastic bottles. While Kilford examined the bottles, he sent Coxon back up the bathroom to grab some toilet roll to pick up the bulk of Crapper's handiwork, which could then be flushed away. Kilford looked at one bottle.

"Bleach? God no! That'll probably turn their carpet white. Bingo! Carpet stain remover." They got on their hands and knees wiping and scrubbing. Crapper, assuming all was forgiven and that this was a new game, gambolled around them, play biting at the cloths.

"Alf," said Bull. "Sort Crapper out mate, he's a bloody nightmare."

"Just shut up and scrub!"

Ten minutes later they stood surveying their handiwork. Kilford was satisfied the carpet was clean, but afraid it looked damp. Hopefully, it wouldn't be noticed. Then Crapper barked as there was a fumbling at the front door which partially opened. "Who's there?" Came a familiar, tremulous voice. With what struck Kilford as admirable presence of mind, Burns scooped up the rags and bottles and darted into the kitchen.

"Er… it's alright Councillor," said Bull. "It's just us… the police."

The door opened fully and the Councillor and June Down crossed the threshold.

"We didn't expect you to be still here," said the Councillor.

"Oh, and you've brought a dog," said Mrs Down. At this point, Crapper, tail scything the air, planted his front paws on Mrs Down's thighs. Kilford clenched his fists and uttered a low, strangled cry.

"Get down!"

"Oh, he's alright," said June stroking Crapper's head.

"He's lovely. We used to have one called Roy, a German Shepherd, just like him."

"Aye, spitting image," said the councillor, smiling and joining in ruffling the fur on Crapper's head.

"What's he called?" asked June.

Bull began: "Cra…."

"Cranberry," cut in Kilford.

"Cranberry? That's a strange name."

"Yes… he… er…."

"He was born on Christmas Day," said Bull.

"Oh, how sweet."

"Is he a good police dog?" asked the councillor.

"Not really," said Kilford, reflecting on the previous ten minutes.

"Why's that?"

"He's too… docile and too… trusting."

"Yes, and too affectionate," added Bull.

"We'll probably have to retire him."

Crapper, who, as Kilford had learned, had a well developed eye for the main chance, looked winsomely from the Councillor to June, his head cocked to one side.

"Oh, the poor thing!" exclaimed June and squatted to hold Crapper's head in her hands. Crapper obliged by licking her face. She laughed with a girlish joy and looked up at Kilford.

"I don't suppose," she said. "I don't suppose, we could adopt him?" Kilford smiled.

"I think we might be able to arrange something."

CHAPTER NINE

Besnik pulled up at the kerb. He was driving a black Mitsubishi L200 Warrior. It was a vehicle he had an immense pride in and his ownership of it was the fulfilment of his deepest ambitions. It was a beast, a man's car, that only millionaires could own at home and he had worked hard for it.

He rolled the window down and craned his neck to look at the houses lining the road. They were dilapidated semis, pockmarked pebbledash and overgrown gardens, some in worse repair than others, but none could be called desirable. He had parked outside number nineteen. According to the piece of paper in his hand, Teethy Irving lived at number twenty one.

He nodded towards it and turned to Leka sitting beside him.

"This is the place."

Leka leaned forward and opened the glove compartment, from which he took a Makarov 9mm: snub, black and wicked. He held it in his hand, hefting it.

"Put that back!" snapped Besnik. "You should not have brought that, you dick! Don't you know, in this country now, they put you away for five years just for having a shooter."

"Five years? And you don't even have to use it?"

"That's right."

"Pussies!" snarled Leka and threw the pistol back into the glove compartment. He reached for his door.

"Wait!" said Besnik.

A man had come out of number nineteen and was heading down the garden path. He walked with the aid of a stick and, as he came out of the gate and turned towards them, Besnik could see that his right leg was prosthetic.

"Is that him?" asked Leka.

Besnik shook his head.

"No. Nobody said our man has one leg. Wait until this one has gone."

§

A dirty needle had cost Adam Pugh, or Pegleg Pughie, his limb four years ago. The experience had made him marginally more careful about sterilising his needles, but hadn't done anything to lessen his heroin habit. Hence his visit to Teethy Irving. He'd broken the rules by coming to Teethy's address but the dealer hadn't been answering his phone and Pughie was growing desperate. The visit had proved to be a waste of time and that worried him, so, head down, he didn't pay any attention to the big, black pickup parked a few yards away but he looked up when someone called his name.

"Pughie!"

Coming towards him on the pavement was a slight figure in joggers and sweatshirt, baseball cap raffishly sideways on his head.

"Ow y' doin' Mazza?"

"I'm a'reet man. You been to see Teethy?"

"Aye, but the fucker's out. Bloke next door says every other Sunday, he goes off the Peterlee to see his bairn. Not back 'til tomorrow morning."

"Bollocks!" said Mazza.

Pughie turned. He thought that he'd heard Mazza's sentiments echoed from the open window of the big, black vehicle to his right. There were two blokes inside. The one nearest turned to his companion and spoke in what sounded like a foreign language. Then the window purred up, the engine started and the pickup drove away.

Had Pughie understood Albanian, he would have known that the driver had said: "Then we come back tomorrow."

§

Kilford and his family watched as a man in a straw boater passed them driving a one horse carriage which rattled over the cobbles. Beth, her eyes like saucers, gawped, but then her attention was captured by the arrival of a double-decker tram, which came clattering round the corner to stop on the road a few feet away from them. The Conductor, a watch chain spread impressively across his waistcoat, stepped onto the road and invited those waiting at the stop to shuffle aboard.

Kilford and his wife and daughters were among them.

On this rare Sunday off, he had taken them to Beamish Open Air Museum a few miles outside Durham. The three-hundred-acre site, which recreated life in the rural North East and its pit villages in Edwardian England, had been Natalie's choice of day out, as it complemented a school history project she was working on. They had ridden from the museum's reception building to the pit village on an old bus, had been inside the mine, the Co-op store, the bank, dentist's, school, chapel and café. Now they were returning to the reception area and gift shop. They boarded the tram and the girls wanted to go on the top deck, but when they reached it, they found only room for three, so Kilford volunteered to go back downstairs. There he squeezed onto a seat beside a middle-aged woman, who shot him a resentful look, before moving her bag to accommodate him. Kilford nodded his thanks and immediately took out his phone. He rang Bull who was at work, splitting his time between manning the major incident intel hub, updating the sex offender files and liaising with the probies in the OP.

"How's it going?" asked Kilford.

"Sod all happening. Teethy doesn't seem to be active today."

"Obviously not the kind of man who would work on the Sabbath. Stan and Ollie behaving themselves?"

"Why aye. I issued them with a carrier pigeon for today. Reckon they can't drop that down the bog." Kilford chuckled.

"Anyway," said Bull. "Have you made arrangements to hand Crapper over to the Councillor and his missus?"

"No way! I've got that dog on an intensive house training course. I've promised Pooch a twenty-year-old malt if he can teach him not to dump indoors. Then he goes to the Councillor. Pooch 'll do it, he can work wonders. That bloke reminds me of Barbara Woodhouse."

"That'll be his tweed skirt and sensible shoes?"

"Aye, summat like that."

They chatted for a few minutes until Kilford felt a tap on his shoulder. He turned to see Natalie standing behind him. She was rolling her eyes to indicate that behind her, and over her shoulder, Beth was coming down the tram's spiral staircase, followed, Kilford could see, by the red trainers and lower legs of the white jeans Vicki was wearing. He realised that they were arriving at the museum entrance and the tram was slowing.

"Bull, got to go, see you tomorrow."

He pocketed the phone, ruffled Natalie's hair in affectionate gratitude and rose from his seat with an innocent smile for Vicki and Beth.

§

On Monday morning Ratty rolled out from under his fetid sheets with a groan. He felt like shit: cold, his mouth dry and his skin itching like a bastard, but he had stuff to do, people to see.

Ratty had told Kilford he hadn't been in touch because he'd been busy. He had. He'd been off his head on H, that new gear, Devil's Dandruff, deedee. The days had passed in states of euphoria, between longer periods of lethargy and sedation. But, towards the end of each of these periods of nodding, Ratty had been increasingly gnawed by a worm of anxiety. He was worried about Eva.

Wrathall was a sick, mad bastard and it was only a matter of time before he dropped her in some serious shit. Every time this anxiety arose, it prompted Ratty's next fix. Now, however, this serious shit had happened. Now Wrathall had only got her involved in a shagging murder. Ratty had almost resolved that he had to do something before his last conversation with Kilford. Now he knew he had to act, he had to see Teethy Irving.

He went into the bathroom, emptied his bladder and even brushed his teeth to try to freshen his mouth. He then threw some clothes on and went into the kitchen. He couldn't face food, but he poured half a dozen Dulcolax into his hand and washed them down with a few mouthfuls of coke. Thanks to the smack, Ratty hadn't had a bowel movement for the best part of a week, so he'd been dosing himself with laxative for the past twenty four hours, as yet without result. But, an hour later, when he alighted from the bus near Teethy's place he could feel something stirring in his insides. Ten minutes after that, when he was walking up the garden path to Teethy's, he was farting repeatedly and ominously.

The house had originally been one half of a council house semi, but had been bought and converted, illegally, cheaply and amateurishly, through plasterboard partitioning, into five separate flats. When Ratty knocked on Teethy's door on the ground floor, it shuddered in its frame. There were sounds of a drawer being slammed and footsteps from within and then the door was opened ajar and Teethy's wary face peered out.

"A'reet Teethy," said Ratty, shuffling from one foot to the other.

"Ratty,"

"`Ow's it going?"

"Canny. What's up?"

"Er… can I come in, like?"

Eyeing him suspiciously, Teethy stood back to let Ratty enter, closing the door behind him. Once in the room that contained a bed and a few pieces of furniture, Ratty was conscious that he'd not come prepared with any sort of cover story, or any cunning way of bringing the conversation around to Wrathall, without arousing Teethy's suspicion and the threat of his interest getting back to Wrathall. Also, the increasingly urgent churning in his guts made it difficult to think.

"So… er… `ow's things Teethy?"

"Like I said, they're canny."

"That's cush." Ratty took a packet of cigarettes from his hoody pocket, extracted one and offered another to Teethy. He lit them and dropped himself into a threadbare armchair.

"Look Ratty, I had to go to Peterlee yesterday, I've got shit to do. What?"

He stepped back as Ratty, his eyes suddenly widened in alarm, got rapidly to his feet again, dropping his fag onto the carpet.

"Teethy man, can I use yer bog?"

"Fucking 'ell! Go on, it's next door."

Like a startled rabbit, Ratty darted back out into the hallway and then into the adjacent toilet cubicle. Teethy swore, picked up Ratty's cigarette, which he extinguished, before putting the still generous stub behind his ear and closed the door through which Ratty had just exited. Then he grimaced at the explosive noises coming though the thin partition between his room and the toilet.

But these were drowned by a crash as the door he had just closed was kicked in.

Teethy's first reaction was that he was being raided and he felt a stab of relief that his stash wasn't kept in his flat. Relief gave way to unease as he contemplated the characters in the doorway. One was a huge bastard with black eyebrows going right across his receding forehead. The other was a thin, nasty looking bastard. No way were they bizzies.

They stepped into the room. Teethy took a pace back.

The big one followed and pointed at Teethy's face. "Hey, it's Bug's Bunny!" he turned to the other and laughed. His companion gave a thin smile. The big one turned back to Teethy.

"You are Teethy, yes? Teethy Irving?"

Teethy swallowed and backed up again.

"I've done piss all. What's I supposed to have done, like?"

"Hey, Mr Teethy, if you've done piss all, then there's piss all to worry about. We're looking for a Karl, Karl Wrathall. You know where he is, I think." Teethy shook his head.

"Don't have a clue lads, honest."

The big man shook his own head sadly and then, in one swift movement, lunged at Teethy, grabbed him by the neck and shoulder, yanked him forwards and threw him against the wall he had been facing, his head smashing into it with such force that it dented and splintered the plasterboard.

§

Ratty who had been sitting on the toilet, listening transfixed, jumped when the wall of the cubicle to his right shuddered under the force of a powerful impact. Pieces of plasterboard were forced inwards, jagged splits running from a central point, marked by a small hole. Ratty gasped, stood and hauled his pants up. He opened the lavatory door, desperate to make his escape from whatever shit was going down next door, but he closed and bolted it again when he saw the door to Teethy's was wide open and his escape attempt couldn't go unnoticed.

He stood, holding his breath as he listened to the sounds coming from next door, now much clearer, thanks to the head-shaped dent in the plaster board. He heard feet scuffling, foreign voices swearing, then thumping and Teethy squealing his protests. Ratty dropped to his knees and put his eye to the newly created hole. Through it he watched the two men throw Teethy onto his bed. The big one leaned over Teethy, holding him down by his shoulders. The other forced Teethy's head down with his left hand and in his right he held something up. Ratty could just see that it was a hammer, before it was brought down against Teethy's mouth. There was a sickening crunch and pieces of something flew upwards. Ratty clenched his own teeth in sympathy.

"Tell us where he is!" roared the big man.

Teethy's reply was muffled and bubbling.

"We have no time for this. Cut him."

The other man dropped the hammer, put his hand into his jacket pocket and pulled out a Stanley knife. He extended the blade. Teethy screamed as this was put under his chin. The thin man's wrist jerked, blood poured down Teethy's T shirt and he screamed louder. The knifeman began working the blade round Teethy's jaw, ignoring Teethy's howls.

"We tear your fucking face off," grunted the big man and inserted his fingers into Teethy's wound, blood gushing over his hand. Ratty watched as Teethy flailed helpless in their grip, a dark stain spreading from the crotch of his pants.

"Stop!" Teethy gasped. "For Christ's sake, stop. Please.

He's shacked up in a flat in Hendon."

"We need more than that, prick."

"I've only been there once. Aah fuck! You drive past the gates of the Wear Docks in Hendon. Carry on until you come to a row of shops. There's a launderette on the end, its above there. I swear to God."

"Good boy. Who's he with and what's his wheels?"

"A lass called Eva. And they've got a silver Sierra with a knackered back end."

The big man took his hands from Teethy's chin that was gouting crimson and patted his cheek. He wiped his bloody fingers on the duvet.

"Good boy. You got those last two right. You go to top of class."

Ratty's wide, staring eye, glued to the hole in the plaster board, watched as the thinner of the two men pocketed his Stanley knife and hammer and then he and his companion left the room, whistling, as though they'd just completed a spot of DIY. Ratty listened to them as their footsteps went down the hall and he heard the front door open and close. He stood trembling for a couple of minutes to be sure they weren't returning, before he left the toilet and crept back into Teethy's room.

"Teethy... you all reet mate?"

"Uugh... Mmm," gurgled Teethy, two fistfuls of glistening, bloody duvet pressed to his lower face. He was writhing and shivering on the bed, his pupils rolling upwards under the eyelids. He looked in a bad way. Ratty scrabbled in his pocket for his phone. With a trembling forefinger, he dialled 999.

"Ambulance! Fucking ambulance! There's a poor bastard with his face half cut off and his gob smashed in. Two foreign nutters have had a go at 'im" Ratty stammered out the address, declined to give his own name and, with a last shuddering look at Teethy Irving, he fled.

§

Wonderwall was on the radio, Bull was tapping away on his keyboard, putting his IT and creative skills at Kilford's disposal in designing a Canine Operative Ownership Transfer Form DG3977. They hoped that this would give Crapper's adoption a sufficient air of official authority to satisfy Councillor Down.

Kilford was in a good mood. Yesterday's family day out in Beamish had built some much needed credit at home, it looked like he had solved the Crapper problem and he was involved in a major case. He, Bull and Blockhead were alone in the office. Knackers and Shifty were downstairs, manning the intel hub in the major incident room. Kilford and Bull had put in a stint earlier in the morning. The investigation was at the hard graft stage of information gathering. Wrathall's girl had been ID'd as Eva Devlin from Newmarket and Suffolk Constabulary were collecting background information. The force in Cleveland were giving a hard time to all drug dealers of West Indian background in Middlesbrough to unearth a link to Wrathall and Durham were conducting follow up interviews with all the witnesses to the robberies on their patch in which Wrathall's involvement was suspected. Durham were also following up a tip off from one of Knacker's informants that Wrathall was holed up in Seaham. Blockhead was unenthusiastic about this.

"This snout of Knacker's," he was saying to Kilford. "Brian Glenning?"

"Aye."

"What about him?"

"He's full of shit much of the time, but I didn't want to discourage her."

Kilford opened his mouth to reply, but his mobile rang. As he picked it off his desk, Blockhead leaned across to the turn the radio volume down. Kilford nodded his thanks and looked at the caller display.

"Ratty," he said. "What's up?"

The voice on the other end was breathless and shrill.

"Have you heard about Teethy? Teethy Irving?"

"No mate, what's the score?"

"It's horrible man, I tell you, it's a frigging nightmare."

"Ratty, just calm down and tell us what's happened."

"I'm fucking telling you man, it's Teethy, he's been cut up really bad, had his bastard face carved up."

"Hang on a minute Ratty." Kilford put the phone to his chest and turned to Bull. "Just have a look on the IS screen and tell us if there's a job in for Teethy Irving. Ratty's telling me he's been attacked, seriously." He spoke into his mobile: "Hang on a minute." Bull clicked on his mouse, tapped on his keyboard, wrinkled his nose and peered at his screen. After a few seconds he had a result.

"He's spot on. There's an ambulance on the way... job says male badly assaulted by unknown males... came from an anonymous caller."

"Ratty," said Kilford. "How come you're onto this?"

"I saw it man. And before you ask me, I've no shagging idea who they are, but they're after Wrathall, they made Teethy tell 'em where he is."

"Which is?"

"Oh shit man, it was fucking horrible. I can't remember every word... Hendon! He said somewhere in Hendon!"

"Right. Keep your phone switched on."

Kilford rang off and told Blockhead and Bull what he'd just heard. Blockhead slapped his desk and got to his feet. "Right, we need to get on top of this. I'll update the boss and get Shifty and Knackers back up here. Yous two get down to Teethy's and see if you can speak to him before he leaves in the ambulance."

Kilford and Bull scooped up mobiles, car keys and jackets and headed for the door. Before they were through it, Blockhead called them back and handed over a couple of radios.

"If there's any chance of you running into Wrathall I want you plugged in."

Once they had left, he headed for the DI's office to brief him. Rocky heard him out, contemplating him over the top of his reading glasses. He rubbed his hands.

"Right, things are moving. Get onto Traffic and Firearms and put 'em on standby. Ask Firearms to make their way to the Sunderland area, update 'em on the incident at Teethy's address and make 'em aware it could be linked to the wanted persons Wrathall and his lass, Eva."

"Okay boss. What about the Major Incident Room?"

"Leave that to me. I'll ring down to Unwin and give him an update. I'll try not to get him too excited."

§

Barely twenty minutes later, Kilford and Bull pulled up on Teethy Irving's street. Bull had to park a few doors down, as the roadside outside the address was occupied by an ambulance and a marked police car. There were knots of people hanging around outside the house, most of them young, thin and pale. They drew deeply on cigarettes and their rodent eyes were darting, trying to avoid those of the detectives, but keen not to miss anything. Kilford noticed Ratty hovering on the edges of one group. Neither he nor the informant made any acknowledgment of the other's presence.

"Doesn't miss a trick does he," remarked Bull.

"That's what we pay him for, the sly so-and-so." As they reached the ambulance, they recognised a uniform dayshift officer, PC Cullen. Kilford was pleased to see him, he was a no-nonsense veteran, who could be relied on to have preserved the scene. He approached them, his radio crackling on his chest. "Hello boys, glad to see yous. Y'see the vultures are circulating." He nodded towards the bystanders. "Teethy's in the back of the ambulance. He's in a bad way. Looks like he's had a falling out with Hannibal Lecter."

"What's the scene like?" asked Bull.

"Like an abattoir. Blood all over the place, even on the walls and some spray on the ceiling. There's a footprint on the back door and I've secured the house.

SOCO are on their way."

"Good job Cull," said Kilford. "We're going to have a word with Teethy."

"Aye well, good luck with that."

Kilford and Bull tapped on the rear door of the ambulance, which was opened by a young female paramedic. They showed her their warrant cards and introduced themselves. Over her shoulder, they could see a groaning Teethy, lying back receiving attention from her male colleague. "How's he doing?" asked Kilford.

"It's a nasty assault, but it's not life threatening."

"Can we have a quick word with him?" She frowned; thought for a moment. "Two minutes max... and just one of you." The two detectives looked at each other.

"You do it," said Bull. "I'll speak to some of this lot and see if anyone saw anything."

Kilford nodded and climbed into the back of the ambulance. The paramedics made room so he could stand by Teethy. Teethy's chin was covered in a dressing but his mouth was uncovered, revealing shattered teeth. His eyes were unfocused and when he spoke, his voice was slurred. "Who did this Teethy?" asked Kilford.

"Dunno… foreign fuckers."

"Can you describe them?"

"Big bastards…."

His voice was getting weaker and Kilford judged he wasn't going to get anything useful in the way of description.

"This have anything to do with Karl Wrathall?" Teethy nodded.

"Wanted to know… know where he is."

"Where is that Teethy?"

Teethy closed his eyes. Kilford gently shook his shoulder, until the female paramedic reached over to restrain him.

"Come on Teethy," urged Kilford. "They'll do for him if we don't get there first."

Teethy opened his eyes and whispered, Kilford had to lean over him to hear.

"In Hendon. He's in Hendon… past the Docks… row of shops… launderette."

Teethy's eyes closed again.

"That's your lot," said the paramedic.

Kilford nodded his thanks and exited the ambulance.

He scribbled a summary of what he'd learned from Teethy while he waited for Bull to re-join him. "Nobody's seen sod all, nobody knows sod all," said Bull.

"There's a surprise."

"And Teethy?"

"We'll be calling him Gummy from now on. Some bastards have smashed his teeth in and looks like they've tried to cut his face off. They were foreigners looking for Wrathall who, according to Teethy, is in a flat above a launderette, or near a launderette, in Hendon. I've got vague directions."

"Let's away then."

"You drive and I'll ring Blockhead."

Kilford called Blockhead and updated him on Teethy and the details he'd given them on Wrathall's location. Blockhead told him that he would update Traffic and Firearms and told him to stay in touch. Meanwhile, he would set Knackers onto researching launderettes in the Hendon area.

After speaking to Blockhead, Kilford used his radio, identifying himself by the call sign for DSU, Zulu and his collar number 2258.

"Zulu 2258 to LB?"

"Go ahead," answered Control Room. "I've an update for the assault at Donwell this morning."

"Go on."

"The suspects are believed of foreign nationality and are travelling to the Hendon area and may be trying to locate Karl Wrathall who is currently wanted for murder. We have no details on any vehicles at this time for the suspects but believe Wrathall may still be in possession of a silver Ford Sierra with rear end damage."

Then more voices came through the speaker: "Tango 1340 can you show me in company with 1102 attending that job?"

"Golf 8197 in company with 110 en- route."

"Delta 32 I'm travelling from Gateshead." Bull turned to Kilford.

"Bugger me Alf! If Wrathall's in Hendon, we're going to find him. We've got every department in the Force heading there." Kilford laughed.

"Not asked for the helicopter yet, Chubby."

"Go on, Dare you."

Kilford spoke into the radio again.

"Zulu 2258... LB... is India 99 available?"

A pause, then: "En route."

The pair laughed, with amusement and excitement.

§

Ratty watched the ambulance pull away, its siren gathering volume and urgency and then he saw the two detectives drive off. He cast a quick glance back at Teethy's place and the crowd who were already beginning to drift away, then he pulled his hood up, hunched his shoulders and began walking in the same direction the detectives had gone.

After calling an ambulance and running from Teethy's flat, Ratty had pelted down the street, desperate to put as much distance between himself and the two foreign nutters as possible. But, after running two blocks, his poor physical condition had overcome his terror and he'd had to stop and lean against a garden wall, drawing great, wheezing lungful's of breath. It was while he was recovering that he had thought to ring Kilford.

Now, that duty was done and he'd witnessed the results of his calls, Ratty had vivid flashbacks of what he'd seen in Teethy's flat. He had to stop, clutch a lamppost and retch. He coughed and wiped the back of his hand across his mouth. Fuck! He needed some smack – badly. Teethy could be a bit of a twat, but he hadn't deserved that. If it had been Wrathall, that would've been different. At least that bastard had it coming, once those foreign head cases caught up with him. Aye, that bastard had stolen his lass. Eva! She was with Wrathall! When those bastards caught up with him...!

Ratty scrabbled in his pocket for his phone and then his trembling fingers called up the familiar number.

After a couple of rings, a hesitant voice answered.

"Yeah?"

"Eva, it's me. Listen, yous need to get out of where you are."

"What? What are you talking about Ratty?"

Ratty heard an angry voice in the background.

"Who's that?"

"It's just Ratty."

"Bollocks to that! Give it 'ere."

Then Wrathall's voice came on the line – loud and clear: "What you doing, belling our lass?"

"Teethy's had his face cut off and they're coming for you now!"

There was a brief silence from the other end, then the call was terminated.

§

Wrathall stared blankly at the phone in his hand. Eva reached out, took it from him and tucked it into the pocket of her jeans. That seemed to break a spell, his eyes came into focus and he looked at her.

"Grab the money! I'll get the gear." She blinked.

"What? Karl, what you on about?" She looked around the one room flat. It was unfurnished, the window, which overlooked a yard and a litter strewn back alley, was cracked and there were obvious damp patches on the wall. But, for all that, Eva had been prepared to squat on her old duvet and call it home, at least for a few hours. She was wasted, she felt sick and she needed to shoot up some of that dedee, needed that rush, then that mellowness. Karl obviously did too. Look at him, his pupils like pinholes, shaking – he needed to chill.

"Just fucking come on!" he shouted and grabbed up the bin bag that held the heroin, then snatched up the car keys from next to it. He glared at her, until, with a groan, she picked up the carrier that contained the cash. He seized her by the forearm and bundled her out of the room and down the bare wooden stairs. They spilled out onto the pavement and she stood blinking, shielding her eyes, while he scanned the street, before dragging her to the Sierra parked outside the launderette.

§

"That's them!" cried Leka.

Besnik didn't take his eyes from the road, but took his foot off the accelerator slightly, letting the Warrior cruise past the shops and parked cars.

"You sure?"

"Yes, yes! We passed a launderette and a silver Sierra was parked outside. He was getting into it, the guy in the photo Morrison got from the police."

"Well done Leka."

Besnik pulled the Warrior's wheel to the right and nipped through a gap in the oncoming traffic to turn into a side street. Then he pulled onto the forecourt of a bodywork repair shop to give himself the room for a U turn, which brought them back to the junction with the road they had just left – in time to see a silver Sierra tearing from left to right across their front.

Besnik pulled out through another gap in the traffic to follow the Sierra, this time prompting two or three horns to honk in angry protest.

"The back – it's all dented," he said. "It's them."

The Sierra had to brake when it met the slower moving traffic ahead and Bresnik remained a comfortable distance behind it. He could make out two figures in the front seats, the driver big and the passenger smaller, possibly a woman. It turned left at the next junction, onto a quieter road and the Warrior followed. Then the Sierra took another right, followed immediately by a left turn.

Giving the steering wheel rapid turns, Besnik swore. "Fuck! He knows! The bastard knows we're following him."

Sure enough, the Sierra suddenly accelerated away and Besnik had to take his speed up to fifty to keep pace. The Sierra took a sudden left, its tyres squealing, a man crossing the road leaping for the kerb. The Warrior followed it as the Sierra took another corner, this time clipping a parked Micra. Here there were more people on the pavement and they watched the Sierra careering down the street, followed by the big black Mitsubishi. A mother protectively pulled her two children close and an elderly man shook his fist.

Five minutes later Besnik heard a siren.

"Shit!" he said and took his foot from the accelerator to stab the brake. The Sierra receded into the distance but the Warrior was doing little over thirty five when the police car, a Volvo V70, drove into view in its rear view mirror. Besnik slowed further and pulled into the side to let the patrol car past in pursuit of the Sierra.

"You're letting them get away!" protested Leka. "Yes, I am letting them get away. You know why? Now the police are here and you brought that fucking gun." He looked over his shoulder and began a three-point turn. "Some other time, I think."

§

Kilford and Bull were driving towards Hendon when his phone rang. It was Blockhead,

"Alf, where are you?"

"We're just coming through Pennywell."

"I've been monitoring comms and it looks like Wrathall's surfaced."

"Hang on, I'll put you on speaker so Bull can hear. Go on."

"Lads, Traffic are behind the Sierra, he's not stopping and he's all over the place, he's driving badly and their struggling to stay with him… he's mounting pavements and going through no entries to get away… hold on…they've lost him… shit! It's a loss, loss, loss." Kilford swore and struck the dashboard.

"What's his general direction? These radios are shite."

"Looks like he was heading for the west of the city. There are units travelling from everywhere. Lads, we've got to get him. We can't let the bastard get away this time. This is our best chance."

"Okay, we'll head towards his old man's. He must know that area like the back of his hand."

"Just do your best boys. And try to get your radios working."

Kilford rang off and Bull indicated to turn towards Farringdon. Kilford was swearing and cursing Wrathall's pursuers for having lost him. Bull, phlegmatic as ever, shrugged and pointed out that, unlike Wrathall, their guys couldn't drive like maniacs and endanger the public. Kilford knew he was right, but he still seethed. Wrathall always seemed to be one step ahead, it was like the evil bastard was leading a charmed life. Kilford couldn't think of a time he'd wanted to nick somebody so much. He pulled his phone out again. He'd ring Blockhead back to see if there was any more sightings. He knew Blockhead would have been on the phone immediately if there had been, but he had to do something. He was calling up the number when Bull jammed his foot down on the brake and Kilford lurched forward in his seat, his head hurtling towards the windscreen before the seatbelt yanked him back. "Sodding hell Bull! What the… '

He didn't need to finish. Bull had braked as a car had come belting out of a side street to their right. It was a silver Sierra, with a damaged rear end. "Yesss!" cried Kilford, punching the air.

Impassive, chewing gum, Bull said nothing, but put his foot back on the accelerator and closed on the Sierra. Kilford rang Blockhead to tell him they had found Wrathall, along with their location and direction. Blockhead was saying something, but Kilford stopped listening, mesmerised by the scene he could see unfolding ahead.

There was no traffic in front of the Sierra, which was doing about sixty. They were approaching a junction controlled by traffic lights, which were changing to red. Wrathall wasn't slowing, he wasn't going to stop. But Bull had to, or at least slow down. Shit! The bastard was going to get away again.

The Sierra shot through the red light and was almost across the junction, when a Transit coming from the left and braking hard, smashed into the rear wing, spinning the Sierra around, so that it was hit again in the rear by a Mondeo coming the other way. Bull pulled up in front of the Sierra, boxing it in.

Kilford saw movement in the front of the Sierra. The driver's door opened and a big bloke – Wrathall! He was getting out of the car. Kilford released his seat belt and jerked his own door open. As Wrathall set off at a run up the road to the right, shoving pedestrians out of his way, Kilford started in pursuit, his arms pumping, bellowing: "Stop! Police!" He was terrified that Wrathall would grab somebody. He pictured a petrified hostage, knife at their throat.

Kilford was fit. Wrathall clearly wasn't. The distance between them closed: fifty feet, then thirty, then down to twenty. Then it was over.

Wrathall stopped and turned, panting, a knife in his hand, his eyes hard and expressionless. Kilford didn't stop, couldn't. He went barrelling into Wrathall in a violent collision that sent him flying backward onto the pavement, Kilford on top of him. Kilford gasped at a jab of pain in his left knee and had a sudden realisation that it was his old football injury. But he had other things to worry about. He jammed his right forearm against Wrathall's windpipe and, with his left hand, he tried to grasp Wrathall's right, which was flailing around, in search of the knife which lay only inches from his scrabbling fingers. He was aware of people shouting, screaming and footsteps running.

Kilford grunted with the effort of holding the writhing figure beneath him, who, even out of condition, was a big bastard. Kilford wasn't confident his left hand had the strength to restrain Wrathall whose right was getting closer and closer to the knife.

Or at least it was, until Bull planted his size twelve shoe and his not inconsiderable weight on it. "You're locked up mate," he said, bending to apply his cuffs. "You alright there Alf?"

CHAPTER TEN

Kilford pulled up in a distant corner of the car park at the back of Sunderland nick. He surveyed the area through his rear view mirror, to ensure there was nobody wandering around who might recognise him and want to chew the fat. He had been signed off on the sick and was supposed to be recovering at home and, while it would be fine in most cases, he didn't want to run the risk of a senior officer catching sight of him and asked awkward questions, or somebody like Shifty, who certainly couldn't be relied on to keep his mouth shut.

After a couple of minutes, Kilford caught sight of a familiar figure making his way across the car park towards him. It was Bull and, by his side, trotting on a lead, was Crapper. As they drew close, Kilford opened his door climbed awkwardly out of the car and limped to the back to open the tailgate for the dog, who was bounding, whooping and trying to lick his face. Eventually, with much patting and stroking and "good boys", Kilford managed to secure the dog in the back and he resumed his seat while Bull got into the passenger seat.

"How's the knee?" asked Bull.

"Still swollen and hurts like a bastard if I put too much weight on it, but it's not like it was on Monday night and Tuesday when I couldn't move it."

"You shouldn't have walked on it after we collared Wrathall."

"Aye, thanks Doctor. Hindsight's a wonderful thing." In fact, in the immediate aftermath of Wrathall's arrest, adrenaline had cloaked the pain in his knee. Within seconds of Bull putting the cuffs on him, a patrol car had pulled up and two uniform officers had secured the prisoner, allowing Kilford and Bull to return to the Sierra, where they'd found Eva, still strapped in the passenger seat, alternately sobbing and giggling. At her feet had been a plastic carrier bag which, on examination, was found to contain about thirty five thousand pounds. It was at this point that the pain in Kilford's knee had hit him.

Kilford jerked his head towards the station.

"So, how's it all going in there?"

"All the usual actions: taking witness statements, transcribing interviews, compiling search team evidence, you know the score. Blockhead's taken responsibility for the file of evidence."

"Tell me about the Wrathall and Eva interviews." Bull shrugged.

"On Wrathall there's not a lot to tell. Tam did the interview with Budgie, to give Durham a look-in. Wrathall just sat there with his brief and didn't say sod all, didn't even speak to acknowledge he was in the room, just sat and stared at the wall. Y'know Tam, he's seen it all, but even he says Wrathall is one cold, creepy bastard."

"And Eva?"

Bull gave a half laugh.

"Can't shut her up. Full and frank admission, but claiming that she was acting out of fear and duress."

"Probably was."

"Yeah, but unlike Bob Marley, she didn't just check the places out for Wrathall and drive him, she took an active part, she actually entered Ryhope Post Office and did the stuff with those towels to get him access to the rear of shop.

"The CPS have authorised charging both, at this stage, with murder and conspiracy to rob. They've been remanded into custody - Wrathall to Darlington and her to Low Newton. The cash found in the Sierra is linked to the Ryhope Post Office with matching serial numbers. There's a long way to go to secure a conviction but, on review of evidence, we're looking at getting all three of 'em in the box together as conspirators, with Bob and Eva turning Queen's evidence."

Kilford nodded. It sounded good, but he was experienced enough to know that it wasn't watertight and that a decent barrister could still pick holes in the case. He was about to say as much to Bull when he glanced in his mirror and spotted a figure exiting the rear of the station: female and blonde, it was Knackers. If she spotted his car, she'd be over like a shot, all concerned and solicitous, which he didn't feel he could handle, certainly not in Bull's presence. He made a show of looking at his watch.

"I've got to go mate. I told the Councillor I'd drop Crapper off at ten."

Twenty minutes later, Crapper was receiving an enthusiastic welcome from the Downs. June smothered him with hugs and kisses and plied him with treats and, although the dog did give Kilford one fond farewell glance, he sauntered happily into his new home.

"Will you come in too Mr Kilford and have a cup of tea?"

Kilford politely declined and then June noticed his NHS issue metal walking stick.

"What have you been doing to yourself?"

"It's just a sprain Mrs Downs, it'll heal."

"Well in that case you should rest it."

"That's just what I plan to do. I've got one other little job to do and then I'm off home."

This little job was a less pleasant one: attending the funeral of Mark Matterson, the postmaster's son Wrathall had killed. It wasn't something Kilford wanted to do, or had to do. But it was something he felt he ought to do.

It was a well-attended service and Kilford had to squeeze in at the back of the crematorium's chapel. The Matterson family were plainly well known and respected and a large part of Ryhope had crowded into that chapel to pay its respects. The deceased's immediate family were occupying the front pews but, from what Kilford could gather from whispered snatches of conversation around him, the postmaster, Sam Matterson, was still in intensive care.

At the end of the service, Mrs Matterson stood at the entrance, supported by a couple of relatives or neighbours, and acknowledged the commiserations of the exiting mourners. As Kilford hurriedly muttered his sympathy, he registered her face: red, raw and ravaged with grief. She still looked dazed, reeling under the sudden, unforeseen pain of a hammer blow that had come from nowhere. Kilford hobbled away, leaning heavily on his stick, but ignoring the pain in his knee, only aware of an all-consuming anger. He'd seen this misery before and he knew he'd see it again: lives ruined and trashed through no fault of the victims. But what really got to him this time was thinking about Wrathall and the certainty that he wouldn't give a shit.

§

Kilford was fit and healthy and his knee healed well, so that it was barely a week and a half later that he was walking back into the DSU with only a slight limp. There was some good natured banter from Blockhead and Bull and Knackers was full of sympathetic attention.

Kilford was grateful when Blockhead told him the boss wanted to see him.

He made his way to the DI's office, tapped on the door and entered at the invitation bellowed from inside. Rocky didn't acknowledge him for a second, but continued writing, before looking up at him.

"You're back then?"

"Yes boss."

"Knee alright?"

"It's canny boss."

Rocky grunted and applied himself again to the papers on his desk. He then glanced at Kilford, as though surprised to see him still there.

"Well, go on then, piss off back to work."

"Yes boss."

Kilford turned and was half way through the door when he heard over his shoulder: "Oh, and well done. Tell your chubby mate the same."

"Thanks boss."

"Aye, now piss off."

§

Back in the DSU, Kilford's account of this conversation was greeted with laughter but little surprise. Then, after catching up on some gossip, he logged into his computer to tackle his email backlog and other routine admin. After an hour and a half of this, he and Bull discussed the status of their various informants. Top of the list was Ratty and they agreed that a meeting was called for. Kilford dialled his number and, to his surprise, it was answered after only a couple of rings.

"Hello mush." Ratty sounded subdued.

"We need to meet."

"Aye, whatever."

"Today good for you Ratty?" Kilford looked inquiringly at Bull, who nodded.

"Canny, aye."

"Right, we'll pick you up in Castletown, usual spot, in an hour."

Ratty agreed and ended the call. Kilford looked at his mobile, frowning. "What's up?" asked Bull.

Kilford shook his head. "Ratty: he didn't sound his usual chirpy self."

"We'll see if we can't cheer 'im up."

Castletown, on Sunderland's western edges, close to the A19, was near enough to Ratty's home turf for him to get there easily by bus, but still far enough away to make it unlikely he'd be spotted climbing into the car of known police Detectives. All the same, Kilford and Bull had to sit parked up for five minutes until the coast was deemed sufficiently clear for Ratty to rapidly approach the car, open the rear door and slip into the seat behind Kilford. He had barely slammed the door before Bull had turned on the ignition, slipped into gear and pulled away. Kilford swivelled in his seat to turn and inspect his informant.

Ratty had never been able to boast film star good looks, but Kilford was struck by how much worse he was looking than when he'd last seen him. His hair was lank and greasy, his skin was white, where his well-bitten nails hadn't scored it with scratches, and he seemed to have lost weight.

"Usual question Ratty," said Kilford. "What are you like at the minute?" Ratty shrugged.

"I don't know mush, I reckon I'm using a tenner bag a day."

"Aye, that's what you reckoned last time," said Kilford, unconvinced.

Bull drove them to Lambton Park, a large open area straddling the banks of the Wear and the border with Chester-Le-Street. It was a straightforward matter there to find an isolated picnic table and benches, where they could sit and talk without being seen or heard. Bull provided Ratty with a cigarette, which he pulled on hungrily. It was a mild day, but Ratty gave a slight shiver and pulled his hoody closer around himself. Bull and Kilford exchanged a glance. "First thing Ratty," began Kilford. "Teethy Irving's not being co-operative, won't make a statement, or a complaint… won't say a dicky bird." Ratty shrugged.

"Teethy don't like the bizzies."

"We've never tried to cut his face off, or perform dentistry on him with a hammer."

"'E'll be shitting it… what they might do to 'im if he speaks."

"What about talking to us – me and Bull, on the QT? You persuade him he can trust us."

"I'll see what I can do."

"C'mon then Ratty," said Kilford, "tell us about Teethy. Who is 'they'? Who did it?" Ratty shuddered.

"It was fucking 'orrible."

"Who did it?"

"I don't know. Honest. Never seen 'em before. I swear."

"When you rang for an ambulance, you said they were foreign. Were they black, white, brown?"

"White. They had foreign accents, like Russian or summat, I dunno."

"Descriptions?"

Ratty told them what he could remember about the appearance of the two men. Then, at Kilford's prompting, he explained why he'd been at Teethy's and how he had been in the toilet when the assault happened.

"So, they wanted to know where Wrathall was?"

"'S right."

"Did they say why? Who sent them?"

"Nah."

"Did they ask him anything else?"

Ratty started to shake his head, but then stopped and raised a finger.

"They wanted to know what he was driving and who he was with. Aye… that's right… and when Teethy told 'em, it was a silver Sierra and he was with Eva, one of 'em, the one who did all the talking, said something like: 'Well done, we knew that.' It was like it was a test."

Bull looked up sharply from his notebook. He and Kilford exchanged another look.

"You sure about that Ratty?" asked Kilford.

"Positive mush. Positive."

While Kilford and Bull considered this, Ratty spoke again: "Er… I was wondering, that fifteen hundred quid you promised me for Wrathall…."

"What about it?"

"Whether I could have it like?"

Kilford sighed. "Ratty, we're not allowed to hand over that amount of money all in one go to a known user. You shoot up fifteen hundred quid's worth and end up dead in a gutter and it's down to us. No, we'll pay you instalments of a hundred and fifty quid." After some grumbling, Ratty accepted this and, an hour later, they were parked back in Castletown and the two Detectives were watching Ratty, hood up and head buried in his shoulders, stumping off down the road, two ten-pound notes in his pocket given to him by Bull in return for a signed receipt, for his expenses.

That was twenty pounds that would certainly be used to buy two bags of heroin.

"You reckon he's telling the truth?" asked Bull.

"Why would he make it up? What could his angle be?"

"You can never tell with that wily little sod."

"If it is true, there's only really one place those two heavies got their information."

"Police. Either somebody on the major incident team, or DSU."

"If it's DSU, then it's the old tail wagging dog routine," said Kilford. "And we both know what that means."

"Shifty – bastard - Blair."

§

Ratty might have looked like he was waving the white flag in his battle with heroin but, contrary to Kilford and Bull's expectations, he came up with a result on Teethy only a couple of days later.

"'E'll speak to you," he said, as soon as Kilford answered his phone. "Just you and your mate. But he's not making no statement or any of that shit. I told him you'd traced me off the call I made for the ambulance. I told him you were cush with me, but he knows nothing about our other business, like." Through Ratty, they arranged to pick Teethy up from a bus stop in South Hylton and they took him to an industrial estate near Dalton Park, off the A19. As it was raining, they tucked the car away in the car park of an empty workshop unit and stayed in the vehicle. Teethy wore a baseball cap and had a scarf pulled up to cover his lower face. Kilford asked him to describe the assault, but Teethy's voice was so muffled it was hard to make out what he was saying. Kilford asked him to remove the scarf. Slowly, and with trembling fingers, he peeled it back, to reveal a mouth that was missing its two front teeth and whose lips were still cut and swollen. Beneath his chin, a row of stitch marks described an ugly, livid line.

"Nasty," observed Bull.

Kilford was less interested in Teethy's scars than in his behaviour. His eyes were darting and feral, as if expecting imminent attack from any direction and he was shaking and hugging himself.

"You alright Teethy?"

"I shouldn't have come! I shouldn't have fucking come! This is the first time I've been out in two weeks and it's doin' my head in. I'm a pissing wreck man."

As if to demonstrate, he held his hand out, palm down and fingers stretched: it was quivering so much it looked blurred to Kilford.

"Teethy, just calm down, you're safe enough with us son."

"Safe!" screamed Teethy. "I'll never feel fucking safe again!"

Then he screwed his eyes shut, hugged himself tighter and began rocking backwards and forwards, racked by violent sobs.

As interviews go, it wasn't a great success and the two Detectives learnt nothing from Teethy that they hadn't heard from Ratty. In the end, afraid that he might enter a state of complete nervous collapse they gave up. They urged him to seek professional help and offered to run him to hospital, but he shook his head angrily, so they dropped him off back in South Hylton and watched him stagger away towards the bus stop.

Bull shook his head.

"He's well messed up. We're no closer to knowing who did it to him – and we probably never will be." Kilford breathed hard a couple of times through his nose and swore.

"No, but we do know who this is all down to – that bastard Wrathall."

§

The next morning Kilford had an appointment at the hospital for some physiotherapy on his knee, so it was late morning by the time he arrived at work. He knocked at the DSU office door and was admitted by Bull.

"Morning fat chops," he said, entering and returning the greetings of Knackers and – with less warmth – of Shifty. Kilford had been brooding and was now convinced Shifty had been responsible for the leak that had led to the assault on Teethy. "Where's Blockhead?" he asked Bull.

"He's asleep. Well, he reckons he's working out of Rocky's office, the boss is off for a few days." Kilford smiled. Their DS was notorious as an enthusiastic participant in his rugby club's many social events and was often the worse for wear.

"Rough again is he?"

"As a badger's arse and he's in a shit mood 'cos he's just got a letter from the CPS. It's not good he reckons."

Before Kilford could answer, there was another knock at the door and Shifty opened it to reveal Blockhead, who did look tired, unshaven, red-eyed and generally hung-over. He lumbered into the room and dropped himself heavily into a vacant chair.

He sighed.

"Right phones on silent my little cherubs, I want to go through what we've got against Wrathall and his lass."

"Are the CPS bumping their gums like?" asked Kilford. "Aye, to be honest they're not happy, so let's see what we've got nailed on against Wrathall. I want the evidence tighter than a spaceman's boot."

"Suit," said Bull.

"What?"

"Suit. It should be spaceman's suit."

"Aye, whatever. Do I look like I work for frigging NASA?"

He closed his eyes and rubbed them with the thumb and forefinger of one hand while the chuckling subsided.

"Right, this is how I see it," he said. "We've got Bob Marley turning against him and his lass Eva spilling her guts on tape, but we know any half decent defence team are going to try and tear both of them apart. We don't know how they'll come across under cross examination in the box, so it's not the best. Let's face it, at the end of the day, they're just another pair of smack heads. Which, in slightly more technical language, is what the CPS are pointing out. "Yeah, okay, Wrathall fits the description on all the jobs and we've got Eva's fingerprints on the outside of the wrapping for the bath towels. There's the thirty grand recovered from their car when they were arrested and some of the serial numbers are a match."

"Then it's a result!" said Knackers.

Blockhead shook his head.

"It's okay, but we need more. The key thing is, there's nothing, apart from Eva's word, tying him to the actual murder at the Post Office."

"CCTV?" said Bull.

"Grainy footage of the man in black – nowhere near good enough. Get me more."

"We can't make up the frigging evidence man!" protested Bull.

Shifty would, thought Kilford bitterly, alarmed now at the real prospect of Wrathall getting off.

"Look, I'm just saying that what we've got may well not be enough and the CPS aren't convinced," said Blockhead. "I'll reply to this poxy letter and get us a bit of breathing space while they're all on remand. I'll draw up some actions for you and we'll take it from there. Okay?"

Kilford spent the next couple of hours working alone on routine work, but he wasn't concentrating. His mind was churning over the Wrathall case. He was determined that they couldn't fail on this job, because to do so would allow the most dangerous, violent person he'd ever met to walk free, and he knew enough about Wrathall now to know that he'd only continue to wreak havoc on lives.

Kilford didn't want that, he didn't want to face that failure, because failure didn't sit easily with him. As a trainee professional footballer, it had been drilled into him to win at all costs and failure, whether that be failure to clean a bath or remove dust from the top of a door frame, or on the pitch, brought punishment - physical and mental – from the coaches, running you until you were exhausted and spewing, or just being eaten by the nagging fear that your best was never going to be good enough. Well, he wasn't going to fail with Wrathall, no way.

Around midday, the rest of the team got up to go their separate ways for lunch, Bull to the canteen, Knackers to the shops and Shifty to some undisclosed destination – probably to make an unauthorised call to one of his dodgy narks. "You coming?" Bull asked him.

"Eh? No, not just now Bull, there's something I want to finish up here. I might join you in a few minutes."

"Your knee still bothering you?" asked Knackers. "Are you not walking properly yet? I can get you something."

Kilford smiled his appreciation and shook his head. He waited until they had gone and then switched on the VCR in the corner of the office and took out the box of CCTV tapes from the robbery scenes. He found the one from the Ryhope job and started watching it, for the twentieth time. He saw Eva enter the post office and go to the counter with her parcel, then another figure – Wrathall – came into the shot and dived over the counter as soon as the hatch was opened. Minutes later, he came out from behind the counter, clutching a bag of cash, walked quickly towards the camera and the shop entrance and left the screen.

Kilford swore. What was it about this that was bugging him? He rewound the tape and watched it again, and again. He glanced at his watch and realised half an hour had passed, the others would soon be back. God, he hoped Bull or Shifty got back before Knackers, he didn't want another of those awkward conversations. What was that she'd said about him walking properly? Kilford sat bolt upright in his chair. That's it! Walking properly! That's what had been nagging him.

He rewound the tape and reviewed it again.

§

An hour later, the team and Blockhead were all in the DSU office, sitting before the VCR. Kilford held the remote and he played back the footage of the Ryhope robbery.

"Well, what do you see?" he asked, when it finished.

Shrugs. Blank looks.

"Nothing we haven't seen a hundred times," said Bull. "Okay, watch these."

Kilford then played the tapes of the Seaham and Peterlee robberies. When they had finished he turned to the others again.

"Well?"

Again a general head shaking.

He sighed. "You dozy bastards. Okay, I'll give yous all a clue: just concentrate on the way he walks." He played the Ryhope tape again. This time, only seconds into it, there was a murmur of recognition from Knackers. He hit pause and looked at her. "He walks funny, he does something with his left leg," she said.

"Good. Now watch again."

He restarted the tape and played it to the end. "I see it," said Blockhead. His left foot pauses as he lifts it, it's like a stutter."

"Aye, but isn't that just the tape?" asked Shifty.

"It's on all of them."

Kilford played them the Peterlee and Seaham tapes again and, now they knew what to look for, they could all see the robber's distinctive gait.

"I knew there was something," said Kilford. "It's been driving me mad, but I couldn't work out what it was until today."

"You're right Alf, well done," said Blockhead. "Er… but what the hell does it mean? What can we do with it?"

"It means he's different in the way he walks and that could identify him," said Bull. "That could be the last nail in his coffin."

"I dunno, I haven't come across this before and I'm going to have to think about it. I'll make some inquiries with the FIB and see if there's any mileage in it."

FIB, or the Force Intelligence Bureau, were Northumbria Police's technical experts, who researched and provided specialist gadgetry, particularly for surveillance, but also kept up to date on general developments in law enforcement technology and forensics.

Blockhead concluded: "Anyway, well done Alf for sticking with it." Kilford smiled his acknowledgement, but he was too anxious to know whether his discovery would make any real difference to feel any satisfaction. That would only come when he'd nailed Wrathall.

§

Harry Morrison took a couple of mouthfuls of beer, gave a satisfied sigh and put it back on the bar. It was his firm opinion that this pub, the Princess Louise in High Holborn, served the best pint in London, not that that was saying much. He looked round with approval at the ornate Victorian décor, frosted glass booths and mirrors, wood panelling. The few other drinkers in the bar on this weekday afternoon looked like professionals – what would once have been called yuppies.

He was just raising his glass for a second time when, in the mirror at the back of the bar, he saw the reflection of a familiar figure approaching. He turned to greet him.

He nodded: "Tel."

Terry - Tell - Firman grasped his hand and gave a warm, wheezy chuckle.

" `Arry, my son. `Ow are you keepin' ?"

Tel, now well into his middle age was short and, when once he would have been called stocky, it looked more to Harry, that he was now turning to fat. He still wore his brown hair, which showed flecks of grey, in the mullet style, which had been fashionable when he'd adopted it in the 1980s. But nobody was going to take the piss out of "Mad" Tel Firman for his hairstyle. At least not anybody who knew him.

Harry bought Tel a pint of lager and they retired to one of the booths.

"It's great to see you again 'Arry," said Tel. "I don't come north of the river for anyone you know."

"I appreciate that Tel."

"So, you up for a few days?"

"I brought the wife to see a show, take her mind off Graham and all that shit. She's off in the West End at the moment with my credit cards."

Tel laughed. "Good for 'er. So what show did you see?"

"Mamma Mia."

"'Eard about it. Any good?"

"Not bad. At least there's some tunes you can sing along to, or whistle, not like the wailing crap that passes for musicals these days."

"You're a cultured man 'Arry, always were."

"Aye, well I can't afford to be too cultured, not as I'm fifteen grand down."

Tel raised his hands, palms out.

"'Arry my son, I'll see you right on that score. You can stand on me for that. I mean, I'm here aren't I?" He leaned over the table and lowered his voice. "'Ere, how about I refund fourteen thou and keep a grand for exes?"

"Bollocks!"

Tel sighed and leaned back.

"Ah well, you can't blame me for trying."

"No, you fulfil the contract Tel – and if you do, I'll pay you another two grand bonus." Tel raised his eyebrows.

"And why would you do that 'Arry?"

"If Wrathall goes down, it'll be because my lad puts him there. He'll want to pay that back. Even if he doesn't go down, he'll still want revenge – on my boy Graham and me. I'm not going to sit and wait for that. Another thing, if Graham has to do time, he'll be marked as a grass and he'll need protecting. Making an example of Wrathall is the best protection I can give him. You fix that for me Tel." Tel smiled.

"I suppose I do have my reputation to think of." They clinked glasses in a toast.

CHAPTER ELEVEN

The next morning Kilford and Bull returned upstairs to the DSU office after an interview with a sex offender – a former teacher and lay preacher - who had been convicted for secretly taking photographs up women's skirts. He'd been done for outraging public decency and ordered to be placed on the Sex Offenders' Register. As he sat behind his desk, Kilford was still shaking his head in wonderment at what seemingly ordinary people got up to. He acknowledged Knacker's greetings and wearily ignored Shifty's leering question.

"What have your pervs been doing now then lads?"

Bull didn't ignore Shifty but instructed him to piss off. This prompted Shifty's irritating cackle and Kilford was sure Bull would have hit him, if they hadn't then been interrupted by a knock on the door. Shifty got up to admit Blockhead, who had been attending the weekly admin meeting with his fellow CID sergeants. From the bounce in his step, Kilford could see that he was in a good mood. He revealed why, turning to Kilford and Bull.

"Right, you two, it looks like we might be onto something. I've spoken to FIB about this walk business and they've looked into it. Seems there's an expert in London…."

Blockhead turned to his own desk, picked up a sheet of paper and consulted it.

"A certain Dr Andrew John Crummie who specialises in something called biometrics. They've had a chat with him and he said, yes, you can identify someone by their gait."

"What, like their garden gate?" asked Shifty with a grin, which faded under the withering glares of Blockhead and the rest of the team.

"The science is new," continued Blockhead, with a last dirty look at Shifty, "but, let's face it, we need something and CPS are willing to give it a go. Dr Crummie says he's happy to view the tapes and might be able to say if it's the same person on those tapes as on comparable footage of a known individual."

"What comparable footage?" asked Shifty. "We haven't got any and how are we going to compare it to Wrathall while he's tossing it off in a cell in Darlington nick?"

"I've discussed that with FIB and the CPS and there could be a way round it, but we'll cross that bridge when we come to it. But for now, we've got to get moving on this, so yous two....' he looked at Kilford and Bull, "get your coats on and get those tapes down to London ASAP." He took Kilford's notebook from his desk and scribbled in it, copying from his own sheet of notes. "Here, that's his address and phone number, but I'll ring him and let him know you're on your way. I want you back tomorrow mind, and no shenanigans tonight."

"As if," said Bull.

"Do we need to run it by the boss?" asked Kilford, putting his jacket on and picking up his notebook and phone.

"He's off today. Anyway, he'd only say...." Blockhead waved his hands in an ` altogether now' gesture and the team chorused: "It's the worst it's ever been!"

§

They were on the A19, nearing York, with Bull driving, when Blockhead rang Kilford's mobile to tell them that Dr Crummie had agreed to see them and view the tapes at 10am the next day. They had been booked into the Pentland Hotel near Waterloo Station for the coming night.

"Waterloo?" said Kilford. "That means we'll have to drive right through the centre of London to get there."

"Aye well, it's the only place they could get you in at such short notice – apart from the Savoy," said Blockhead. "But the Pentland has parking, so that clinched it."

"Aye, I'll bet it did."

Cursing he rang off and Bull, who'd got the gist of the conversation, cheerfully pointed out that when they reached the capital, it would be Kilford's turn to drive.

As a result, by the time they checked into the Pentland, Kilford was ready for a stiff drink.

Negotiating London's traffic had been fraught. The last hour had taught him that, whereas, at home, on a busy road, a driver indicated to ask permission to change lanes, here, it meant he was changing lanes, like it or not, because nobody ever gave way unless forced into it.

But, after a call home to Vicki and the girls, a few pints and a decent Italian at the expense of Northumbria Police, he was feeling better. By the following morning, after an early night and a decent sleep, he was fully recovered.

During their full English, Kilford consulted his London A to Z and a tube map. Dr Crummie's surgery was on Devonshire Close, off Harley Street. He and Bull could easily take the Bakerloo Line from Waterloo to Regents Park tube station, which was only minutes from Devonshire Close. He explained this to Bull.

"Let me look at that," said Bull and, taking the A to Z, he examined it, rubbing his chin.

"It's only a kick in the arse away man, it's a nice enough day and we've got plenty of time, we could walk."

"What's wrong with the Tube?" Bull shook his head.

"I hate the bloody Underground."

"Why?"

"It smells."

Kilford rolled his eyes and sighed.

"Okay, we'll walk."

Twenty minutes later, they were gazing up at Nelson's Column when Kilford's phone rang. It was Rocky.

"Hello boss," said Kilford.

"Right you arsehole!" boomed Rocky's voice and a flock of startled pigeons took to the air. "Where are you and your chubby mate at?"

"We're in Trafalgar…"

"Right, get back to my office, I want to see yous urgently."

"Boss, it's going to be late afternoon before we can get back."

"Bollocks! It'll take you ten minutes to get back from the Sulgrave. You can come in and then get back there to whatever you're doing."

Kilford grinned.

"No boss, we're not in Trafalgar Walk, we're in Trafalgar Square, in London."

There was a brief silence before the DI spoke again. "You better be bloody winding me up. What are you doing down there?"

"Hasn't Blockhead spoken to you this morning?"

"Clearly not. Now you talk to me and this had better be fucking good or I'll tear yous both a new arsehole."

"Boss… boss… I'm losing you… hello… hello…." Kilford winked at Bull, hit the disconnect button and put the phone back in his pocket.

"Reception's terrible," he said.

"Worst it's ever been," agreed Bull.

§

Dr Crummie's surgery was in an elegant red-brick house, part of a Georgian terrace. An equally elegant young receptionist showed the detectives into a wood panelled waiting room furnished with plush leather armchairs and offered them coffee, which she served them in china cups with saucers.

"I'd go to the doctors more often if it was like this," said Bull, when she'd left the room.

"Aye, I wonder if she'd take a look at my knee."

"Oi, you'll be making Knackers jealous."

"Piss o...." Kilford interrupted himself with a fit a mock coughing as the receptionist re-entered the room with a dazzling smile to tell them that Dr Crummie was ready to see them.

"He finished his earlier appointment sooner than he anticipated," she explained.

"It's okay, you can bring your coffees through." Carefully balancing their cups and saucers, they were shown through to the consulting room of Dr Crummie, a tall grey-haired man with tortoiseshell glasses. He shook their hands and invited them to sit.

"I understand you have some tapes for me to watch?"

"Yes sir," said Kilford. He opened his briefcase and took out a cassette which he handed over.

"They've all been copied onto the one tape. Everything's on there and it's obvious who the subject is. We'd just like your opinion on the way he walks and whether that's distinctive enough to identify him."

"Let's take a look." Dr Crummie smiled and took the tape and swivelled at a right angle in his chair so that he was facing a combined TV and VCR, which Kilford hadn't noticed before. He switched it on and slotted the cassette into it.

They watched the footage of Wrathall's robberies. Dr Crummie sat with his fingers steepled before his mouth, saying nothing. When the tape had finished, he jerked forward and rewound it, then sat back and watched it again, still without comment, but this time scribbling some notes on a pad. He watched the tape through another couple of times, then ejected it. He rose from his chair.

"Excuse me a moment," he said.

He left the detectives alone in the room. Bull looked at Kilford, his eyebrows raised. Kilford shrugged. Seconds later, Dr Crummie reappeared and sat back behind his desk, leaning forward, his hands clasped.

"Well gentlemen," he said. "I don't have to tell you that the footage isn't of the best quality." Kilford and Bull nodded glumly.

"However," he went on, "it's good enough for me to be able to say two things with confidence. One is that it's the same individual in each of the recorded episodes because, secondly, he has a characteristic gait, as you had spotted. I won't bore you with the medical science, but it's likely the result of a congenital condition or possibly, a childhood injury."

Kilford leaned forward in his seat.

"That's brilliant Doctor. So, if we got another recording of this individual, one which was certified as being of our suspect, would you be able to say whether it was the same as the bloke on these tapes?"

"Provided the quality was good enough and that it clearly showed him walking, I'm sure I would, yes." Kilford and Bull thanked the doctor, who invited them to sit in reception with more coffee while he made a copy of their cassette from which he could make more detailed notes. Once that was done and they had thanked him and shaken hands and Bull and Kilford were back out on Devonshire Close, they punched the air and slapped each other on the back. Then Kilford rang Blockhead to tell him they had a result. "That's great!" said the DS. "I'll tell the boss, which should keep him happy."

"Chew your arse this morning did he?" asked Kilford. "He wasn't best pleased that I forgot to tell him I'd sent you two down to London."

"You should have told him: there's nice to know and need to know."

"Yeah, thanks Alf, that would've gone down well. Listen, I want yous to do me another favour while you're down there. Drop in on Eva's mam in Newmarket. Cambridgeshire have spoken to her, but they're not really up to speed on this. You see if Eva told her mam anything about Wrathall. It might be useful. I'll text you her address."

An hour later they were in their car making their way to the M25. It was Bull's turn to drive, so he was doing the swearing, while Kilford was examining the road atlas.

"Bloody Blockhead," he said. "Newmarket's well out of our way. It'll take us over an hour to get there."

"Let's hope Rocky doesn't ring us while we're there. He'll think we've gone to the races."

The interview with Eva's mother didn't produce anything useful. All they learnt was what they already knew: that drugs in general, and Wrathall and Devil's Dandruff in particular, were particularly effective at wrecking lives.

Mrs Devlin invited them into her large, plush, detached house, with its large well-kept gardens in the middle of an estate of similarly exclusive houses. Sitting in a tastefully – and expensively – furnished sitting room, they explained the purpose of the visit. Mrs Devlin expressed her willingness to co-operate, began to talk about her daughter – and then burst into tears.

Still sobbing, she showed them photos from the family album of Eva as a little girl, then as a teenager, a happy, pretty girl who was obviously part of a loving and supportive family.

Then, however, the father had run off with his PA, Eva had made some bad friends, culminating in a disastrous relationship in her first months at university with a boy from Sunderland. Then it had become apparent that she'd picked up a drugs habit, she'd dropped out of uni, and gone to live with her boyfriend. Visits home had become less frequent but appeals for money were constant.

"I told her, 'Eva,' I said, 'I'm not giving you any more money unless you get help, go into rehab'. Then she stopped ringing. And now this, now she's in trouble with the police and she's going to go to jail." She ended this with a wail and she threw herself onto the sofa, burying her head in a cushion. Kilford and Bull exchanged horrified looks. Kilford got up from his chair, patted her on the shoulder and made soothing noises while Bull muttered something about making a nice cup of tea and escaped into the kitchen.

Half an hour later the detectives were hurrying thankfully down the drive to their car.

"What a bloody mess," said Kilford.

He was silent for much of the long journey back, depressed, thinking about Eva and about his own daughters.

§

Ratty gnawed at his thumbnail, then reached under his shirt to scratch his chest before running his hand through his lank hair, then resumed work on the thumbnail. He was on edge, he needed some smack, but he was out and unlikely to score until that evening at the earliest.

Fuck it!

He was alone in a flat in the Sulgrave. He was borrowing it for a few weeks under an unorthodox arrangement that was unknown to the local housing association and which it certainly wouldn't approve. Fuck them too!

So Ratty had a roof over his head, but he didn't feel settled. It was weeks now since Wrathall had been arrested and that had lifted a dark cloud from the Sulgrave. But Ratty was torn between relief at being able to move around the estate without the threat of Wrathall spotting him and giving him a kicking and unease about Wrathall's forthcoming trial. Ratty was no lawyer but he'd enough experience of court to know that any decent defence barrister would try to extract the name of a snout in open court to undermine the prosecution case. Ratty trusted Kilford as much as he trusted any bizzie, but if a judge ordered that he be named, that was it – he was fucked.

Ratty was also nagged by regret that Eva had also been nicked. And not just regret – also the realisation that, with his key role in getting her lifted, he hadn't exactly played a blinder.

"Stupid bitch! It was her fault." He told himself, but it didn't make him feel any better.

No, the only thing that could do that was H. But that was in short supply for him, until he got some cash. And that new stuff, Devil's Dandruff, cost an extra couple of quid a wrap.

Problem was, as Ratty was honest enough to admit, he hadn't been too energetic lately. Yeah, he'd been overdoing the brown and that wasn't good for shifting his arse. He had to get things together. Make one big effort, Do something worth doing. Yeah, why the fuck not? Wrathall had done that shit hadn't he? Not timewasting on some poxy shoplifting and shit. Yeah, sod it! Why not take over where that bastard Wrathall left off?

§

After Kilford and Bull's trip, weeks passed, during which they wrote up a report of their meeting with Dr Crummie, which went to Blockhead and then went up through the channels to the CPS. Meanwhile, Blockhead liaised with FIB to explore the possibilities of getting covert footage of Wrathall while he was on remand. The first response was that he would have to get the permission and co-operation of the prison governor. He duly wrote to the governor, who pondered the matter for a week and then told the DS that, while the surveillance was alright by him, they really would need to get Home Office clearance. The DI offered his analysis of this.

"Fucking arsehole is covering his fucking arse." As far as the rest of the DSU were concerned, this went on behind the scenes and Kilford, who'd learned the hard way to be philosophical about the bureaucracy of the police and criminal justice system, concentrated on his sex offenders and his other informants.

He was getting increasingly worried about Ratty, who hadn't been in touch for some time. Kilford tried ringing him but the number was unobtainable, which sounded alarm bells. On a couple of occasions Kilford and Bull drove around some of the areas that they knew Ratty frequented, hoping to find him, but without luck. Ratty's reward was now authorised and it was up to Kilford and Bull to pay out their source, which, experience taught them, would usually generate more intelligence.

But the Wrathall case was always at the front of Kilford's mind, so when Blockhead came into the office one day, like an overweight Neville Chamberlain, triumphantly waving a piece of paper, Kilford looked at him eagerly.

"Is this about Wrathall?"

"Too bloody right it is. The Home Office have only said yes and FIB are good to go."

"So when do they do it like? And how?" asked Bull.

"That's not for the likes of us to know," said Blockhead. "With covert surveillance the less people in the loop the better. Last thing we need is a sodding prison riot."

Kilford cast a wary glance at Shifty. If that bastard leaked this....

"But those guys in FIB have some incredible kit," continued Blockhead. "They once showed me one of those little coat hangers that you can hang on the hook on your car door. You know the kind of thing? Well, it's got a pinhole camera concealed in it, so you can park up a surveillance car, hang up your jacket and film while you're innocently sat there smoking and reading the paper."

They heard nothing more for another week and then a small parcel arrived for Blockhead. It was from FIB – video footage taken in HMP Darlington three days earlier. The whole team and the DI crowded round the VCR to watch. It lasted about thirty minutes and showed a handful of prisoners in an exercise yard, strolling and chatting. The camera, which appeared to be positioned a few feet above the prisoners' heads, concentrated on one individual – unmistakably Wrathall in his prison coveralls – who did little talking but ambled round the yard with his distinctive limping walk. The film had been edited so that the faces of the other prisoners were blurred and only Wrathall's was distinct. At one point, in a chilling reminder of one of the robbery videos, he seemed to stare blankly at the camera. The video was accompanied by a statement, signed by a senior prison officer, stating that the subject in the video was Karl Wrathall, quoting his prison number, and that it had been taken on the day in question.

Blockhead ejected the tape and brandished it.

"I think we've got the bastard."

"Well done," said Rocky rubbing his hands.

"Right, now let's get moving on this. Get a copy of that on Red Star down to your doctor in London. There's no call for you two clowns to go off on another of your jollies."

Kilford held out until the afternoon of the following day but then, having confirmed with Red Star that the parcel had been delivered and signed for, he couldn't wait any longer and picked the phone up to call Dr Crummie. The dazzling receptionist put him straight through.

"Mr Kilford, good afternoon, how are you?" said the doctor.

"I'm very well doctor thank you. Er… I just wondered whether you received the parcel we sent down yesterday."

"Yes, thank you. I watched it several times yesterday evening."

"And…?"

The doctor chuckled down the line.

"I was engaged in writing you a report when you rang."

"And…?"

Another chuckle.

"Essentially my report states that I can say with a high degree of confidence that the person in the robbery videos is the same person on the tape that I took delivery of yesterday. And yes, before you ask, I'll be willing to testify to that effect in court as an expert witness, if required."

"Thank you very much Doctor. I look forward to receiving your written report and we'll be in touch. We really appreciate this."

Kilford hung up and shared the good news with the team who burst into cheers. But their triumph was short-lived.

Later that afternoon Blockhead made a call to the CPS to update them. Initially his tone was upbeat and confident, but Kilford and the rest of the DSU soon detected a note of irritation and before long this had escalated to swearing and Blockhead's face turned an even deeper shade of red. Finally he slammed the phone down.

"Wankers!"

"Problem?" asked Knackers.

Blockhead threw his pen onto the desk and sighed.

"Yes, there's a fucking problem. According to the CPS, Dr Crummie's evidence might help but it's not exactly a game changer. This biometrics stuff hasn't been used in court before, so it's not like DNA or fingerprints."

"But the bloke's an expert!" said Bull.

Blockhead shrugged.

"So one doctor says you can identify a man from the way he walks and it can't be anybody else and the jury look at each other and go, `oh yeah?' Then the defence get their own expert to say you can't rely on a walk and this is untested science and Crummie's work hasn't been peer reviewed and blah bloody blah. Naah, we might have put another small brick in the wall but it's still down to relying on the word of two junkies who've got every incentive to testify against Wrathall. It's not looking good. That bastard could still walk – no pun intended."

§

Ratty was hunched inside his hoodie, hurrying along.

It wasn't a cold day but he couldn't stop shivering. Fact was, he was struggling. A little shoplifting and theft from cars was paying for enough H to stop him climbing the walls – but only just. And he'd even sold his mobile. He had to get his hands on some real cash and soon.

He found a phone box a few streets from the Sulgrave. It stank of piss, but at least it worked. He entered it, picked up the receiver, looked up and down the street and then punched in the number he had scrawled on a scrap of paper. The phone rang a couple of times and then it was answered and he fed in a couple of coins.

"DC Kilford, Intelligence Unit."

"Dan, it's me, Ratty."

"Ratty! Where've you been? I've been trying to ring you."

"Yeah, phone's been on the blink."

"Well get it fixed. You're no good to me if I can't get in touch. You got anything for me? You want to meet?"

"Er… things are quiet at the moment."

"We should definitely meet. I want to know what state you're in. You sound in a bad way. No wonder you're not picking up anything worth passing on." Ratty opened his mouth to reply but the beeps demanded more coins so he slammed the receiver down.

"Fuck it! Fucking bastard!"

He left the phone box and hurried back to the Sulgrave. He climbed a set of stairs and walked along a walkway to a battered door. He banged on it and then bent to shout through the letterbox.

"Oi, Zippy! It's me: Ratty."

There was a noise from inside and the door was opened to reveal an emaciated, pasty figure in his mid-thirties with a shaven head and wearing joggers and a sweatshirt that hung off him. This was Floyd 'Zippy' Lewis, a long term Sulgrave resident and local legend for his car thieving skills.

"Ratty."

"Zippy."

"You want to come in like?"

"Aye. Ta."

Zippy stood back to let Ratty in before hastily closing the door. They walked through to his main room and flopped into two tattered armchairs facing each other. "Y'all right Ratty? You look a bit rough mate."

"Aye, cush. Got a bit o' cold or summat. You got any gear?"

Zippy shook his head. Ratty didn't believe him, but he didn't have the energy to pursue it and knew it wouldn't do him any good if he did.

They both stared into space for a couple of minutes, Ratty shivering and Zippy scratching himself.

Finally, Ratty broke the silence. "You want to make some money? Good money?"

" Course. What is it? A motor?"

"Naah. Well, we'll need wheels, but it's for an off-licence job. We do it over."

"What? Like a robbery?"

"Aye."

"Oh shit, Ratty!"

"It'll be a piece o' piss man. I promise. You on?"

"How much?"

"Dunno. Reckon it could be a few grand easy." Zippy swallowed, passed his tongue over his lips and nodded. "Aye, alright, I'm on."

"That's brill, fucking brill. You got a knife Zippy?"

CHAPTER TWELVE

James Ward looked out of his living room window at a miserable October evening, at a howling wind which was driving the near horizontal rain. But, whatever the weather, the view through this window always brought him quiet satisfaction. Harton Village Green presented the kind of scene that might feature on a Christmas card, surrounded as it was by charming cottages and their cheerful lights.

Opposite, on the other side of the green, the lights were still on in the village shop, called – imaginatively – The Village Shop. He knew that Dorothy, the manager, would be closing soon. Good luck to her. She was getting on and must be a good couple of years past retirement date.

James himself had retired from teaching five years ago, when he and Mary had moved here, to their dream cottage in their dream village. They'd made the right choice. It was a good place to spend your retirement years. He smiled at the view and then turned to move across the room to turn the light off. He had enough light from the TV and there was no sense in wasting electricity, not at today's prices. But he wouldn't close the curtains yet, there'd be no nosy so-and-so walking past to peer into their home in this weather.

He sat in his favourite armchair, from where he could still see The Village Shop and settled down with a glass of beer to watch Spooks.

Mary was visiting her sister in Seaburn, so he'd have a peaceful hour or so to himself. He smiled again.

§

Ratty brought the car to a halt a few yards short of the shop. It was a red Micra, a real old biddy's car and Ratty approved of that, it was like a sort of disguise.

Zippy had nicked it from outside a house in South Shields. He'd stuck some spare plates on it. They weren't off a Micra but they'd do for the time they needed it.

They got out of the car and Ratty handed Zippy a ski mask.

"Stick that on as we go into the shop."

"I'm not putting that on Rats!"

"Just do it man! It's too late to lose your bottle now. It'll be a piece o' piss – straight in and out. And it's only one old bird."

"But… masks! It'll bring on me asthma man!" Ratty shook Zippy's shoulder.

"You'll be picked out by the cameras man. You're well famous, you know that Zippy?"

Zippy's mouth broadened into an uncertain beam. He tittered and took the mask.

§

As he waited for Spooks to start, James glanced through his window. A small car was pulling up almost outside the shop. Two figures got out. They looked like young men. He was sure they weren't local. They were heading for the shop doorway. Doreen wouldn't be pleased; she'd be just getting ready to cash up. One of the men reached into his jacket pocket and took something out, he argued with the other for a moment and then passed the object to his companion. Then they both pulled on masks and entered the shop.

As the door closed, he saw something glinting in the hand of one.

James reached to take the telephone handset from its position next to the TV remote. He dialled 999 and proceeded to give a running commentary on the scene he saw unfolding across the green.

§

In the Northumbria Police Control Room, Yvonne Riley spoke into her headset microphone.

"LB to any PR. Can anyone attend Harton Village Shop. Robbery in progress."

PC Steve Lochran, who was sitting next to his colleague PC Jock Campbell while they were parked up completing some paperwork, came straight back.

"2248, I'll attend LB. I'm round the corner in the Turk's Head carpark in company with 1341."

"We've got two males who've entered the store at the front wearing balaclavas, one male believed in possession of a knife."

"2248, is the caller still on the line?"

"Yes, males still on the premises but out of sight."

Twenty seconds later Steve Lochran brought the Fiesta to a screeching halt behind the Micra. He had barely stopped when a figure wearing a ski mask came running out of the shop.

"1341, at scene, runner towards Westoe wearing balaclava and dark clothing."

Both officers got out of the car to see inside the shop, a second male wearing a mask, running towards the door.

"2248, one male still in premises. Any back up?" The officers entered the shop door as the masked figure reached it. They pushed him backwards and he stumbled against a rack of wine, slipped and fell. His hand went to his jacket pocket and Lochran and Campbell drew their truncheons and struck him across his arms and shoulders until, with a squeal, he raised his hands in surrender. Lochran forced him to roll over onto his stomach, while Campbell pulled his arms back, forced his wrists together and cuffed him. Lochran reached into man's coat pocket and removed an eight-inch kitchen knife.

Gasping and his heart pounding Lochran bent towards the prone figure and panted into his ear: "You're arrested on suspicion of robbery - you bastard. You don't have to say anything, but it may harm your defence if you don't mention now something which you later rely on in court."

There was a grunt from the figure on the floor. "1341, one detained at scene. We need a van to transport the prisoner."

As Campbell made the call, two more uniformed officers entered the shop. Assured by Lochran that he and Campbell had their prisoner secured, they moved down the store to search the premises. Gently pushing open a door behind the counter, they found the huddled, weeping figure of Dorothy Findlay. Around her feet lay a several bags of cash. One of the officers went back to tell Lochran and Campbell what they'd found.

"2248, we'll need an ambulance to check out the IP not life threatening."

"Let's get the old eye-in-the-sky," muttered Campbell.

"1341, LB is India 99 available?"

"En-route and Delta section en-route.

Last direction of travel for the one outstanding?"

"1341, towards Westoe Village," said Campbell and whispered to Lochran with a thumbs up,

"Chopper and dogs – brill."

"2248, do you want me to add this onto the SOCO log?"

"2248. Yes we'll get a keyholder on scene." He looked over his shoulder at the dying sound of a siren and to see the flash of more blue lights. "Ambulance on scene."

"Right, let's take a look at our wee pal," said Campbell and turned the figure onto his back before pulling him into a sitting position. He took the top of the ski mask and dragged it from the robber's head, to reveal, a white, scratch-scarred face under hair that was standing on end in sweaty peaks. Campbell had seen enough smackheads to know, from the glazed eyes, that this one was out of it.

It was Jordan Ratcliffe, universally known as Ratty. He looked at the officers and, momentarily, his eyes focused.

"Yeah…you've got me bang to rights."

He sniggered and added: "It's a fair cop."

§

While Ratty and the Northumbria Constabulary were getting reacquainted, Zippy was living up to his nickname by haring away from the village green. As he ran, he tore off his ski mask and threw it. The wind snatched it and carried it across the green. Zippy ran into the outskirts of the village and then into the fields beyond. The clatter of an approaching helicopter drove him back towards cover and towards Harton. He climbed over a low fence into a garden and crouched in some shrubbery for a few seconds, rain dripping down his neck, until he was sure he had not been heard from inside the house. The helicopter grew louder and he realised he had to move in case it drew the curious householders into their garden. Zippy crawled across the wet lawn to a garden shed, which he found unlocked. Carefully he opened the door and stepped inside. He picked a dustsheet from a workbench, crawled under the bench and pulled the sheet over himself, shivering in his wet clothes, to wait until things calmed down.

From his hiding place, Zippy could hear the chopper, but nothing else. He couldn't hear Ratty being taken from The Village Shop and being put in a cage in the back of a police van to be taken to South Shields Police Station. He certainly couldn't hear the details of Ratty's arrest being outlined to the custody sergeant in the Custody Suite, Ratty then being informed of his legal rights and told that his detention would be authorised and that a doctor would be called, before he was led to his cell.

Nor could Zippy hear – although it would have been of more interest – a search of the area around the village by the dog section and all available uniformed officers. One delta officer, Adam Fletcher, did find a sodden black ski-mask on the far side of the green. He held it out to his Cocker Spaniel Beano, who gave it a half-hearted sniff. Fletcher walked Beano around the green to see if he could pick up a scent but there seemed to be nothing, so a thankful handler and dog headed back to their warm, dry van, stopping by the shop to hand the ski mask over to the SOCO team who had just arrived. They judged the mask to have been worn by the second offender and therefore significant and entered it into the incident log. Arrangements were then made for the Micra to be uplifted and recovered under the stolen motor vehicle scheme, to be examined for any forensics such as fingerprints and DNA by SOCO officers the following day in daylight.

§

Zippy remained unaware of all of this, as he dried off under his dust sheet. He did however listen to the sound of the helicopter growing fainter, until it disappeared altogether. Then Zippy gave it another couple of hours before he crawled out from his hiding place and left the shed, so to make his long, weary way home, cursing Ratty with every step.

§

Kilford got into the office the next morning at eight. Knackers opened the door to him and she was half way through her smiling good morning when she was interrupted by a familiar annoying cackle. It was Shifty who was at his desk looking at his computer.

Kilford returned a quick, answering smile to Knackers, before – despite himself - turning to Shifty. "What's so funny?"

"Look at the incident logs," said Shifty. "Your boy's been locked up on a nasty job in Harton last night.

Sounds like he's stuffed to me."

"Who're you on about?" asked Kilford, with a bad feeling in the pit of his stomach.

"Ratty the super grass – known outside these four walls as Wayne Langley. Knifepoint robbery on an off-licence. Old woman alone in the shop, one outstanding. Straight out of the Wrathall playbook.

The Boss is going ape shit about it."

Kilford closed his eyes and rubbed his chin. Ratty! Wanker! What the hell was he thinking? Kilford had worked hard on him over the years, turned him into a useful source, who'd provided useful intel and Kilford felt some responsibility for the little tit. He should have seen this coming. Shifty cackled again.

Kilford rounded on him.

"I don't know why you're so pleased about it – you twat!" He turned to Knackers and muttered an apology before returning to Shifty.

"He's the same snout who gave us Wrathall. He put himself out for us. Your snouts ever do that?"

There was a knock on the door. Knackers opened it to let Bull in. Bull looked from Kilford to Shifty, who were glaring at each other, the atmosphere tense.

"What's up, little fellah?" he asked Kilford. "Only looks like Ratty's got himself locked up for a knifepoint job."

"Oh, for Christ's sake! What a dick!"

"Shifty here thinks it's a right laugh."

Bull contemplated Shifty for a full thirty seconds until the other looked uncomfortable and began to fiddle with objects on his desk.

"Y'know Shifty," said Bull at length,

"if you fell down in front of me right now with a heart attack, I'd just step over you. No, on second thoughts,

I'd just sodding walk all over you."

Shifty blustered about people not being able to take a joke and then became intent on his computer screen. Knackers turned away, hiding a smile. Bull looked at Shifty for a few more seconds and then turned to Kilford.

"Let's pull the incident log up and look at exactly what the little tosser's been up to before we go see the boss. Kilford nodded glumly and they consulted the log to read the grim details of Ratty's latest adventure. Then they made their way to Rocky's office, knowing that they'd be held responsible for their source going rogue.

"I can't believe he could've been so bloody stupid," said Bull.

Kilford shook his head.

"We should've seen it coming. We could see he was going off the rails."

"Look, it's not our fault man, we can't nursemaid him twenty-four seven. I suppose that tosser Shifty couldn't wait to pass on the good news."

"Hadn't got my coat off." Bull shook his head.

"One of these days I'm going to punch that sweaty bastard's lights out."

"Make sure you let me know before you do."

They approached the DI's office. The door was ajar and he must have heard them talking, because Bull's hand was barely on the handle before a voice roared from inside.

"If that's yous two arseholes, you better get in here" Kilford and Bull exchanged a smile and replied in unison: "On our way boss."

"Don't even think about taking the piss! The pair o'yous get in here now!"

For ten minutes, Rocky raged about the mess Ratty had got himself into, the possible legal complications, the questions that would be asked upstairs, the loss of a valuable source, who had turned rogue snout. How many times had he underlined the importance of looking after snouts, of not taking your eye of the pissing ball?

Eventually however, the storm blew itself out in the face of the Detectives' dogged defence, pointing out that they had tried to maintain contact with Ratty, but that had proved impossible, how all potential risks regarding that source over recent weeks had been examined, discussed, reviewed, risk-assessed and duly recorded on Ratty's file. Without saying so, the DI grudgingly seemed to accept they had not been at fault.

"Anyway, Wayne Langley is well and truly stuffed. First thing, I spoke on the phone to the DS who's dealing: he's coughed the job over night without a brief being present, which isn't like him. He'll be charged with robbery this morning and placed in front the magistrates this afternoon and remanded into custody. He's looking at a long frigging stretch this time"

"Can we have authority to go and do an exit interview with him?" asked Bull. "What, for old times' sake?"

"Boss, there were two on the job and there's still one person outstanding," said Kilford.

A spasm of irritation crossed the DI's face.

"Don't you think I hadn't thought of that?" He clearly hadn't. He tapped his pen on the desk a couple of times.

"Alright, you can, but don't be promising him anything. Is that understood?"

"Like a text which he's entitled to?" said Bull. "Get your arses over there after he's been charged and see what he says and get back to me. Is that clear? I want the name of his bastard pal. Them upstairs will be chewing my balls off if they get any inkling our best snout, who gave us that bastard Wrathall on a plate, is doing knife point robberies. Now move it!"

§

Shortly after midday, Kilford and Bull were sitting at a table in an interview room at South Shields Police Station. There was a knock at the door and Bull opened it to let in Ratty who'd been escorted from his cell by a member of the custody staff.

Ratty walked in and sat down on the other side of the table and his escort withdrew. Kilford and Bull stared at Ratty without speaking. Kilford was struck by his appearance and demeanour. He looked grey but sweaty, with dark circles under his eyes, his hair lank and uncombed. He was trembling and held his hands over his stomach, as if in pain.

He looked at the detectives with a weak smile.

"Looks like I'm fucked on this one boys."

"Conspiracy to commit robbery?" said Bull. "I'd say that's the understatement of the year Ratty."

"What were you thinking of mate?" asked Kilford. "We've been trying to find you for weeks now. We've been ringing but no answer. You've still got money owed from the Wrathall job."

Ratty grimaced and shook his head.

"The gear's got the better of me, that's the truth, man. I'm rattling my tits off here, I'm really struggling… and with Eva going away, me head's been done in."

"How much gear are you using at the minute?" Ratty gave a brief, humourless laugh.

"As much as I can get. I tell you, it's out of fucking control, that's why we blagged that shop, I was off me head." He put a finger in his mouth.

"And I think me bastard teeth are falling out as well.

I'm sorry lads."

Bull jabbed his forefinger at him.

"Your best bet is to put a guilty plea in from the start and we can sort out a text. Remember what we said about texts when we started working with you?"

"Is that the letter to the judge?"

"That's right mate," said Kilford.

"Don't worry, it'll be a good one, you've put up loads of good jobs and Wrathall will be the icing on the cake.

Plus, you never got any cash for the job."

Ratty's eyes widened in alarm and Bull added quickly: "Don't worry mate, no one will know, apart from the judge and it should get you a lighter sentence. You're still going down though, you realise that don't you?"

"I suppose I deserve it after last night."

The detectives let this hang for a moment, as Ratty contemplated his own stupidity in rueful silence. Then Kilford leaned over the table.

"Ratty, we need to know who you were with last night. The boss is chewing our arses off."

Ratty jerked back in his chair and held his hands up. "Lads I can't say! It's too tight - you know what I mean."

Now Bull put his elbows on the table. "What if we told you we recovered a balaclava… nearby… discarded… forensics and that…." Ratty frowned.

"The old biddy's in a bad way, Ratty," said Kilford gently. "Shock."

"I can't give you his name man!" The detectives stared at him. Ratty sighed.

"Alright then, it was Zippy. He'll be expecting a knock anyway."

Kilford and Bull in unison and disbelief said: "Zippy Lewis?"

"I know, I know… don't know what I was thinking.

Fact is, I was just desperate, y'know?"

"Here's what we'll do," said Bull. "We'll stick his name in the hat, or even the balaclava, and see what comes of it. You never know, we might strike it lucky if we go down the forensic line first. Zippy's DNA's bound to be on file, so we'll point Forensics in his direction. How's that sound."

Ratty shrugged. "Cush… I s'pose." Kilford shook his head.

"Zippy! If you had to make a choice from the cast of Rainbow, you'd've been better off taking George or Bungle than sodding Zippy"

Ratty laughed and it struck Kilford there was an edge of hysteria to it, then Ratty suddenly grew serious. "Lads, see if you can get me a doctor out. Honestly, I'm going up the bastard wall, here."

"We'll sort that out for you," said Kilford. "You'll have to go back to your cell now mate. But, listen, like we said, we'll sort out a text for you for your Crown Court appearance, but you've got to keep that under your hat. Don't even tell your brief, for your own safety's sake. If it gets out, you're history. Y'know that don't you?" Ratty nodded.

"Good. Well, okay mate, thanks for all you've done and best of luck."

Bull tapped on the door to summon the custody officer. Kilford and Bull watched Ratty go shuffling back to the cells, then sighed and shook their heads, knowing their former source was looking at a long custodial sentence, text or no text.

It wasn't until the following afternoon that Kilford and Bull were able to see their DI and inform him that Ratty's accomplice had been Zippy Lewis. It was agreed that, in order to protect Ratty as their source, Zippy's name would be put forward as a suggested match for any DNA found on the ski mask, which, while considerably shortening the whole matching process, would make it look as though Zippy had been identified through forensic channels rather than by Ratty.

As Kilford and Bull were leaving Rocky's office, he treated them to one of his grudgingly given well done episodes.

Still grudging or not, it was welcome and they returned to the DSU with a spring in their step and smiles on their faces.

§

There was fierce competition between the three CID teams in Sunderland, with the rivalry being particularly fierce between DSU and the Proactive team.

This was partly because Proactive was led by the highly ambitious DS Paul Evans, who was eager that his crew be seen as the best in the station. He allowed them to use their own informal sources, whom they ran in their own way, not passing their intelligence through the correct channels, in other words the DSU. This was more than a simple turf war, it often caused real problems for DSU, with crossed wires and subsequent cockups. The DI was aware of the problem and had warned Evans, causing more bad blood.

But the Proactive team DS would have been unpopular with DSU anyway. He wasn't just ambitious, he was cocky with it and that cockiness often bordered on arrogance. He also had an inflated sense of his own importance and that was a weakness DSU exploited. A big, broad-shouldered man, Evans was balding, wore heavy, black-framed glasses and boasted a set of large horse-like teeth that seemed too big for his mouth and were always bared in a humourless grin. It had been Bull who had first noticed the DS's uncanny resemblance to Bingo, from the children's TV animated puppet show Banana Splits. To Evans' fury, the nickname became an instant hit throughout the whole station and the DSU team would sing the Banana Splits signature tune whenever he was observed walking past the office through the one way glass separating it from the corridor. On one occasion, a hearty rendition too many of "La, la, la; tra, la, la, la" had driven Evans to complain to the DI, who had raged at DSU for their "fucking childishness". But it did little to stop the taunting of Bingo.

In the week following Ratty's arrest, relations between DSU and Proactive team were made even more fraught. The pursuit of Zippy Lewis and another job involving a car theft ring meant that Bull blew the team bugle twice during the week, drawing envious snarls from the Proactive team. So, the DSU team were in a mood to expect retaliation on the afternoon following Kilford and Bull's meeting with Rocky. Then Bull's desk phone rang.

"DSU office. Can I help you?"

Bull heard an American accent booming through the handset.

"Hi there. This is Special Agent Joe Stricker from the Federal Bureau of Investigation, Washington DC. May I speak to an officer dealing with male sexual predators?"

Bull rolled his eyes and put his hand over the receiver. "It's those Proactive tossers again with one of their wind-up calls. Pretending to be bloody Eliot Ness or something this time."

The others shook their heads wearily. "Just hang up," said Knackers. "I would." But Bull uncovered the receiver.

"Well howdy there Special Agent Stricker. It's Sherlock Holmes here. How can I be of assistance, to y`all?"

"Good morning, or rather afternoon, Mr... uh... Holmes. I'm calling to inform you about a Dutch national who will be arriving at Newcastle Airport in possession of indecent material relating to young boys."

"Well that's great news and thanks for the fucking tip off," said Bull and hung up.

"Tossers!"

§

Things looked bad for Ratty. Newly arrived in HMP Darlington, he was facing months on remand awaiting trial. If that wasn't enough, worse was the fact he was sharing his twelve foot by eight-foot space with, Angry Anderton, another smackhead who seemed to have free access to H. That wasn't helping Ratty. Ratty watched as his pad mate dropped his trousers and carefully remove his stash of heroin, wrapped in cling film, from his rectum. Then, from somewhere, he produced a small roll of foil and a lighter. He placed the brown powder on the foil then gently heated it from underneath. It turned into something like toffee and bubbled, dancing on the foil. Angry beckoned Ratty, who needed no invitation, and they bent over to inhale the fumes, chasing the dragon.

After his hit, Ratty lay on his bunk sleepy and euphoric. He thought about Eva and about how they might have had a half decent life together – but for all this shit.

The only slim hope he had to hang onto was that text being prepared by his handlers in Sunderland for his trial. He'd worked well with those two bizzies, Kilford and Miles, over the years. Like they'd told him: he'd given them good stuff and he knew for a fact it had led to a load of their target criminals being sent down and the recovery of Class A drugs and firearms. He trusted them – as far as you could trust any coppers – and he was confident that they'd come up with something to make the judge less inclined to see him as the kind of head case, junky low-life the Prosecution were bound to paint him as.

He was still turning this over in his mind in the early evening, as he trudged round the prison's yard for his thirty minutes' exercise, along with a couple of dozen other remand prisoners. He shivered and fought a wave of nausea. He wondered: would Angry come through again after? If he didn't, there'd be a mare of a night in store. If he did, the whole bastard cycle was just going to go on and on. Christ, what a life!

Ratty felt a heavy hand clamp itself onto his shoulder. He started to turn, expecting another prisoner wanting a light of a fag. Then he heard the voice and his guts leapt, even before he saw the cold staring face. "Need a word in your shell Ratty and we haven't got much time," growled Karl Wrathall.

CHAPTER THIRTEEN

"Fuck me Karl I didn't know you were in here mate." Ratty's trembling and nausea suddenly got a whole lot worse. He attempted a weak smile at Wrathall who stared back.

"Yeah, I'm in here, but hopefully not for long. But while you've got the pleasure of my company, I've a little job for you."

"In here?"

Wrathall took a firm hold of Ratty's forearm and drew him closer and leaned so that his mouth was inches from Ratty's ear, as he whispered: "No, not in here you twat. I gather you're at court next week, pleading guilty to a knifepoint robbery - bit like mine. Correct?"

"Aye... but...."

Wrathall's grip tightened to a sudden painful squeeze, making Ratty squeak. Wrathall's lips drew closer. "Don't go using that word with me Ratty, it really winds me up - and you don't want that."

"Wh... what word?"

"The word 'but'. I don't want to hear no fucking buts. Understand?"

Ratty swallowed and nodded.

"You were wearing a balaclava," continued Wrathall. "There was an old biddy in the shop just before it closed. Correct?" Ratty nodded again.

"Eva - your lass - is going to plead guilty to all charges, dropping me right in the shite," hissed Wrathall. "But you can make up for that Ratty. You're not much shorter than me. Understand where I'm coming from?"

"Er… not a shagging clue Karl. Honest."

"Don't worry, it's simple – so fucking simple even you'll be able to understand it. When you appear at court next week you can cough to all my jobs, including a murder. You fit the bill see?

D'you get it?"

"What! I can't do that man! I haven't a scooby about your jobs. Murder! You're having a laugh!

Ow!"

Ratty gave a low yelp as Wrathall gave his forearm a vicious twist.

"Do I look like I'm laughing Ratty?" Wrathall reached inside his jacket and produced a sheaf of folded papers. He thrust it into Ratty's face.

"I told you, this is simple. You read this, it'll tell you about every single job from beginning to end. I've included everything you need to know, it's as if you were on the plot. It's a bit of homework for you. You learn that off by heart."

"Oh, for shit's sake! I can't do that, I'll get lifed off man."

Wrathall stuffed the paperwork inside Rattys jacket. "You'll be out in ten. But let's be clear, you piece of shit, if you don't do it, you're not going to survive in here for ten days. It's as simple as that. Be a good boy and do as you're told, or you're a dead man walking. You know it's a piece of piss for me, there's some hard people in here who'll do me a favour and I've got enough of the screws in my pocket to look the other way. So, what d'you say Ratty?"

Ratty couldn't say anything. He nodded.

§

The full DSU team were in the office at nine the following morning, already at work - studying the incident logs; reading emails, updating source files. They all looked up when there was a loud and familiar bang on the door. Blockhead sighed, hauled himself from his chair and opened it.

"Morning boss," he said.

A red-faced Rocky gave his DS only a curt nod before striding into the room waving a sheet of paper. "Right you arseholes! Who's Mr Sherlock-fucking-

Holmes out of you lot?"

Silence.

"No one wants to cough the job then? Well listen, I've just had a Special Agent Stricker on the phone from Washington DC. Seems very conscientious and hardworking our Mr Stricker – it being about four in the morning over there, so that just adds to my pissing embarrassment. Apparently he was speaking to Sherlock Holmes last night in this unit. However, Sherlock used ` profane'" Rocky made inverted commas in the air with his fingers " language and hung up on him. Ring any bells?"

There was some coughing and shuffling of papers.

Kilford spoke.

"To be fair boss, we thought it was a wind-up."

"Oh that's all right then! I'm just grateful it wasn't the Home Secretary. I knew it would be you or your sodding mate here." He made an angry gesture towards Bull.

"It was me," said Bull quickly.

The DI glared at him, breathing hard through his nose.

"It's no frigging wind up. Read this printout he's just faxed me and when you've read it, you two get along to my office. This better get sorted before it goes upstairs."

"We'll sort it boss," said Blockhead.

After a last glare round the office, Rocky thrust the document into Blockhead's hand, turned on his heel and left, slamming the door behind him.

Nobody spoke as his footsteps stomped off down the corridor. Kilford grinned.

"Alf, this isn't funny," said Blockhead, before he started laughing, followed by the rest of the team.

It was Blockhead who first got himself under control. Wiping the back of his hand across his eyes, he said: "Come on guys and gals, we'd better get this sorted. Now that Bull's single-handedly torpedoed the special relationship."

There was more laughter while he read the faxed document that Rocky had left.

Blockead read the sheet, frowning and pulling on his lower lip with his thumb and forefinger. When he'd finished, he removed another page which had been stapled to the back of the document.

"Okay," he said. "We've not got a lot of time with this.

Here's what we've got. A Dutch national called Dirk De Jong is arriving at Newcastle Airport from Cairo at 10.15. He's believed to be in possession of indecent images of children for distribution. Looks like he's a major player in a worldwide paedophile ring who exploit young boys in Luxor in Egypt. Looking at this, the FBI have picked this up from phone taps. This photo of him is shite but apparently he's sixty two years old, slim build and believed to be over six-foot tall. Here, have a look at him. We've got an address of 66, Fenham Terrace, Penshaw – So it's on our patch."

"We haven't got a lot of time," said Knackers.

"What's the plan?"

"Bull and Alf, make your way to the airport ASAP and see if you can spot him as he comes out of arrivals. If you see him, follow him and let's hope he's going to Penshaw, or we're in the shite. Knackers, you go to the magistrates' court and get a warrant for 66, Fenham Terrace. Shifty, research this bastard and wait for Knackers to get back."

"Should we go for our arse kicking first?" asked Bull. "Eh? No, there's no time for that. I'll speak to the boss and calm him down... but lose this bastard and it'll be more than an arse kicking for yous lot."

Kilford and Bull grabbed their jackets and left the station at a run. They got into their car and Bull had the engine started and gear engaged before Kilford had his seat belt on. They exited the station with tyres squealing and proceeded to break all speed limits, overtaking and weaving in and out of traffic in an effort to reach Newcastle Airport in sixty minutes. En route Kilford put in a call to Special Branch and, after hurriedly explaining their problem, gained permission to park outside the airport terminal.

Kilford spent the rest of the journey advising Blockhead of their arrival and examining the poor reproduction of a photograph that the FBI had faxed, along with the written description. They pulled off the airport roundabout with just eight minutes to spare.

At around 10.20, people began coming through the exit doors. After about a dozen had come through trailing their suitcases, Kilford jerked forward in his seat and nudged Bull. A tall, thin, tanned man with neatly combed silver hair, looking to be of late middle age, strode through the doors, carrying a tatty, brown leather briefcase and a small suitcase. Bull and Kilford gave a quick glance at the photograph.

"That's him!" said Bull. "That's definitely him Alf."

"I think you're right. Let's see where he goes from here."

The tall male walked with a confident stride directly in front of their unmarked car and made his way towards the taxi rank. The detectives craned their necks to follow his progress.

"Let's pray he's going straight home or you're in the shite mate," said Kilford.

"Me in the shite? I thought we were a team."

"Hey Chubby, I never pretended to be Sherlock Holmes. I never even spoke to Special Agent Shyster."

"Stricker."

"Whatever… 'Ere we go! He's got a taxi."

The man, believed to be Dirk De Jong climbed into the back of a taxi, which then pulled away from the rank and towards the airport exit, followed by Kilford and Bull.

The taxi turned onto the A696 heading south east. This was expected as it was the direction for most centres of population and transport links. The more tense moment came ten minutes later when they hit the roundabout junction for the A1. Everything depended on De Jong – if it was him – going south and home to Penshaw for which address Knackers hopefully had a search warrant. If the taxi headed north towards Northumberland or straight on for Newcastle and Tyneside they were in trouble. At the roundabout the taxi started to indicate right – it was going south.

"Thank God for that," breathed Bull.

Kilford made another call to update Blockhead who told them that not only had Knackers got the warrant but she and Shifty were already parked outside 66 Fenham Terrace in Penshaw, waiting for them. The taxi was heading south but that was no guarantee it was bound for Penshaw.

As Kilford cheerily pointed out to Bull: there were a lot of other destinations on the A1 between them and London. There were tense moments until they followed the taxi off at the correct junction and then at every subsequent roundabout and junction, Kilford fielding calls from Blockhead demanding updates all the way. They relaxed a little as

Penshaw Monument grew nearer. It was an imposing structure built in the style of an ancient Greek temple on Penshaw Hill and dominating the country around and the sprawling settlement of terrace houses that stood at its foot. Now Kilford felt confident enough to ring Knackers. "We're heading for your location, will be there in five, look out for a black taxi."

The taxi pulled into Fenham Terrace and came to a halt outside number 66. Bull pulled up right behind it, just as Kilford saw, on the opposite side of the road, Knackers and Shifty get out of their Fiesta and walk to De Jong as he was paying his fare. They were joined by Kilford and Bull.

"Mr De Jong is it?" said Knackers.

The man, who had been leaning to pay the taxi driver, straightened and turned, taking in the detectives. He looked puzzled, focused his attention on Knackers as the taxi pulled away and said: "Yes."

"I'm Detective Constable Hartnack from Sunderland Police Station and these are my colleagues," she said, indicating the three detectives who were staring levelly at De Jong.

"We're in possession of a warrant to search your premises, to search for articles in connection with the possession of indecent images of children. Do you understand?"

"No... well yes, but you won't find anything." He spoke in clipped, accented English. He looked at each of the detectives in turn. "I've just returned from my holidays."

"You've got nothing to worry about then," said Bull. "So let's just go inside your house and get started shall we?"

De Jong shook his head as if in disbelief and led them to the front door of his house, a modest brick terrace with a tiny front garden. He unlocked the door and ushered them into a house that appeared clean and well maintained. He lead them down the hallway to the kitchen and, en route, Kilford glanced into the lounge, which was well furnished in a Scandinavian pine and chrome style and with well-stocked book cases. In the kitchen, De Jong placed his suitcase and briefcase on the floor and turned to face the detectives. Kilford studied him as Knackers explained the details of the warrant and what he could expect to happen next. There was a hint of cockiness about the Dutchman, an arrogance Kilford had seen before in well-educated suspects, a conviction that that they were more than a match for any slow-witted police officer.

This seemed to wind up Shifty, who demanded brusquely: "Right, before we search the house, let's have a look in your case."

De Jong reached down for his suitcase and opened it on the work surface.

"You will find nothing, but, go ahead, please, be my guest."

Shifty unzipped the case, which was full of basic clothing, toiletries, trunks and a pair of flip-flops. These were taken out one by one and placed neatly on the work surface. When the case was empty De Jong looked round at the detectives.

"I told you you'd find nothing," he smirked. "You want to search the rest of the house now?"

"Let's have a look in your briefcase first, sir," said Kilford. "If you don't mind."

De Jong frowned and pursed his lips before placing the briefcase on the surface next to the suitcase.

Shifty pointed to the combination reels.

"Can you give me the numbers to open it please."

"Four, five, one, three, on both sides," said De Jong. His tone was a touch less confident and Kilford could detect a sheen of sweat developing on his upper lip and forehead.

Shifty aligned the numbers and clicked open the case, revealing paperwork, a passport, foreign currency and a pair of white underpants. Nothing illegal or even incriminating.

Shifty rummaged through the items with increasing impatience. Kilford knew all the team had a growing sense of foreboding that this wasn't going to be a successful search. Pity the TSG weren't there. When it came to searches, they knew what they were doing.

De Jong was brightening.

"You see: still nothing."

"We haven't started yet," growled Bull.

Kilford reached over and took the pair of underpants. He held them with the thumb and forefinger of each hand, displaying them.

"Bit on the tight side for you Mr De Jong, wouldn't you say?"

De Jong shrugged angrily. Bull reached past him and picked up the now empty briefcase and began shaking it from side to side. There was a distinct sound of something moving. He and Kilford exchanged a glance and then Bull clutched at the case's loose lining and yanked. The lining ripped away from the frame and a couple of dozen colour photographs cascaded onto the work surface and several slid onto the floor. Knackers bent to pick them up. She put them with the rest on the surface and spread them out. They showed naked figures: middle-aged white men on beds with Middle Eastern looking boys in their early teens and younger. She picked up one photo and pointed to one of the subjects – clearly De Jong.

"Holiday snaps?" she said.

De Jong's tan couldn't hide the fact that blood was draining from his face, which now shone with sweat.

"It is not what it looks like. I can explain."

"You certainly can. In due course."

Knackers cautioned De Jong, concluding: "I'm arresting you on suspicion of being in possession of indecent images of children. Do you understand?"

De Jong seemed to physically shrink. He nodded and, with head bowed, allowed himself to be handcuffed by Knackers, who, with

Shifty led him out to their car to be taken back to Sunderland Police Station, where the inquiry would then be handed over to Tam's Reactive team. Kilford and Bull remained at De Jong's house, liaising with Blockhead to organise a TSG team to undertake a thorough search of the premises.

§

It was mid-afternoon by the time the pair returned to the station, steeling themselves for another bollocking from their DI. Instead, they were surprised to find an upbeat atmosphere in the office. Senior management it seemed, had got wind of a successful operation performed by their command on behalf of the FBI and Blockhead had spun a convincing narrative about the excellent work the DSU had done in responding to information received only just before the suspect had landed at Newcastle Airport. No mention of Special Agent Stricker's conversation with Sherlock Holmes the previous day.

In the end, the search of De Jong's house produced more indecent images of children and a seized laptop which yielded mobile phone numbers, email addresses and names linked to an international paedophile ring. After several interviews by Tam Macfarlane's reactive team, De Jong was charged and subsequently sent to prison for a lengthy custodial sentence.

But that lay months into the future. That afternoon,

Kilford and Bull had just been brought up to date by Blockhead when Rocky arrived in the office, rubbing his hands together vigorously and chuckling. "I knew it was a smart move to give yous two responsibility for sex offenders."

Kilford and Bull wore thin smiles and nodded.

"Anyway," continued Rocky, pointing at Bull, "you can have the pleasure of ringing your pal Special Agent Stricker to give him the good news." Bull sighed and nodded again. As he was leaving the room, Rocky paused at the door.

"You two did well."

"It was down to Bull," said Kilford.

"He found the photos." He explained about the search of the briefcase. The DI nodded at Bull.

"Well done Chubby."

After Rocky closed the door, Bull heaved another sigh, picked up the phone and asked Blockhead for the FBI number.

Kilford patted Bull on the shoulder.

"Nice one Sherlock."

For the rest of the afternoon Kilford, Bull and Blockhead worked on the paperwork for the De Jong case to present Reactive with a complete package. It was six thirty when they finished.

"Fancy a pint?" asked Bull.

Kilford grimaced.

"I'd love one mate, but as we've got a reasonably early finish I can earn myself some much needed brownie points if I get off home."

Kilford smiled to himself. In fact, he was well in credit on brownie points, having bought a puppy, a black Lhasa Apso with a white front paw, which he had introduced to an amazed and delighted family the previous night. Vicki had actually whispered in his ear that she was proud of him. Tonight the Kilford family were due to convene to select a name for the newcomer from a shortlist drawn up by the girls – with their mum's oversight. Kilford, as excited by the new arrival as they were, was determined not to miss it.

"You can count me in," said Blockhead.

They logged out of their computers and Kilford was reaching for his jacket when the phone on their desk rang. Kilford swore and picked it up.

"Source Unit. DC Kilford speaking."

"Alf, its Jean in the front office. I've got a call from Darlington Prison. The caller won't give me his name and is asking to speak to you."

"Put him through please Jean and I'll speak to him." Kilford covered the receiver.

"Incoming call from Darlington nick. Wonder who this'll be."

Blockhead and Bull, who were on their way to the door, stopped, curious.

A familiar voice came over the line.

"Dan? Is that you? It's Ratty here."

"Yes, it's me mate. How's it going?"

"Thank fuck! It's been doin' me 'ead in trying to get to a phone. Listen, I'm in the fucking shite mate."

"That's the understatement of the year Ratty. Even with a good text you're still looking at five years."

"I'm looking at shagging twenty years now! That bastard Wrathall has got to me in the exercise yard. He's telling me I've got to go to court on Monday next week and cough that I'm the blagger on all his jobs, including the murder. I fit the description, my lass is charged with the jobs and I'm sitting in here, charged with a same bastard type of job which I'm pleading guilty to. I'll get lifed off mate. He's said if I don't do what he's said I'll be killed in here."

Kilford sank into his chair, looked at Blockhead and Bull and shook his head.

"Your're right, you are in the shite... hold on a minute... you're at court next week...?" Ratty interrupted, now with panic in his voice.

"Listen man! He's scripted up the jobs, everyone one of 'em in detail, so when I go to court I'll know the jobs inside out."

"Where are these scripts now?"

"I've got them in my pad... I've had to read through 'em so I know the score."

"Listen Ratty, we need those scripts. I'll have to think of something... you just make sure they're not too well hidden. Are you listening to what I'm bloody telling you?"

"Aye, but how the fuck are you going to do something before next week?"

"Trust me, you just do as I... hello... hello, Ratty? Shit!

He's been disconnected."

"Was that Ratty?" asked Bull. "What's going on?" Kilford told them. Bull and Blockhead swore and joined Kilford sitting at the desk. They looked dazed.

"What a bloody nightmare," said Blockhead.

"You do realise what this means?" said Kilford. "Our star intel source, who was instrumental in us collaring one of the nastiest, most violent offenders we've had to deal with in a long time, is going to have to frame himself for the crimes he helped solve."

"And Wrathall walks," said Bull.

CHAPTER FOURTEEN

"How the hell," groaned Blockhead, "are we going to sort this out?"

"We've got to get hold of those scripts," said Bull. Kilford rubbed his chin.

"That's easier said than done. If we arrange to search Ratty's cell for the scripts it'll look well dodgy and come back on Ratty. He'll be dead."

Blockhead and Bull dropped back into their chairs. The three detectives looked at each other. Bull toyed with a pen on the desk, Blockhead tugged at his earlobe and sucked his teeth and Kilford stared at his lifeless computer screen. Blockhead broke the silence.

"Okay, here's what we do. We organise a search of every cell on Ratty's wing… make it look like a routine search for drugs or mobiles or something. What d'you think?"

Bull nodded: "Don't see why it shouldn't work. What d'you think Alf?"

"Yeah," sighed Kilford.

"I agree we need to get those scripts, if only to see what's on them. After all, it's all about Wrathall's jobs, according to the bastard himself. But where does it get us then? What does it prove?"

There was another silence and again, after a minute, Blockhead broke it.

"What exactly did Ratty say about these scripts?" Kilford shrugged.

"Can't remember his exact words, but he said Wrathall had gone into great detail about all his jobs so Ratty could make it sound like he'd done them."

"Odd that... wouldn't have had Wrathall down as the literary type."

"Yeah, well, maybe there's a sensitive, artistic soul beneath that outer layer of being a complete and utter shit."

"`Hang on," said Bull.

"We did know that Wrathall likes to write."

"Eh... what you on about?" asked Kilford. He looked at Bull, his brow furrowed. Then, as Bull grinned back, realisation dawned.

"Of course! Who's a clever chubby bastard then?" Blockhead looked from one to the other.

"What the hell am I missing here?" Bull explained.

"When we went to Wrathall's old man's place looking for him – and that, by the way, is one really weird old bastard – we found a big pile of letters Wrathall had written him from Bradford."

"Letters in Wrathall's handwriting," added Kilford.

"Signed by the man himself."

"Get a handwriting expert to say Ratty's script and those letters were written by the same person and that's another nail in Wrathall's coffin."

A grin widened across Blockhead's face. He sat forward in his chair and punched the air. "I'm going to ring the boss. He's going to love this."

"Let's hope so," said Kilford, taking up his jacket again.

"Now, I'm off. I've got a dog to name."

§

Rocky did love it.

The next morning he stood before the DSU team rubbing his hands.

"Right, we're going to have to move quick on this. The search of Wrathall's dad's house won't be a problem. Alf, you and Bull go on that, as you've seen the letters and know where they are."

"Yes boss," said Bull.

"We'd better brief the TSG about the old man's little family. They're tough lads but that might freak them out."

"Eh?"

Bull and Kilford explained about Old Man Wrathall's mannequins. Rocky stared, then rubbed his eyes and shook his head in bewilderment.

"I thought I'd heard it all. Anyway, I'll speak to the governor at Darlington and arrange to meet him this morning. Wrathall's caused some misery in this area, so I don't anticipate a problem there. Cliff, you get onto the CPS and arrange an urgent meeting to get an adjournment for Ratty's case next week and don't take any shit off them – we need some elbow room on this." The DI was consulting his page of notes when Kilford spoke.

"Boss, I take it we're going to try and fix the searches for the same time. If Wrathall gets wind that we've searched his dad's house that script might disappear, or, if we do the prison first, he might get word to his dad."

Rocky peered at him over the top of his glasses.

"Do you think I hadn't thought of that?"

"Well... 'course boss, I knew you would, but..."

"What do I tell you arseholes every day?"

"It's the worst it's... no, sorry, not that one... fail to plan, plan to fail."

"Exactly. Those searches have to go down together. Not only that, we need them both done today, even if it means staying late. I want the scripts and letters in our possession before either of them goes walkabout. Is that clear? Good. We'll meet again at three this afternoon to see where we're at."

§

Ratty was on his way back to his cell with Angry. They had been in the exercise yard. Ratty was shivering. It hadn't been particularly cold outside, but he was getting used to being indoors – and he badly needed some gear. He was hoping that Angry would provide, so he was working hard at keeping on the right side of his cellmate, laughing at his jokes and listening intently to his interminable, rambling, pointless stories.

Angry was well into one of these as they mounted the concrete steps leading to their wing. Ratty, his arms wrapped around his body to keep warm, was aware of Angry's low droning and contributed by the occasional murmured grunt to indicate that he was enthralled by whatever he was rambling about.

"So, I said to 'im…." Angry was saying, as they entered the landing walkway.

But Ratty never did find out what Angry had said because at that moment, as they passed an open cell door, Ratty was grabbed from behind and pushed through into the cell. He did hear a voice close to his ear growling: "Fuck off Angry, you've seen nowt."

Ratty was bundled into the cell, spun round and forced back against the bunk. He was staring into the face of his assailant, a short man, who had obviously made good use of the prison gym facilities to develop formidable biceps, pectorals and the characteristic V-shaped torso of the bodybuilder. His head was shaven and he sported a neat goatee beard, but Ratty's attention was mostly taken by his eyes, which were icy blue and unblinking. Then his gaze was drawn to the shiv that Goatee held up to his face, a green, plastic toothbrush, whose handle end had been filed to a wicked, jagged point. Slowly, Goatee lowered this and pressed the point into the underside of Ratty's chin. "There's no point shouting Ratty, 'cos if the screws hear you, they'll do piss all about it. Y'know what I'm saying?"

Ratty nodded.

"I've got a message from Karl. He just wants to remind you that he's counting on you. You cough to those jobs when you're at court, or you'll get shivvie here through your scrawny little neck. You got that?"

Ratty nodded again – and bleated for good measure.

"Good."

The shiv disappeared and, seemingly simultaneously, Goatee's hands gripped either side of Ratty's head and banged the back of it hard against the bunk frame.

Ratty yelped.

"Now, you just fuck off back to your cell Ratty and get swotting."

§

At the three o'clock meeting in the DSU Blockhead explained that Bull and Kilford had sworn out a warrant to search Wrathall's dad's house and that the TSG had been alerted and would be in the station at five for their briefing. He also reported that he and Shifty had attended a meeting with the CPS, who had raised no objections to adjourning Ratty's trial for a week.

The DI nodded his approval and then told the team that he and Knackers had been to see the governor of HMP Darlington who had been eager to co-operate. He was going to detail four of his most trusted prison officers to conduct a drugs search of Ratty's wing at six that evening and they would be primed to look for handwritten documents in Ratty's cell. He had also agreed to arrange to transfer Wrathall to another prison the following day to prevent him renewing his pressure on Ratty.

After the meeting, Kilford sat at his desk to do some paperwork. He chose the most routine tasks he could find, because, although normally good at compartmentalising and concentrating on the job in hand, that afternoon he couldn't tear his mind from the Wrathall case.

They had found and nicked that bastard and stopped him in his tracks. They'd got the evidence against him, but now he had pulled a flanker and it looked like he could not only get off with it, but actually put Kilford's best snout in the frame for it. This had put things on a knife edge, where it was going to be a case of either win it all or lose it all – and which it was to be depended on what happened that evening.

Briefing the TSG wasn't like the last time. They were sitting in the same room and, once again, Kilford was at the front, going through the job details and the same impassive faces gazed back at him. But there were no helmets, protective jackets or heavy boots, just blue coveralls. There was also no undercurrent of tension, they knew they weren't going on a job where there was likely to be any trouble. It was just a routine house search.

It was also different, when, at ten minutes to six, Kilford and Bull drew up outside Wrathall's dad's house in Farringdon. The TSG van parked about fifty yards behind them, out of sight.

Kilford and Bull made their way up the garden path and knocked on the door. A few seconds later, they could hear shuffling on the other side and then it was opened to reveal the suspicious, resentful features of Wrathall Senior.

"Oh, it's you again," he said. "What do you want this time?"

Bull produced the warrant.

"Mr Wrathall, we have here a warrant to search these premises for articles in connection with a series of robberies. Do you understand?"

"You'd better come in then," said the old man, as though they were there to read the meter. Bull stepped in while Kilford went back to the road to wave to the TSG, to let them know they could now join them.

The TSG team filed into the hallway while Wrathall Senior retreated to his front lounge to sit in front of a TV whose volume was turned up high. As the TSG sergeant passed them, Bull tapped him on the shoulder and pointed to the pile of manila envelopes on the telephone table. The sergeant looked at them and then at Bull and Kilford, his eyebrows raised. The detectives nodded and the sergeant produced a clear plastic bag into which he placed the envelopes. The team then spread out around the house, upstairs and down, methodically searching. Kilford and Bull listened to floorboards creaking and drawers being opened and then exchanged grins when they heard barely muffled exclamations and swearing from upstairs.

"Looks like they've met the family," said Kilford.

§

About twenty five miles to the South, Ratty was lying on his bunk, hands clasped behind his head, digesting his evening meal and trying to ignore the feeling of nausea that it had brought on. It helped to take his mind of his stomach by reflecting on Wrathall and his threats, but soon Ratty was thinking he'd rather throw up. He was saved from this dilemma by a sudden commotion on the landing outside his cell – heavy footsteps, then banging and shouting.

"What the fuck's goin' on?" said Angry, sitting on his own bunk.

Before Ratty could venture an opinion, there was a rattling at the cell door which was then thrown open by two of the senior screws.

"All right you two, on yer feet!" shouted one, an officer called Mawson.

"Stand by your beds! Cell search."

"What yer lookin' fer?" asked Ratty, swinging his feet to the floor.

"Hunt the slipper, what d'you think? Mobiles and drugs."

The screws strode into the cells, each making for a bunk. In swift, practised movements, they pealed back the sheets and duvets and pulled off the mattresses. Underneath Ratty's was the sheaf of papers Wrathall had handed to him. Mawson picked it up and brandished it under Ratty's nose. "What's this then Ratty?"

"Dunno. Never seen it before."

"Tooth Fairy left it, did she?" He peered at the documents. "You been writing your memoirs Ratty? I think I'll hang onto this. I've always wanted to know your life story."

"Suit yourself mush, nothin' to do wi' me." The rest of the search was perfunctory and half-hearted, taking barely a couple minutes. Then the screws left and marched off down the landing, to go through the motions on the rest of the landing, provoking noisy protest from the other cons.

Ratty breathed deeply and thought: "Dan Kilford, I just hope you know what you're fucking doing."

Three hours later, in the DSU, Kilford was playing Snake on his Nokia, with great care and concentration, while Bull was folding a thin sheet of foil, which had covered his bar of chocolate, into progressively smaller squares and rectangles, after having first smoothed out all the wrinkles on its surface. Blockhead, had his feet on the desk and was leaning back, staring at an upper corner of the room. Kilford's phone bleeped his latest Snake failure. He sighed and pocketed the Nokia. "Where's the boss?" he asked Blockhead. "Down the pub. Said to update him if anything happened."

Bull tossed his square of foil towards the wastepaper basket and missed. He slapped his palm onto the desk.

"It's nine o'clock. How long does it take to search a bloody cell?"

"They couldn't just search Ratty's could they?" said Blockhead. "That'd look too obvious."

"Aye… `suppose."

There was a tap on the door and all three men jumped to their feet. Kilford got there first. He opened it and was staring at Knackers who, in return, was giving him her best dazzling smile and was brandishing a transparent evidence bag. Shifty stood behind her shoulder, leering.

"Look what we've got here boys," she said walking into the room and placing the bag on her desk. The door was allowed to swing shut and everyone crowded round the desk to examine the bag, which contained crumpled sheets of A4 paper bearing handwriting.

"Everything go to plan?" asked Blockhead.

"As well as it could've, apart from the waiting" said Knackers. "We hung around outside of the landing for ages until they finished the whole search and finally a screw came and just handed over the letters. We've got a note of his details for a statement. We bagged the papers and came back here."

"Did the screw mention Ratty?" asked Bull.

"Naah, not a word," said Shifty.

"C'mon," said Blockhead, "let's get these papers separated into individual bags and compare the handwriting to Wrathall's letters."

The five detectives sat around Kilford and Bull's desks and began sorting, working fast, not speaking. Kilford had to force himself to slow down, to be methodical, but he was excited, knowing that they were on the brink of a major breakthrough and from their gleaming eyes, he could see that the rest of the team felt the same.

Once all the sheets were bagged separately, they were spread out across Bull's desk and then Wrathall's letters to his dad were laid out on Kilford's desk next to them. The detectives pored over them. Kilford looked from one set of scripts, where the large letters sloped to the right with exaggerated loops and curls, to the next.

They were precisely the same.

"Well, I'm no handwriting expert, but I'd said we've got a result here," said Blockhead.

"I agree," said Kilford.

"Deffo," said Bull.

Knackers nodded, but Shifty was shaking his head. "Yeah, okay, it's the same handwriting and we know it's Wrathall's, but what does it prove?"

"Oh come on man!" protested Bull. "Why would Wrathall write down details of a series of robberies if he wasn't behind them?"

"Shifty's right, they're not a clincher – on their own," said Blockhead. "A half decent brief can still argue that Wrathall only wrote down the jobs because, although he'd been wrongly accused, he was afraid he was going down for them and wanted somebody else to take the rap. Not a nice thing to do, but no proof that he was the robber."

"Oh, for shit's sake!" cried Bull.

Kilford closed his eyes and shook his head. This couldn't be happening. He wasn't going to let this happen. He shut out the voices of the others arguing and picked up one of the scripts from Ratty's cell, his eyes following the words, his mind churning. He read one line, stopped, re-read it. He looked up, not focused, blinking.

"What's up Alf?" asked Bull. "Seen a ghost?" Kilford looked at Blockhead.

"On the Peterlee job – where was the safe located?"

"Out back somewhere. Remember, the CCTV showed him dragging the old biddies out there."

"Whereabouts out back?"

"Dunno. There was no CCTV out there."

Kilford spoke while scanning the note again: "Did we release any details to the press about the severity and details of the assaults at Peterlee?"

"Not that I recall." Blockead ruffled his hair in exasperation and shouted: "Alf! What are you getting at man?"

"Look at this... and this. Wrathall's gone to town with these scripts. He's telling Ratty where exactly the safe is, at the back of the premises, to the left when you go through the door, under some shelves. He mentions kicking one of the old biddies in the face. We'd never have disclosed that."

"Would we hell," breathed Blockhead, taking the evidence bag from Kilford and gazing at it with something like reverence.

"Brilliant! Well done Alf, the boss is going to be over the moon - as you football types might say. Right, that's enough for tonight. First thing tomorrow, we go through this lot and see what other detail Wrathall has in there that only he could know and we'll check on the location of that safe, go to Peterlee if necessary. If this all stacks up, what we have here is pure gold."

"It's better than that," grinned Kilford. "It's a signed confession."

CHAPTER FIFTEEN

Kilford sniffed, grimaced and lowered the passenger window of Blockhead's Astra by about an inch. Blockhead took his eyes briefly from the road to glance across.

"You hot, Alf? I can turn the heating down."

"No, it's okay, I just need some fresh air."

What he needed was air which didn't contain so much of Blockhead's aftershave. It was pungent at the best of times but today the sergeant was wearing enough for his entire rugby team. Kilford knew why but thought it best to keep it to himself. Blockhead was, after all, his sergeant.

They were driving to Newcastle to meet the CPS barrister in her chambers by the Crown Court to discuss the Wrathall case. Blockhead had jumped at the chance for this conference. The barrister, Penny Heaton-Niles, was no Rumpole. On the contrary, she had flowing, silken blonde hair, long, shapely legs, high cheek bones and limpid blue eyes. She also had a cut-glass accent expressed through a husky voice.

Hence Blockhead's overloaded aftershave.

To take his mind off that, Kilford started summarising their evidence.

"Right, so on the Peterlee job, Wrathall has described the exact location of the safe at the rear of the premises - which we've confirmed - and also mentions kicking a member of the staff in the head. Neither detail was made public. Add to that the fact that he describes the parcel used in the Ryhope Post Office job, detailing its poor wrapping and that it contained bath towels."

"Again, details not disclosed," said Blockhead. They went over other evidence, including the cash seized from Wrathall's Sierra. The documents seized at HMP Darlington and at Wrathall Senior's house had been swabbed for DNA and dusted for fingerprints before being sent to a handwriting expert. Since those searches, at Rocky's request, Wrathall had been transferred from Darlington to HMP Bradford. The handwriting results had come back as positive – the letters and the documents in Ratty's cell had been written by the same hand. An expert from Forensic Science had also provided a statement that Wrathall's fingerprints were on both sets of documents. They drove over the Tyne Bridge. Kilford smiled. He knew many Mackems – natives of Sunderland – who would feel physically sick crossing this iconic structure, symbol of their ancestral enemies in Newcastle. But Kilford had played for Newcastle United and his loyalties had become divided. As for Blockhead… well, he wouldn't understand, he was into Rugby.

They parked in a multi-storey and walked down to Newcastle's Quayside, where the imposing, modern Crown Court building looked out across the Tyne and Gateshead on the opposite bank. A keen breeze was blowing up the river, from the North Sea and though the egg slicer struts of the Millennium Bridge.

They turned up by the Crown Court and found the doorway, in a block of classic style sandstone buildings, to Penny Heaton-Niles chambers. The detectives went to Reception and introduced themselves. Blockhead was there in his role as OIC, or Officer in Charge of the case and file submission and Kilford had responsibility for the intelligence generated by the CHIS, Covert Human Intelligence Source, namely Ratty, aka, Wayne Langley.

They were directed to take seats in reception, while Penny Heaton-Niles wrapped up another meeting. Kilford picked up a gardening magazine and raised it to hide his grin at Blockhead straightening his tie and smoothing his hair.

Two minutes later Penny came in, full of smiles and apologies, to usher them through to her office. She was stunning in a tight black business skirt, so Blockhead was too tongue-tied to manage more than an incomprehensible babble while Kilford returned the pleasantries and reassured her that they had only just arrived.

In her office, she provided them with coffees and then got straight down to business, opening the files of evidence against Karl Wrathall, Eva Devlin and Graham Morrison, aka Bob Marley. These files contained information such as: the defendants' details; their criminal records; summaries of the evidence against them; details of exhibits, such as money recovered, the CCTV tapes, Wrathall's letters and the sheets recovered from Ratty's cell. There were also witness statements and transcripts of interviews. There was also – and this was what most interested and concerned Kilford – confidential information, including intelligence.

The intelligence was recorded on the form as classified and highly sensitive, and the information they contained was thoroughly edited to protect the real identity of the informant. This even had to be kept from Penny, as prosecuting counsel. Given that these identities were a closely guarded secret in Sunderland nick, known only to the DSU and Rocky, they would certainly not be disclosed to a lawyer, who might be prosecuting one week, but defending the next. For the snouts concerned, this was literally a matter of life and death.

Penny started to go through the files, referring to a list of questions she had prepared. She had hardly started before she paused, wrinkled her elegant nose and said, in a low voice: "Excuse me, it's a little stuffy in here, I'll just open a window."

As she got up to do this, Kilford looked down and bit his lip, marvelling at the universal appeal of Eau de Blockhead.

She resumed her seat and they continued going through the files.

"Hmm, these scripts found in the cell, I think we can present these as indicating a desperate man trying to get another to take the blame for his crimes," she said.

"I'm sure you can, Penny," said Blockhead.

She smiled. "Tell me about the background to this cell search."

"We heard about the existence of these scripts in the prison from a source," said Kilford. "The whole wing was searched and they were found in the cell of the prisoner Jordan Radcliffe. He denies any knowledge of how they came to be in his cell and declines to make any statement."

Penny nodded and made notes, frowning. Kilford knew that she would be uneasy about unnamed sources. Barristers dislike unknown sourced intelligence being introduced into cases, seeing such undercover work as a dark art, about which a defence counsel could raise doubts in the mind of a jury. She looked at the two detectives.

"Was your original source, mentioned in the form "A" (intelligence report), the getaway driver in the first two robberies, or any of the other crimes?"

"No," said Kilford and Blockhead in unison.

"Is the source Graham Morrison?"

"No."

"Eva Devlin?"

"No."

"Okay," she said closing the file. "That's good enough for me, but you," she pointed at Kilford "can expect to be cross examined by defence counsel on your source."

§

Kilford and Bull were in the DSU discussing a tip they had received from a snout that a known drug dealer, Darren Goss, was operating out of a farm in the Hetton-Le-Hole area.

"Dunno how we're going to OP that," said Bull. "No Councillor's bog seat to get probies to stand on round there."

"Yeah, well, we'll think of something," said Kilford.

His mind wasn't focused on Darren Goss, but on Karl Wrathall, whose trial was scheduled to start that morning. Blockhead was due to attend. While Kilford was contemplating this, Shifty answered a knock at the door to admit the sergeant. Blockhead was calling into the office on his way to Crown Court to pick up various papers prepared by Kilford and Bull. He was wearing a well-pressed, charcoal grey suit, shirt and tie. The top button of his shirt wasn't fastened and his neck bulged over the collar. The suit also looked as though it had been made for a thinner man. He stood by his desk, aware that four pairs of eyes were fastened on him.

He waved his hand down his side to indicate his suit.

"Well, what d'you think?"

"Too tight," said Kilford, to sniggers from Bull and Shifty.

"Eeh, don't listen to them," said Knackers. "You look ever so smart."

"Thanks. Anyway, you bastards, this is my lucky suit… never lost a case with this on. Ha'way lads, give me a bit of confidence. I've got a lot on my plate to worry about."

"Looks like there's been too much on your plate recently, looking at how tight those kegs are," said Bull, nodding at Blockhead's trousers.

"Aye, whatever you do, don't go dropping anything when you're on the stand, if you bend down, it could be a disaster… judge'll be pissing himself," said Kilford.

After an exchange of curses and followed by laughter, Blockhead left, accompanied by Knackers, who was to be his assistant at Crown Court. In the station car park, they loaded the files into his Astra, then she got into the passenger seat, while he carefully manoeuvred himself into position behind the steering wheel. As he drove towards Newcastle, he was muttering about "the bastards" under his breath, but he was glad to have had something to take his mind off the trial. Even for an experienced copper, court could be nerve-racking. In no other job is somebody's work subjected to thorough, forensic, hostile analysis and the first day of trial was always particularly bad – then almost anything could happen.

From the point of view of the stress levels of the police officer in court, the best case scenario was always a plea-bargaining, but that was never going to happen here. Wrathall was looking at a lengthy sentence and, for him, none of the police team would have been happy with anything less than a murder conviction. No, Wrathall's best chance lay in his defence barrister being able to tear apart Eva's and Bob Marley's evidence.

At the Crown Court, Blockhead and Knackers made their way to their designated police room, sat at a table and began unpacking and organising their files. After a few minutes, there was a tap at the door and Penny Heaton-Niles entered.

"Hi Penny," squeaked Blockhead, rising from his chair.

She looked at him, appearing distracted and flustered. She had a document in her hand, which she waved at him.

"DS White, you're not going to believe this. I've just been served this typed letter by the defence, which appears to be from Governor Gibson at HMP Bradford.

Do you know anything about it?" Blockhead swallowed.

"I haven't a clue, what's it about?"

Penny looked at the sheet, scanning it.

"Governor Gibson believes that Wrathall is an innocent man and has been framed by you and your team. He goes into detail... mentions abuse of process... unsolicited comments... that major witnesses, namely Morrison and Devlin, have been pressured by yourselves by making promises of lighter sentences. He finishes by saying that your intelligence is fabricated and that there are no actual informants. DS White, please tell me none of this is true."

Had this beautiful, blonde barrister walked into the room and detonated a hand grenade, the effects could hardly have been less devastating. Blockhead gawped at her. His throat, already under pressure from his shirt collar, felt even more constricted and his mouth was dry.

"May I?" he eventually croaked, holding his hand out for the letter.

She passed it to him and he examined it, struggling to comprehend. It looked genuine, on HMP Bradford headed paper and with an official stamp under the signature of Governor Gibson. Blockhead passed a hand over his forehead. If any of the allegations in this document were true, there would be massive consequences for DSU and for him personally.

He swallowed.

"Where... er... does this leave us? I've never come across anything like this before."

"You and me both," said Penny, shaking her head. She pursed her lips and rubbed her chin. "Right, this is what we'll do. We'll seek an adjournment until tomorrow. I suggest you take this away and look into it as a matter of urgency. If this is genuine, it's a game changer – and I don't mean for the better." She left the room, but Blockhead barely noticed. He dropped back into his chair, with a suddenness that brought a painful reminder of just how tight his trousers were, but it snapped him out of his shocked paralysis.

He shook his head.

"I don't sodding believe this."

"'Course not," said Knackers. "It's complete bollocks, Bull and Alf would never…"

"Eh… no, there's no question of that."

But he knew there would be questions. The kind of things detailed in that letter weren't unheard of in the murky world of police intelligence, where even the straightest coppers could be tempted to bend the rules to nail a known villain. Even if Bull and Alf were pure as the driven snow, eyebrows would still be raised and questions asked among the top brass. And that would not reflect well on Detective Sergeant Clifford White.

§

Within forty minutes they were back in the DSU and, as they had called ahead to alert the team, everybody, including the DI, was assembled, waiting for them. Without saying a word, Blockhead took the letter from his briefcase and handed it to Rocky. The DI started to read, while Blockhead dropped into a seat and sank his head into his hands.

"So much for your lucky suit then," said Bull. Blockhead raised his head and fastened his gaze on him.

"Why don't you just –"

"Shut up you arseholes while I'm reading this will yous!"

They subsided into sullen silence while Rocky finished reading the letter. Then he threw it down onto the desk.

"Right, this needs sorting out today. I want this tosser Gibson spoken to on the phone and then I want him visited to see what the shagging hell he's playing at. Is that understood?"

"Boss," said Kilford.

"What?"

"After Block… the Sarge rang through, I got on the phone to Bradford and I spoke to the governor's secretary, a lass called Sarah. She told me he's off for a week and back tomorrow."

Bull, who had picked up the letter and had been reading it, flicked the edge of it with his stubby forefinger,

"There's something not right about this. Alf, how do you spell, committing?"

"What?"

"The word – committing. How d'you spell it?" Kilford shrugged and spelt it out.

"And, intelligence?"

"I, N, T, E, double L, I, G, E, N, C, E."

"What is this?" growled Rocky. "A spelling test?" Bull pointed to the letter.

"If this letter's from the governor, he can't spell." Rocky snatched the letter from him and scanned it again.

"Shit! It's not often I can say this, but you're right, y' chubby so-and-so. This letter's bollocks. He can't even spell sergeant – the dyslexic bastard." The DI rubbed his hands together.

"Alf! When did this bloke… Gibson… when did he go on leave?"

Kilford looked at his notepad. "Er… his secretary said a week ago. Yeah… he's taken five days and he's back tomorrow."

"This letter is only dated Friday, so he wouldn't have been there to sign it. And Wrathall's back in Bradford!" He put the letter on the desk and whipped off his glasses.

"Right, I want Shifty and Knackers down at that prison first thing in the morning to see that governor. Take this letter and show him it and find out what the hell's going on here. That bastard Wrathall is behind this, he's got to be. Cliffy, you ring the CPS and update them and tell them we'll have an update at court before lunch tomorrow, let that barrister know something stinks."

Rocky left the office and the detectives got down to their allotted tasks. Kilford breathed a deep sigh. After they had received Blockhead's initial frantic phone call from Newcastle, he'd had a return of that sickening feeling that Wrathall was going to get off, that – with one bound – the toe rag would be free. But, closer examination of that letter showed there was obviously something about it that didn't ring true. Still, on the face of it, it looked authentic and it had clearly come from HMP Bradford. How the hell had Wrathall managed that? There was something almost not quite human about that bastard.

§

Paul Gibson pinched the bridge of his nose and screwed his eyes shut. He tried to recover that sense of wellbeing that it had taken a week in their Anglesey holiday cottage to achieve.

No, it was no bloody use. That feeling of relaxed optimism was gone, not to be recalled. It had been driven away the moment he had returned to his office in HMP Bradford and his strangely subdued PA, Sarah, had told him that two detectives from Sunderland were on their way to see him – urgently. They were here in his office now, sitting in front of him, an attractive, self-possessed young blonde and a shabby, dishevelled character with a sneering mouth and restless eyes. They were both gazing at him, waiting for his reaction to the letter that lay open on his desk.

Gibson opened his eyes and rubbed his mouth. He gestured at the letter as he might at something his dog had rolled in.

"So this, you say, was produced in court?"

"Not in open court yet sir," said Knackers. "But the defence have disclosed it and we assume they will use it."

"But, it's a forgery dammit! I've never seen it before and that's not my signature."

"It is on prison stationery and it does bear the official stamp."

"I can see that, but the fact remains that it's a forgery."

"Can you explain how somebody, acting on Wrathall's behalf, could have gained access to the notepaper and stamp?"

Gibson glared at the closed door, on the other side of which was Sarah's office. She probably had her bloody ear to the keyhole.

"No," he said, loud enough for his voice to carry. "But you can rest assured that I'll find out and then there's going to be hell to pay for someone."

Shifty nodded. "In the meantime sir, do you mind if we take a statement from you, declaring that you have no knowledge of this document?" Shifty grinned. "The statement will of course, carry your genuine signature which will be useful for comparison."

"I'll be happy to. I'll have my secretary take it down and type it up for you."

He used his intercom to issue a curt summons for Sarah, who, within seconds, came trotting into the office, her eyes red-rimmed and wide and her lips trembling.

§

To the triumphant cheers of Kilford and Bull, Blockhead relayed the good news that Knackers had just called through from Bradford. Then he picked up the phone to pass it on to Penny Heaton-Niles. She called him back twenty minutes later to describe how she had confronted the defence team with the news that the letter was really not something they would want to embarrass themselves with by producing in court. The defence lawyer had paled, gulped and agreed and asked Penny not to mention any of this to the judge.

"I just wonder what stroke Wrathall's going to pull next," said Blockhead.

§

With the forged Bradford letter discreetly forgotten by the defence and prosecution teams – and the judge remaining blissfully unaware of its existence – Wrathall's trial got underway.

Kilford and Bull got on with their other work: monitoring sex offenders and running informants. They were especially interested in those who provide intelligence on Darren Goss, the drug dealer operating out of a farmhouse, on whose rumoured and reported activities they were building a thick file.

But they received daily updates from Blockhead and Knackers about events in court. Knackers was particularly keen to give Kilford a breathless rundown on each day's proceedings.

In the first couple of days, the witnesses taking the stand were police witnesses, such as officers who had seized property or conducted interviews. Then came those who had been on the premises which had been robbed. The one who had dominated the court had been Betty Matterson, widow of Sam, who had died in the Ryhope job.

"It was terrible," said Knackers. "She kept breaking down and they had to adjourn. A couple of people on the jury were in tears. I had the sniffles meself."

"What about Wrathall?" asked Kilford. "How did he react?"

"Nothing. Just stared into space."

The next day Knackers told them how Eva and Graham – Bob Marley – Morrison had fared under ferocious cross examination in which, as expected, the defence assaulted their characters and credibility. But, according to Knackers, both of them stood up well and gave as good as they got. The testimony of Dr Crummie, the Harley Street expert on gait, was given short-shrift by the defence, who dismissed it as pseudo science, but Penny Heaton-Niles did her best to make sure the jury got a good sense that it was just one more piece of evidence stacking against the accused.

"She's very good is Penny," said Blockhead, then coloured at the knowing looks and smirks that greeted this.

§

Bull parked the car on the country lane, tucking it in close to the dry stone wall, at a spot where the road widened slightly. He and Kilford had made sure that they were out of sight of the farm on the other side of the tree-topped knoll that lay about three hundred yards beyond the wall.

They got out of the car, looked up and down the lane and then clambered over the wall, in Bull's case, with much scrabbling and swearing. Once in the field, they headed quickly up towards the knoll anxious to reach the cover of the trees. If they were spotted by the farmer or any other associate of Darren Goss, the whole investigation, and the intelligence on which it was based, could be compromised.

They reached the trees, panting, and looked down the other slope. A few hundred yards away lay the farmhouse, nestling in a dip. Kilford pulled the binoculars from inside his hoodie and looked through them.

"This is no good Bull. We can see the roof and the top windows but we can't see the doors and the track leading to the farm, it's all in dead ground. We can't log any comings and goings from here."

"Well, we can't get any closer, not without being spotted." Bull slapped the trunk of the beech under which they were standing. "We'll need to climb this tree and then we'll be fine - that'll give us a good eyeball."

For a couple of seconds Kilford contemplated Bull, then said: "Aye, that'll be the royal we will it? I take it you're not getting up there chubby?"

"You're lighter than me Alf. Be best if I just give you a bunk."

Kilford shook his head in resignation, then put his right foot into Bull's cupped hands and was hoisted up into the beech. He positioned himself on a lower branch, then climbed higher. Straddling this, with his back resting against the trunk, he raised his binoculars.

"Can you see it?" asked Bull.

"Hang on, let me focus. Aye, that's fine, I can see the doors and the lane and – sodding hell!"

At that point, from within his hoodie, Kilford's phone started to ring. Cursing, he juggled binoculars and phone before he succeeded in getting the Nokia to his ear. It was Blockhead.

"Alf, it's me mate. Where you at right now little fellah?"

"Twenty foot up a tree…why?"

Blockhead chuckled. "You can't keep a good man down, that's what I always say. Anyway, stop larking about and get your daft little arse down here – and Bull. They want yous in the box – now."

"Nice to get some notice. We're not exactly dressed for court appearance."

"Doesn't matter, it's a come-as-you-are party. Penny apologises but they've had to change the running order for some reason. Come right here to court straightaway, they're calling yous."

Amid a flurry of twigs, dead beech leaves and oaths, Kilford half climbed and half dropped to the ground, cursing as he felt his knee going. He gave Bull a hurried explanation and then the two of them set off at a run back down the field, over the wall and to the car. By this time, Kilford was in a sweat and, before putting his seat belt on, he wrestled himself out of his hoodie. Then he rubbed his hands down his face and tried to compose himself, ignore his throbbing knee and get into the right frame of mind to face judge, jury and a defence barrister.

Barely half an hour later he and Bull were receiving a hasty briefing from Blockhead, who told them little they didn't know, or could have worked out. DC Daniel Kilford was required to give evidence with regards to intelligence that had been provided to the police regarding a series of offences in the County Durham and Sunderland areas. Kilford nodded, received a pat on the back and was then walking into court. He was nervous, as he usually was when giving evidence. It was always hard to give clear information, without giving away the identity of the source, which the defence barrister would always be trying to tease out, with the added fear that they might already know it. In this case, it was even more fraught with danger: how was it going to look if it came out that the main source was a heroin addict, dealer, thief and was himself recently convicted for a similar knifepoint robbery? To add to all that, Kilford wasn't wearing his suit, but only moss-stained jeans and a T shirt. As he entered the courtroom, despite himself, Kilford's eyes were drawn to the dock where, for the first time since he had been wrestling him on the pavement in Pennywell, he saw Wrathall. The prisoner gazed back, impassive, intent, unblinking. Wrathall was in the box with Eva and Bob Marley, charged as co-conspirators, but Kilford only had eyes for Wrathall. Kilford was sworn in and then noticed the judge peering at him, from over the top of his spectacles – in a manner reminiscent of Rocky, though there the resemblance most definitely ended. Judge Faulkner was dry and precise and did things by the book. "Detective Constable Kilford, before we commence, could you explain to me what it says on the front of your… T shirt?" He said T shirt as though it had only just been explained to him that such a garment existed.

Kilford glanced down at his chest and groaned inwardly. Oh, why the hell had he put this on? He swallowed, shuffled his feet and cleared his throat. "Er… Your Honour, it's not what you think… FCUK… it stands for French Connection UK, it's just a brand name. I didn't have time to get changed… I was told to come straight here."

There was a second's silence and then a low rumble of laughter from around the court room. A slight smile even played across the face of Judge Faulkner, who said: "Well, having cleared that up, you may continue Miss Heaton-Niles."

Penny, with her barrister's wig perched on her hair, gave Kilford an encouraging smile and took him through the intelligence reports in chronological order. These were concise but damning, outlining the occasions on which Wrathall had been responsible for knifepoint robberies in the North East, in company with Graham Morrison and Eva Devlin. In one of these robberies Mark Matterson had been stabbed and subsequently died. The reports further described how Wrathall was involved in the supply of controlled drugs and had frequented the Middlesbrough area, from where he was believed to have obtained his supplies.

This was the easy part and Kilford settled into his role. He also gained some satisfaction from his occasional glances at Wrathall, whose glare seemed to intensify and jaw muscles tighten with every fresh detail of his activities detailed for the court.

Kilford sensed that the evidence from the sanitised intelligence reports was swaying the jury members who were sat forward on their benches, seeming to take in his every word. So, he was anxious not to blow it, when Penny gave way to the defence barrister, a snide little weasel he'd crossed swords with before, called Francis Clegg.

As expected, Clegg began probing about the role of a source handler and the type of person who would be a police informer, clearly trying to install an idea into the minds of the jurors of their inherent unreliability. Kilford was able to bat these questions away with ease, comfortably describing his role and explaining that police informants came from all walks of life and that, yes, most productive informants were criminals. Kilford was experienced enough in court not to add that that was what made them productive. He wasn't even tempted into sarcasm, as, from the line of Clegg's cross examination, it become obvious - to his relief - that the defence had no idea who the real source was and that they probably thought it was Bob or Eva. Kilford could breathe more easily because this was high stakes. It was out of the question that he could ever name a source, even if it was demanded in court and even if the judge ordered him, under threat of being sent down for contempt. Ratty had been sent down for eighteen months – a light sentence thanks to his text – but his life was still in Kilford's hands. "Am I right in thinking, Detective Constable Kilford, that your source is actually present, here in the courtroom today?"

In giving his answer, Kilford followed the usual technique and looked towards the judge and jury. "I can neither confirm nor deny this, Your Honour."

"Would I be correct in saying that your source is a female?" asked Clegg.

"I can neither confirm nor deny this, Your Honour." And so it went on, with Clegg growing increasingly testy but Kilford, sensing that the judge had no issue with his stonewalling, becoming increasingly relaxed. At last Clegg had finished and Kilford was dismissed, As he made his way to the back of the court, he looked straight at Wrathall, he stared back and, as though he was rubbing an itch, drew a finger across his throat.

Kilford returned a grin.

Bull was on the stand next and an exasperated Clegg demanded: "Well, Detective Constable Miles, are you going to be more forthcoming than your colleague and trusted friend? Will you feel able to confirm or deny?"

"No, Your Honour."

Bull was dismissed.

§

The next day Kilford sat hunched in a chair in the court's police room. Blockhead and Knackers were with him, but nobody was speaking. The rules were that witnesses were not allowed to discuss the case until it was over. However, it had been whispered to him that Penny thought he had done very well in the testimony he had given the day before.

His part was done and there was no reason for him to be back in the court building now, but he'd had a call from Blockhead that the jury, which had retired late yesterday afternoon, had, after a morning's deliberations, reached its verdict.

Now that moment was near, Kilford felt physically sick.

His mind went back to Mark Matterson's funeral, to Betty Matterson's grief-wracked face. He saw Eva Devlin's mother collapsing in sobs on her sofa, contemplating the ruin of her daughter's life. This was all down to one man. Kilford had dealt with a lot of nasty villains in his time on the force, but none had got to him like this one. He hated Wrathall and he was terrified he was going to get away with it, that the jury would distrust the evidence enough to let him return to freedom to wreak his own particular brand of havoc. Knackers could obviously detect his tension. She reached over and touched him on the forearm.

"It'll be alright Dan," she whispered.

He returned her a weak smile and was about to speak when Blockhead's phone rang.

"Hi Penny," he said. "Right… right… okay… thanks." He pocketed his phone and turned to the other two.

"We're on. The jury's back."

Kilford's stomach took another lurch as he jumped to his feet. The three of them hurried down the corridors to the court room. They went through the swing doors and Kilford took in the scene. Judge Faulkner was already seated and the jury were filing into their box.

Penny was at her desk and she was grim-faced. "Oh God, she's heard something," thought Kilford. He looked at the dock, at Wrathall – again flanked by Eva and Bob - and he was sure he could see a gleam of triumph in that bastard's eye. Shit! Shit! Shit! The jury were seated. Their foreman, a thin, stern woman, with steel grey hair and a no-nonsense manner, rose to her feet. Kilford had her down as a retired head teacher. He studied her, trying to read her expression. Which way had the jury gone? You could never tell. Sometimes, often, those twelve upstanding citizens would return incomprehensible judgements that seem to fly in the face of the evidence heard in court. What made it worse, was that you never found out why, could never know what had been said and argued in that jury room. Kilford went over the evidence. The testimony of two criminal junkies, no positive ID or forensic. Shit! But the Ryhope Post Office – that had to be sound. There was

Eva's confession and the fact they were arrested together with money identified from the Post Office. Wrathall fitted the description and he'd described the parcel at the job as containing towels, a fact no one else was aware of. He'd described the job in detail in his letters to Ratty and his handwriting was a match and the paperwork was covered in his fingerprints. All this must be enough, surely?

Kilford clenched his fists and strove to remain expressionless. The court clerk said: "Have you reached a verdict upon which you are all agreed? Please answer yes or no."

"Yes."

"Regarding only Karl Wrathall… on the first count of conspiracy to commit robbery at Seaham County Durham, what is your verdict?"

A pause. Then….

"Not guilty."

Despite himself, Kilford looked at Wrathall, detected a gleam of triumph in his eye.

"On the second count of conspiracy to commit robbery at Peterlee County Durham, what is your verdict?"

"Not guilty."

Kilford drew in a deep breath through his nose.

"On the third count of conspiracy to commit robbery at Wingate, County Durham, what is your verdict?"

"Not guilty."

"On the fourth count of manslaughter at Wingate, County Durham, what is your verdict?"

"Not guilty."

Oh God! The bastard was walking free.

"On the fifth count of conspiracy to commit robbery at Hutton-Henry, County Durham, what is your verdict?"

"Not guilty."

Feeling sick, Kilford prepared himself to rise from his seat and leave the courtroom, determined to avoid looking at a triumphant Wrathall.

But the clerk of the court hadn't finished.

"On the sixth count of conspiracy to commit robbery at Ryhope, Tyne and Wear, what is your verdict?"

"Guilty."

Kilford blinked. What?

"On the seventh count of murder at Ryhope, Tyne and Wear, what is your verdict?"

The foreman's eyes turned to Wrathall and, in them, Kilford could read a look of burning anger. She paused. Her lips pursed.

"Guilty."

CHAPTER SIXTEEN

A murder conviction. That was good enough for the DSU and for Rocky. But, a week or so later, came the icing on the cake when Wrathall was handed a twenty year sentence. Result!

The prestige of the DSU soared and Rocky was – for a brief period – held in high regard by the fucking arseholes upstairs.

Kilford felt great personal satisfaction. He was commended by Rocky and enjoyed the professional approval of his colleagues, but, more important than all that, he was satisfied with himself. He knew he'd done a good job, the best he could, and he was happy with that. He was also happy that he'd taken a violent criminal off the streets. Of course, he was sorry that Eva was sent down for four years. He felt for the kid, regretted a wasted life. But he knew that if he got too hung up about all the people he dealt with who'd made bad choices, he'd never sleep at night.

Bob Marley, or Graham Morrison, who had pleaded guilty to the offences Wrathall had been acquitted of, received two years, a light sentence, reflecting his cooperation in testifying against Wrathall. That struck Kilford as fair.

§

There was somebody, however, who wasn't so philosophical. Harry Morrison didn't think his son getting sent down for two years was fair. No, Harry Morrison wasn't happy about that… not happy at all.

§

Wrathall was being escorted back to his cell after seeing his solicitor to plan his appeal. The brief had tried to downplay his chances, but Wrathall wasn't taking no for an answer.

No way was he doing twenty – even if that did really mean ten. Not after he'd seen the smug look on the face of that short-arse bizzie who'd nicked him. He really wanted to wipe that smirk off his face. And there were other scores to settle – Eva, the fucking bitch, she had it coming, and so did that little shit Bob Marley. There were debts to pay and that couldn't be done from inside. No way. If his appeal didn't work, he was still getting out. He'd done it before and he'd do it again.

He and the prison officer reached the foot of a flight of stairs. Then, from behind, he heard a door open and a voice called: "Oi, Wilko!"

He turned. There was another screw standing in the doorway through which they'd just come. He was beckoning to Wrathall's escort. "You wait here," said his screw.

Wrathall nodded and stood waiting while the two officers talked. He looked around at the sound of footsteps behind him. A figure was coming down the stairs. He half recognised the guy, a big swarthy bloke called Arben. He was foreign – Albanian or something.

Arben nodded at Wrathall as he passed him. Wrathall opened his mouth to acknowledge him, but his words were choked off into a grunt as Arben's huge forearm was wrapped around his windpipe. Wrathall fought to prise him off, his fingers clawing and scratching, but a shiv was rammed in hard, a couple of inches under his left ear. He went down.

Within minutes of the frantic, bellowing screws reaching him, Karl Wrathall - convulsing and gushing crimson – had bled out. Dead.

ACKNOWLEDGEMENTS

While the story is firmly based on true life experiences as a detective, the story and characters are entirely fictional.

I express my deepest gratitude to Peter Jackson, without whom, my dream of writing a book would never have come true. Rest in peace my dear friend. To my true friends whom I worked with within intelligence, thank you to the best days of our lives.

To Donal MacIntyre, thank you for your help, support and advice.